FRIENDS OF ACPL

Calvert Casey

THE COLLECTED STORIES

A Book in the Series

Latin America in Translation / En traducción / Em tradução

Sponsored by the Duke–University of North Carolina Joint

Program in Latin American Studies

Calvert Casey

THE COLLECTED STORIES

Translations from the Spanish by John H. R. Polt

Edited and with an introduction by Ilan Stavans

Duke University Press Durham and London

1998

Typeset in Monotype Fournier by Tseng Information Systems, Inc.

Library of Congress Cataloging-in-Publication Data appear

on the last printed page of this book.

Translation of the books in the series Latin America in Translation /

En Traducción / Em Tradução, a collaboration between the Duke–University

of North Carolina Joint Program in Latin American Studies and the university

presses of Duke and the University of North Carolina, is supported by

a grant from the Andrew W. Mellon Foundation.

Contents

Introduction

What every author hopes to receive from posterity — a hope

usually disappointed — is justice. W. H. AUDEN

It has become a commonplace to embrace renegade artists as symbols of our modern condition. Our first response is to ignore them, to deprive their work of any serious consideration. But no sooner do they fall completely into the abyss of oblivion, than our omission becomes apparent. So we change our mind to embrace them profusely and obsessively, as if regretting a terrible sin. Poe, for instance, the master of the macabre, was at first so forgotten that his grave had no tombstone for twenty-six years. When he finally got one, only Whitman attended the ceremony. How ironic, then, that no other American writer today, with the probable exception of Poe's nemesis, Henry James, commands so much public and critical attention. How jarring that after his contemporaries time and again denied his genius, he is today a commodity in textbooks and a magnet to bring the young to good literature. Or take Kafka. His shadowy self, his sense of alienation, of break from the rules of social behavior, made him a pariah, an eternally unhappy person whose work during his lifetime failed to command any thoughtful response from publishers and readers. He even asked his best friend, Max Brod, to burn his entire oeuvre after his death. But we revere Kafka now. We turn him into an idolized rebel because that allows us to recriminate against Western culture, against its mechanisms to normalize individuals, from which all of us like to think we are somewhat disconnected. Kafka and Poe figure as oversensitive and painful creatures inhabiting the margins, individuals suffering from physical and psychological sicknesses we see as nightmarish. "I would prefer not to," cries Bartleby, Melville's famous eccentric, a motto well suited for all renegade artists, scapegoats of a society that doesn't quite know how to react to them. So it sings to them in chorus: Ah sufferers! Ah humanity!

Calvert Casey, an unsettling Cuban, belongs to the same type of artist: the rambler and rebel who prefers not to. Through his shyness and silence, through his perception of reality as a smoke screen behind which Truth is hidden, he dreamed of remembrance, of leaving behind a legacy endorsed by future generations. One nurtures paternal feelings toward one's work, Casey once wrote, hoping it would be safe and protected for the ages. But for too long already, since his suicide in Rome in 1969, his work has remained unfairly trapped in oblivion. Unfairly, I say, because some of Casey's short stories, such as "The Visitors" and "Piazza Margana," are incomparable, of the type that deeply disturbs our conventional views of life. Like "The Building of the Great Wall of China," like "The Pit and the Pendulum," they have a fugitive quality. Every single one of them is less about a character participating in a well-defined plot than about a mood and a state of mind. Casey's testament was to explore through prose the other side of things, that "feeling of irreality" that constantly haunts us.

His presence, by most accounts, was "pallid," i.e., subtle, unfelt by many, as if this renegade artist, this troubled soul, needed to apologize for his actions. And he did apologize, repeatedly. Proof is the instance just before taking his suicidal overdose of sleeping pills, when, already inconsolably depressed, Casey drafted a letter to the Italian police deploring the inconvenience of being found in such a distasteful state. An inconvenience? Or when he agonized about being followed all over Europe by Fidel Castro's secret police, who he believed had orders to annihilate him. Was he paranoid? Was he yet another Cold War schizophrenic, constantly looking back in case someone followed him? His tomb, like Poe's at first, remains unknown. Worse, after his untimely death, an Italian news reporter found in his apartment statues of fornicating Indian gods and pornographic postcards and immediately branded him as a sodomite, a monster of the perverse—this in spite of his attempt, evident in his "Notes on Pornography," to extricate the vicious from the erotic, the superficial from the esoteric. Thus, in death Casey quickly enhanced the anathema that had surrounded him like an unwelcome shroud all his life. He lived and died in a permanent state of eclipse, a larva frozen in time.

Periodically, however, someone somewhere will try to revive him. Literati of a high caliber all tried their luck: Italo Calvino, Vicente Molina Foix, María Zambrano, Luis Goytisolo, Guillermo Cabrera Infante. These hopeful attempts have surely kept Casey's legacy alive. He remains a well-kept secret, a martyr on the road to beatification. But he never quite makes it there, in part because he was a true nomad from a no-man's-land, a visionary from nowhere and everywhere. He made his reputation in Spanish, though he switched tongues with such vehemence, from English to Spanish, from Spanish to English and Italian, that he belongs to no single language and to all at once. And while he found real solace only in Havana, his odyssey pulled him from Istanbul to New York, from England to India to Italy, to the point that no locality was ever truly his. In other words, Casey was the freakish nonconformist we all nurture within, an Irishman from the United States dancing to syncopated Caribbean rhythms, crushed by his own sexual and political identity, always in search of the elusive word and world he could call his own. Is his "I would prefer not to" destined to find a wider audience? Will posterity ever grant him the justice he deserves? Or are we to be disappointed?

To some degree, Casey's close friend, Cabrera Infante, is most responsible for keeping him around, for not letting oblivion triumph decisively over memory. His excellent essay "Who Killed Calvert Casey?" written in 1980, did much to generate a halo of supreme mystery around him. "A decade after his death," wrote Cabrera Infante, "Calvert resuscitates, rises from the dead and from underneath the bookish stone stretches out his bony hand that holds up a few pages to let us know what true literature is, visible in that writing that is his winning pawn: his prose is a communicating vessel: on the reverse is life; on the obverse, death. Calvert Casey lives and dies in each reading and his texts are a Moebius strip of reading: finite, infinite." Known among friends as La Calvita, Cálver, or simply as Cal, he produced a prose that is allergic to the baroque linguistic vices and devices ubiquitous in the Havana of the fifties. His style has a queerness to it that makes it unique but difficult to grasp. The best way to define it, I suppose, is simply to say that it seems wrapped in a thin, white veil. We want to caress Casey's sentences but can't. They are removed, intangible. They are for us but not fully ours. He left us with only a small number of fictional tales, a very small number: seventeen original stories in total, all of them with one exception remarkably short, collected in a couple of volumes: *El regreso*, first published in 1962 in Havana, expanded a year later and enlarged again in 1967, when a Spanish edition by Seix Barral appeared in Barcelona; and *Notas de un simulador*, which appeared in 1969, shortly before Casey's death. Dead at forty-five, Casey seems to have been at the brink of artistic maturity but not quite there. While he tried his luck at a novel in progress — *Gianni, Gianni*, which he announced time and again and seemed to be working on toward the end, with "Piazza Margana" as one of its segments — he either never managed to finish it or simply destroyed it after it was almost completed. What he did generate, apparently with some hesitation, was a novella, "The Master of Life and Death." His personality, obviously, was suitable for the condensed and meteoric, as if he could make himself offer only snapshots of his plight, never a sustained account. Throughout his life, he also published a number of essays in periodicals, for the most part Cuban but also Mexican, many of which were gathered in 1964 in *Memorias de una isla*. They fail to capture us because Casey was not a thinker but a dreamer. He did not master a strategy to develop and critique ideas. Instead, he was adept at turning words into windows to the heart. Each of his stories is an exploration of the act of survival of the weakest in the margins of society. They all read like segments of a fractured novel and an autobiographical one at that, for Casey understood literature as a key to unlock his troubled soul. This explains why the same type of protagonist, a Gregor Samsa *a la cubana*, parades throughout his oeuvre, always bargaining with a small set of motifs. At the brink of maturity but incapable of grasping it — that, to me, is how Casey's legacy ought to be described. How much richer would we have been had he lived a few more years? And yet, his immaturity seems enough. It has weight and power.

Fate was never on Casey's side. In fact, death in many ways was a more suitable alternative than more years of suffering. He suffered from inexplicable periodic pains. Also, not only was he quiet and introspective, but he had a way of vacillating existentially, to make his presence unnoticeable. This hesitation was enhanced by his stuttering, of course, a birth handicap that became his trademark in Havana and was obviously connected to his timid temperament and introverted spirit. And one could also explain his recurrent pains as connected to his verbal impediment, for stuttering remains a most mysterious malady, connected, since the Enlightenment, to an imbalance of forces in the body. At any rate, Casey's nondescript behind-the-curtains style has its counterpart in his legendary stuttering. Luis Agüero, who met him during a *tertulia* in the offices of the weekly *Lunes de Revolución*, under the editorship of Cabrera Infante, once described him as "wearing thick glasses and dressing like a post-office employee." When he was nervous, Agüero adds, his stuttering would make his cheeks red as blood. In the shallow waters of conversation, Cabrera Infante himself claims, Casey would unexpectedly fall, "tripping over the least prominent words, like a rock on his oral road even if it were only an oral cobblestone." Antón Arrufat, another friend, to whom *El regreso* is dedicated, claimed Casey choked on the words he could not swallow.

No matter how we see it, a stuttering writer is an extraordinary metaphor for modernity. Words were both his tool and his trap. He made them his, but they betrayed him. For Casey, stuttering was a way to negotiate between silence and statement, between death and literature. Only in "Homecoming," his most personal story, does a character actually suffer from a language impediment, but throughout all his pages characters tremble and stagger. In fact, each of Casey's tales, I'm convinced, stutters: each stumbles and bobbles and gets lost in its own verbal labyrinth. The reader invariably finishes the tales exhausted, with a feeling of inconclusion. What are they really about? What do they say? And what do they seek? What is it that words conceal? Their characters are constantly disconnected from their surroundings, as in "The Execution," a tale, with a quotation from the Song of Solomon 1:12, somehow reminiscent of Camus's *The Stranger*, in which a man is imprisoned for a crime he never committed and is taken to his death without uttering a word of complaint. This attitude is symptomatic: loners abound in Casey's universe, loners without self-esteem, tormented by a vast galaxy of aunts: a young man prepares the burial of a baby who is his relative; a misfit returns to a park bench hoping to establish human connections that seem ill fated from the beginning; a disoriented adolescent imagines being introduced to his manhood by a prostitute but never realizes his fantasy; an outcast is hypnotized by a group of homeless people who make him feel accepted; a gay man is bewitched by his lover's blood. Hypnosis, fantasy, enchantment: in all these stories, words are only an excuse; they seduce and deceive.

Casey was born in Baltimore, Maryland, in 1924. He was thrown by birth into a verbally mixed habitat, for his father was American and his mother Cuban. Conflicting biographical reports abound: apparently, he grew up in Havana but in 1948 he moved back to the United States. However, when his first published story appeared, he identified himself as having lived and gone to school "in his native Cuba" until 1946. A deliberate mistake? Elsewhere he added that he had worked in Canada and Switzerland until 1950, when he had been a translator for the United Nations, first in New York City and then in Rome. This sense of dislocation, of an itinerant life, permeated his worldview: home was nowhere and everywhere — neither in space nor in words. Baltimore doesn't figure at all in his memory, nor does Paris or the metropolises of other countries he went through: France, Mexico, Czechoslovakia, and Haiti. New York City is mentioned but dispassionately: it is too cold, too impersonal, too aggressive. Only in two cities did Casey feel comfortable: Havana and Rome, Rome and Havana — undeclared mirrors of each other. He would live in Havana but die in Rome or vice versa. Once in the mid-fifties, wandering in Europe without a goal, he experienced an eerie insight. "One morning in Rome," he wrote later, "in a Rome impoverished by the first postwar years, I had a curious vision that might have lasted a few seconds but that I remember quite clearly. The heat was intense. In a café in Corso Umberto I was drinking some liquid that would allow me to continue walking. A noisy crowd, mostly populated by brown faces, descended through the wide Via Barbieri, leaving behind the ivory sculpture with images of dolphins. The sound of people getting onto a bus, their little scenes of violence turned into little scenes of laughter, the intense life of a city curiously cosmopolitan and provincial had the virtue of pushing time back. That city wasn't Rome anymore but another remote city, Havana. The similarities were painful: the ivory sculpture was the old Neptune exiled in a Vedado park after presiding over the dealings of many generations in mornings such as this one. On the arcades I had crossed moments before, I saw a crowd descending in the *portales* of the Calzada de la Reina. The balconies were the same cement balconies of the old avenue where I first contemplated the great spectacles of this world. The emotion this vision produced in me carried along an infinite panic. (I recalled the panic elephants feel when death is near and they are far from the place where they were born.) I was terribly far from Havana. Perhaps I had forever lost the paradise (and also hell) of my first vision. My voluntary exile ended that morning. I had to return to the scene of discovery, where everything is given and nothing is in need of explanation."

When seen from beginning to end, Casey's fate is made only of arrivals and departures. Havana, the scene of discovery, as authentic a habitat as he would ever find, made him believe his homelessness was temporary. It also convinced him that Spanish, his mother's tongue, was his true household. His first story, "The Walk," had been written in English. It was published in the *New Mexico Quarterly* in 1954–55 and was awarded a prize by Doubleday in New York. But his "homecoming" is signaled in multiple ways: he himself translated "The Walk" into Spanish (or, I should say, rewrote it) as "El paseo" for inclusion in the first edition of his debut collection of stories, *El regreso,* published in 1962 by Ediciones R in Cuba; and as early as 1955, at age thirty-two, he began sending material from the United States to the magazine *Ciclón.* Eventually, he switched to Spanish, and the fall of the Batista regime and the incident in Sierra Maestra inspired him, in the early sixties, to relocate to Cuba. This metamorphosis, this heartfelt homecoming, is minutely and movingly described in his 1960 essay "Memorias de una isla," as well as in the story "Homecoming." In the latter, an idealistic young Cuban, exhausted by the "feeling of irreality," by the loneliness of New York, returns to the land of his origins. The autobiographical ingredient cannot be a coincidence: like Casey, the protagonist is guilt-ridden, insecure, lonely, bookish, prematurely bald, and a stutterer. But the story is imbued with prophecy, for his hope quickly turns into hopelessness. Like Joseph K., he is suddenly and inexplicably arrested. In prison he is tortured and, toward the end, he falls off a cliff as he staggers along the place where his torturers have dumped him. More than anything, "Homecoming" is about guilt: by returning to his homeland he dreams of freeing himself from the guilt that possesses him, but the guilt might not bring him to his end, since his death is inflicted on him with complete indifference to his integration into Cuban society.

The resemblance to Casey's own pilgrimage is astounding: he spent only a bit over half a decade in Havana and then left the island, deserting it in 1965 while on a lecture trip to Budapest. The cycle went in reverse: he first resettled in Geneva, working once again as a translator for the United Nations, but eventually he returned to the Via Barbieri and the café of Corso Umberto, relocating in Rome. He continued to live in Spanish but readopted English as his artistic tongue. In the latter he wrote *Gianni, Gianni*. Switching landscapes and languages is a shocking act of self-transformation: by giving up one habitat and code and embracing another, a person undergoes a deep sense of loss and resurrection. For Casey, however, the loss is not a beginning but an end; in him the homecoming carried along its counterpoint: his departure was a return, and his return brought a sense of closure — *la huida y el regreso.*

Casey's Cuban period was incredibly prolific: not only did he quickly move up in the intellectual hierarchy but he published two books and more than two dozen "occasional" pieces — essays and reviews — on Edward Albee, Pedro Juan Soto, Juan Carlos Onetti, and René Marqués, among other authors and topics, originally commissioned by *Lunes de Revolución* and other weeklies of equal quality, a handful of which were collected in 1964 in the volume *Memorias de una isla;* but this period was also marked by a deep ambivalence, as is his whole life. Upon his arrival, he first worked in a department store. Later he became drama critic of Havana's evening daily, *Pueblo.* He frequented a small circle of friends, among them Agüero, Virgilio Piñera, Cabrera Infante, Arrufat, Oscar Hurtado, Lisandro Otero, Humberto Arenal, Miriam Acevedo, Juan

Arcocha, Pablo Armando Fernández, and Heberto Padilla. When *Lunes de Revolución* was closed by the government because its staff was considered politically dangerous and sexually promiscuous, Casey worked in the Casa de las Américas, directing the Colección Latinoamericana book series. He was, to be sure, a supporter of Castro's Revolution, not always openly enthusiastic about its drastic changes, but convinced, no doubt, that Socialism was the only road to a better tomorrow.

However, this enthusiasm soon turned to disappointment. Toward the end of that period, in 1964, he came across Italo Calvino, who at the time was a judge for the Casa de las Américas prize and was reading manuscripts. Their relationship is illustrative of his state of mind. As it turns out, Casey gave Calvino and his Argentinean wife Chiquita a tour of *La Habana vieja* and of the city's cemeteries and churches. "At that time," Calvino wrote later, "he still had high hopes for the Revolution: not to abandon the besieged island, he adapted himself to its miserable life with a tranquil and ironic understatement. One needed to go beyond the layers of his reserve and humor to understand how hard it must have been for a man like him, with his graceful physical appearance and renal colic, the experience of joining the 'volunteer brigades' sent to *la zafra* in order to increase sugar production." But Casey had a moral standard unlike those around him, which left Calvino impressed. Everyone made use of the black market to satisfy basic needs, but not Casey. He ate only what the official food ration allowed and his clothing was reduced to a pair of rotten pants. "That man," Calvino further remarked, "so friendly and courteous, who had opted for Cuba because it was his mother's country, but could have equally chosen his original *yanqui* citizenship, lived the Revolution as a moral experience, both individually and collectively, stuck to his endurance, never asking for benefits or having wrong illusions." And yet Casey described Cuba's "new life" to Calvino as "overcast with thunder." And his Italian friend was impressed — so impressed that at his return to Rome he commissioned the Italian translation of *El regreso,* which Einaudi published in 1966. Did Calvino, himself part Cuban, understand that Casey wouldn't last long on the island? Assuredly, for *Il ritorno* eventually persuaded Casey to return to Rome. Havana had a future, but not for him.

His circle of friends was already ostracized and, what's worse, his sexual preferences obviously turned him into a pariah.

Casey's sexuality might have been nonbelligerent, but it certainly wasn't tenuous. He was open about it and discussed it, in sonorous privacy, with friends like Piñera, Severo Sarduy, and José Lezama Lima. Cabrera Infante tells a revealing episode. One day while walking the Havana streets that join the Parque Central to the Plaza de Alvear, Casey, Cabrera Infante, and Cabrera's wife Miriam Gómez passed along the Asturian Center, with its iron grilles and paving stones. Inside is a magnificent staircase: " 'Do you see that staircase?' asks Calvert, obliging us to look and see once more the familiar steps of the palace, all marble, wide above and opening up even wider below, with balustrades that become stony volutes at its end, coruscating conches." Casey says: "OK, I have to make a confession to you. More a confidence, really . . . The desire, the dream of my life is to go down that staircase. . . . But I want to go down it wearing a flowing crinoline, laced and low-cut, my shoulders bare, my breasts bursting out all over. The sleeves will have to be short to show off my perfect arms. On my long beautiful neck a pearl necklace catches the light, and I wear ruby ear-studs like a drop of blood on my lobe. Also, perhaps a diadem, if it is not very burdensome, of precious stones. My sleek blond hair will fall in romantic locks on my naked shoulders. Have I already told you that my shoulders are naked? You'll see my round shoulders and my splendid back. I would be made up to perfection: arched brows, violet eyes, red garnet lips and touches of rouge, very light, a highlight and nothing more, since my complexion will be translucid. Then decked out like that, I will go down the staircase, step by step, slowly, like a queen, all the lights on my descent. . . . What do you think?"

And what do *we* think? Casey's transvestite fantasies had doom written all over them. He tried all sorts of subterfuges, even marriage, but to no avail, for sooner rather than later, the regime ostracized him. His homosexuality, along with his political disenchantment, pushed him to the limit. Unlike others, he was lucky for, although out of public favor, at no point was he ever imprisoned, as other gays were, nor was he sent to a labor camp designed for *los indeseables*. Exile was Casey's only option and to exile he went. By then most of his oeuvre had been written, including the various stories, "In Partenza" and "Polonaise Brillante," for instance, dealing tacitly — and tactfully — with gays under repressive political systems. *Un cobarde*, a coward? Perhaps, but so were Boris Pasternak and Isaac Babel. Still, in an age such as ours, obsessed with difference, we should be careful not to overinflate Casey's gay identity. He is unlike Reinaldo Arenas in his "civilized" quietness. And even Lezama Lima's erotic totemism seems too explosive for Casey. No, his style was subdued, closer to Piñera's than to anyone else's. His sexual ambivalence (he had gay and straight love affairs) manifests itself in the ubiquitous theme of sexual disenchantment that permeates his work. Carnal encounters are forced on characters, who invariably end up dissatisfied. What is preferable, Casey seems to suggest in stories like "Goodbye . . . and Thanks for Everything," is the creation of an imaginary lover, the best means of escape through love. Fantasy, in short, is the only hope, even the sort of vampire-like fantasy in "Piazza Margana."

Imaginary lovers, imaginary homelands . . . Once in exile, Casey's artistic spark greatly diminished. A state of paranoia overwhelmed him. He feared *El líder máximo*. He was convinced Cuba's secret police was about to capture him. When the translator and editor J. M. Cohen invited him to be part of an anthology published by Penguin in England called *Writers of Fidel's Cuba*, he declined unless the title were changed. His overall objective was to keep as low a profile as possible — or even lower. The truth is that he wanted to vanish altogether, to cease being Calvert Casey, to be reborn under another identity. As a result, not only did he stop writing for periodicals but he almost ordered Seix Barral not to publish the Spanish editions of *El regreso* and *Notas de un simulador,* which were under contract, for fear of attracting too much attention. And so he became a ghost, a Cold War monstrosity, victimized by the general state of fear that made the life of Cuban exiles in Europe utterly unbearable. He traveled to places like New Delhi, Czechoslovakia, London; he used Krakow as the setting of "Polonaise Brillante"; he met Gianni, an Italian gigolo who became his raison d'être. What he never stopped was his enormous outpouring of correspondence to friends (Cabrera Infante, Arrufat, Piñera), some of which has begun appearing in Cuba and elsewhere but still awaits serious consideration. Typically, in a 24 June 1967 letter to Arrufat,

Casey describes the terrible nostalgia that invades him in his exile from Cuba, but he also celebrates Rome as the sole medicine that can cure his longing. He applauds his addressee's completion of a novel and talks about a translation he has just completed of H. P. Lovecraft, "who kept me sleepless in Geneva out of sheer terror," he writes. After two or three lines, he adds: "I reread this letter. With its fury and apocalypses and its essential incomprehension [one could say it is] the letter of a defeated man. I assure you it isn't. While translating Lovecraft (who can be a horrible writer) I had this vision of human life: we are bubbles that suddenly puff, but if we make puff or paff when we vanish it really doesn't matter, and if we don't vanish it also doesn't matter. . . . Will we see each other again? In fact, we have never ceased to see each other, and if we accept that matter is eternal then we were always one, and if going a bit further you can tolerate my pantheism . . . you will understand that we are one and the same, that any separation or difference is only a form of illusion." This correspondence is all about death, but then again, so is his entire oeuvre. Death is always on the way, zigzagging his characters—death and its double, the enervating heaviness of life. What is the capacity to die, Casey's idol, José Martí, once claimed in Mexico, but the capacity to organize? In "Potosí," anthologized in *Nuevos cuentistas cubanos,* for instance, designed as a tale of *lo fantástico* with its surprise ending and set in a cemetery, the un-named narrator wanders around reading inscriptions on tombs—in Chinese, Spanish, and Hebrew. (What the narrator calls Poles in the story are really Jews, and thus Polish is Hebrew.) And in "The Sun" he records the reaction of six characters to a nuclear holocaust two hours and fifteen minutes before the hydrogen bomb is set off.

All this makes Casey Kafkaesque. He shows an affinity for prostitutes and the indigent, as if only in the underworld, the realm of the wicked, could he find his calling. His vision entails an inescapable feeling of alienation, of remoteness that is very much the product of modernity and came to him as a result of his peripatetic journeying, for in essence Casey was nothing but a loose cannon. Curiously, *Memorias de una isla* includes essays on both Martí and Kafka: in Martí, an icon in Castro's regime, Casey cherished the romantic hero obsessed with death, his own and the abstract nothingness of Kierkegaard; and in Kafka, denounced as "an abomination" by Soviet Communism, he also sees his own reflection: an artist of the unreal and nightmarish, isolated from society, alone and lonely. Casey oscillated between the two: he glorified Martí's political commitment but knew deep inside that he himself was anything but romantic, and he treasured Kafka as a symbol of modern pain and wrote about necrophilia, which in his stories goes hand in hand with occultism. One of his most memorable literary performances, and a favorite of mine, is "The Visitors," often ranked by critics among the best Cuban stories ever written. As is usual, we enter a universe of aunts and relatives linked to one another not solely by blood but by inexplicable forces, but we see it through the eyes of a lonely young man. The link between this world and the next is explored through a series of spiritualistic sessions in which the dead punish the living and vice versa. This is a tale of longing and fear, though not a horror story. What is life if not a punishment for sins we are irremediably forced to perform?

During his last couple of years, Casey befriended new people and reencountered old acquaintances: the philosopher María Zambrano and the critic Vicente Molina Foix of Spain, Sarduy in France, Cabrera Infante in England, Calvino in Italy. But in spite of himself, he was truly a defeated man. Mysticism had been an alternative. Sarduy saw his name inscribed in the *Tibetan Book of the Dead*. His nervous suffering and itinerant existential jogging map his slow disintegration. Was he too fragile? Was modernity too heavy a burden on him? When did his character give in to the cruelty of everyday life? What is unquestionable is that a tepid depression kept him *in partenza*. Altogether, this last phase looks like a descent, but Zambrano preferred to describe it as an elevation—an ascent to symbolism. Obscurity and pain surrounded Casey as he began to emanate a halo of light. After a fervent romance, Gianni abandoned him. Love was gone, and so was meaning. Already in the Havana of the mid-sixties, he had talked to people about suicide. "Only through suffering," he told Arrufat, "does our life acquire its true meaning." But how much suffering can a pallid renegade artist handle? In the final count, Casey did have a bitter doom, but he also had his rewards. Not many wandering authors have been able to relocate themselves in another habitat, geographical and verbal, and in the end awake such stubborn admiration among their peers.

Not many have inspired in their land of choice magnetic poems such as the following one by José Triana, written in 1969 at the news of Casey's death, of which this is John Polt's translation:

Like smoke he comes toward you, like
a buzzing will-o'-the-wisp
that runs you over and rips you up.
What arms and legs and wings!
You see him slipping along, more like a sleepwalker
or disoriented perhaps by the shadows,
through crickets jubilant in their madness.
He's probably coming from Istanbul,
from some solitary wrung-out river;
though they say that by Saracen hands,
back in the age of Titus, he perished.
You can make him out among the swallows
with his tenacious lips and shoes.
A monk would send you messages from him
when spring was dreaming wildly
of charcoal, shouts, and salamanders.
In your own adolescent dreams you may
have had an inkling of his biting eyes,
and more than once on dirty steps you thought
you saw him fornicating, drunk.
Someone said they'd seen him in some tribe
choking the autumn's arrows
and that the Sultan of Persia had retained him
among the dwarf attendants of his harem.

We need not speak his name, and we do need to.
What's left of him is still about,
and all disasters find their way into the cabala.
Dawn shifts the shadows, memories
are little drops and stones that importune
the vast house of the abyss.

Ah, falling shadows, falling shadows!
Beneath the water you can see his body.

A Note on the Text

The stories in this collection are in approximate chronological order, ranging from 1954 to, presumably, shortly before Casey's death. "The Walk," originally written in English, was first published in *New Mexico Quarterly* 24 (Winter 1954–55). "Piazza Margana," the only surviving fragment of an aborted novel in progress, *Gianni, Gianni,* also written by Casey in English, appears here for the first time, with editorial emendation of minor lapses in syntax and vocabulary. Except for this fragment, all the other stories in this collection are part of *El regreso* (1st ed., Havana: Ediciones R, 1962; 2d expanded ed., Havana: Ediciones R, 1963; 3d expanded ed., Barcelona: Seix Barral, 1967) and *Notas de un simulador* (Barcelona: Seix Barral, 1969). While several of them underwent modifications, presumably by Casey, our translation is based on the author's latest version, which we take to be the best indication of his artistic judgment. The only exception is the name of a figure in "The Visitors": Franco in the 1962 edition, Félix in the one of 1967. Not convinced that this change is due to Casey's initiative, we opted for Franco. Previous English translations of two of Casey's stories were published in *Writers in the New Cuba,* ed. J. M. Cohen (Baltimore: Penguin Books, 1967): "The Lucky Chance," herein titled "Happiness," and "The Execution." The Penguin text of the latter differs substantially from ours, which we believe to be based on the author's final Spanish version. We omitted the story "La plazoleta," also part of the 1967 edition of *El regreso,* since it is clearly an early and much briefer version of the novella "The Master of Life and Death." Our translation of "A Little Romance" first appeared in *Massachusetts Review* 37, no. 3 (Autumn 1996). Finally, we wish to thank Vicente Molina Foix, whose Spanish translation of "Piazza Margana" was part of a special section devoted to Casey in *Quimera,* no. 26 (December 1982), for his generosity and guidance. José Triana's poem "Calvert Casey: In Memoriam" is used with permission of the publisher of *Quimera.*

Translator's Note

For help in the translation of Calvert Casey's stories,
I am grateful to David Frick, John M. Hunt III, Irma and Ignacio
Navarrete, Julio Ramos, Estela and José Ignacio Rasco, and
always and especially Beverley Hastings Polt, my wife and most
helpful critic. All are, of course, quite innocent of
such flaws as remain in my work.

Calvert Casey

THE COLLECTED STORIES

The Walk

"Come the first of the month," Ciro's mother said, "we will go to Anastasio's and you will try on a pair of long trousers." She remained silent for a few seconds, fumbling nervously for the big soup ladle which lay conspicuously within her reach, on the tablecloth. Having found it, she dipped it into the fuming *potaje*, bringing up the boiled slices of green banana and yucca, and then dipping them again, deliberately and to no visible purpose.

As on previous occasions when the visit to Anastasio had been mentioned, Ciro grew restless and mumbled impatiently:

"Yes, yes, Mother, you've said it before."

She gave a sharp short laugh and added: "You are growing up — you are not a boy any longer. Now, it's decided — come the first of the month, we'll go to Anastasio, and he'll fix a nice pair of blue trousers for you to wear."

Thus released, she ladled out the first course of the family meal, a copious affair which not even the sultry Cuban summer could discourage.

After this latest announcement, Ciro tried as hard as he could not to look at Zenón, his bachelor uncle who was sitting in his place at the opposite corner of the table, since every time mention was made of the long trousers Zenón would cast little confidential glances in his direction. The boy finally gave up, however, and met the other's winking eye. Ciro's uncle hooked his napkin into his collar and started to eat very slowly, gazing down at his plate in a contented trance, only looking up to wink at Ciro from time to time.

Ciro's maiden aunts, two stout pleasant women, were smiling. "He will look very handsome in his new trousers, no doubt," said Felipa, the younger one. She giggled, looking at Ciro with a roguish expression, opened her eyes very wide, and burst at last into open laughter.

"Felipa, Felipa, calm down," entreated her sister, herself giggling. Ciro's young sister was watching them, deep in the semi-stupor of her second teething.

It all worked up slowly but surely, through all those weeks, seemingly endless for Ciro, like a huge balloon inflated with a slow-motion pump. As he went about his daily errands, or left for school in the early morning, or walked into the house after a day out in Altagracia, the playing grounds near his home, Ciro became aware that the center of interest had been shifted from his eldest cousin's latest pregnancy and was now focussed sharply on him. The sudden unmentioned concern had left him in a spotlight, at whose center he stood, assailed by his aunts' giggles and his mother's sudden tenderness. There was an air of placid conspiracy in the family, a tacit understanding, a fat contentment, an ineffable mirth universally shared. It transgressed the limits of the household, trickled down the inner court to the neighbors, flowed past the iron grates of the balconies overlooking the street and poured finally into the entire neighborhood.

As the end of the month approached and the day of the visit to Anastasio grew nearer, a complacent smile had turned up on the faces of all of Ciro's uncles, and even on the faces of their wives and in-laws. He sensed his cousins eyeing him now in admiration.

Too, Ciro suddenly perceived that his Uncle Zenón's stature in the family had grown out of proportion. From a half-accepted and colorless bachelor in a large family of solemn patriarchs, he had become overnight an important figure considered with intimate affection by everyone. His sisters-in-law had suddenly taken to Zenón, with the very unanimity which had formerly marked their tolerance of his manner when they had first been admitted into the clan. On Sunday evenings now, as they mounted the stairs into the stifling front parlor, they greeted him amidst much fanning, wiping the cold sweat that trickled down between their breasts: "It's really Zenón! And how nice of him to spend the evening at home. The wise man of the family — wouldn't give up celibacy for anything." He was offered cigars by his brothers, who no longer found grounds for picking on him, and Felipa often looked his way intently, scowling with an affection never witnessed previously.

On a Saturday afternoon, as Ciro and his mother, back from Anastasio's, turned the familiar corner into the street where they lived and began mounting the slope to the house, he saw his two aunts leaning against the rail of the mezzanine balcony, their elbows propped on two pink brocade cushions. His mother looked up smiling.

"What happened?" the younger aunt asked.

"Everything is in order," Ciro's mother said, standing under the balcony, "Anastasio himself will deliver the trousers tomorrow morning."

"What color?" the other asked again.

"Blue, dark blue," Ciro's mother replied.

An expression of uncontrollable curiosity appeared on the face of Mrs. Figueras, their neighbor. She and Mr. Figueras were standing on their balcony, across the street, and evidently had been unable to grasp what had been said.

"Dark blue," Ciro's aunt hastened to brief them, "Anastasio himself will deliver the trousers in the morning."

"Is that so?" Mrs. Figueras offered, undoubtedly pleased at Anastasio's diligence.

Nothing else was said about the subject and the evening meal was eaten without any allusion to Ciro's attire, a deep unhurried satisfaction having settled over the family. Only once Ciro caught his mother looking at him, gazing down and then suddenly up at him again.

On Sunday afternoon—Anastasio having lived up to his word and repute—Ciro stepped briskly into his brand-new pants, which covered his ankles, deserting forever the loose-fitting trousers which his mother used to tie just below the knee. He washed his hands, combed his hair, and went out onto the spacious roof, where he was to meet his uncle after siesta.

The air was dry; the square red tiles embedded on the roof-floor calcinated slowly under the sun. A maze of flat roofs, occasionally broken by a lonely wash line waving in the distance, and separated by low thick walls, spread out of sight. Ciro sat on a low stool under the thin shade of a wooden trelliswork, waiting for Zenón. He appeared at five, wearing his Sunday finery: white and black shoes, striped shirt and tie, white linen suit stiffly starched, and white stiff hat. A blue sapphire was shining on the small finger of his right hand.

"Ready?" he asked, touching Ciro on the arm. Ciro smiled faintly, caught in the waves of cologne coming from under his uncle's hat and spreading in the hot afternoon.

"Don't be late for supper," Ciro's mother said without looking up at them from her corner of the main balcony.

"We won't, Mother," Ciro answered. His legs were a little shaky as they went down the stairs and into the street. He rubbed his hands against his thighs trying to dry the sweat off the palms, and felt his uncle's hand resting on his shoulder almost tenderly.

The afternoon breeze began to come in soft waves as they walked down the half-deserted streets lined by whitewashed walls, and hushed in the Sunday air. Anonymous women emerged here and there from their doors on a mid-afternoon reconnaissance, staring fixedly at them until Ciro felt uncomfortable. They crossed a big dusty square where a few trees stood dejectedly, walked along a narrow promenade, and slowly entered the old section of town. The sidewalk was very narrow here and they took to the road.

Ciro was seeing the *quartier* for the first time. The streets were no longer asleep in Sunday slumber. People walked, talked, and laughed aloud. On certain corners, large groups of young boys in shirt sleeves congregated and talked. They called each other by their first names, often making obscene gestures as they chattered. Groups of young girls strolled along, arms around one another's waists, deliberately ignoring the loud exchanges. The small coffee-shops were full of men and women seated around tiny marble tables drinking coffee with milk and eating buttered bread. White electric bulbs glared furiously from the ceilings. Some of the customers had taken their chairs out to the sidewalks, from where they shouted their orders to the waiters inside.

Everyone seemed to know Ciro's uncle, and Ciro could hardly recognize him now. A mysterious change had overtaken him when they crossed the promenade. This was a new Zenón, and Ciro tried to think of the restrained man who sat daily at the family table abiding in silence the inane little jokes everybody made at his expense. He had expanded; he stopped here and there, shook hands with many people, laughed boisterously.

They stepped into one of the coffee-shops and joined several people at a table. These were older people, well-fed and pleasantly garrulous, and Ciro was surprised at the ease with which his uncle fitted instantly into the mellow comradeship that linked them together. The uncle gave a short account of his health, and then almost immediately Ciro became, to his embarrassment, the subject of conversation. They patted him on the shoulder, took delight in his physique, felt his biceps and praised his good looks. His masculinity was the subject of firm, slowly delivered statements. The people sitting at the next table looked at Ciro appreciatively, and with some vague affection.

"Is he really your nephew?" one of the women at the table asked.

"Oh yes," Ciro's uncle protested, "but I can assure you: he is almost like a son to me."

"The boy looks exactly like you," the woman insisted, "what are you trying to tell us?"

"We know you, Zenón." An old man sitting next to Ciro was talking now. "You are too modest. Look at the boy's face. The very face of Zenón when I first met him." The woman had left her chair as the old man spoke, and taking Ciro by the chin she proclaimed the resemblance again, this time in an energetic voice.

"I bet he won't be as wicked as his father," she added. Everybody laughed at this. Ciro looked at his uncle, who seemed delighted.

"You are wrong," another woman in the group said. This one was fat and dark. "With his looks, the little one will very soon be well ahead of Zenón." The laughter was general now and attention was centered on their table.

"Don't be sad, Zenón," the woman went on, raising her voice. "Such is life. I bet he'll live up to your name, though." She winked one eye as she turned around to watch the effect of these words upon her audience. There was a roar of agreement. Zenón was clearly delighted. Smiling, he rose and shook hands with everyone. Then, amid shouts of good wishes, he and Ciro left.

They walked for a few minutes along the noisy thoroughfare, and then turned into a quiet little street lined with small one-storey houses. The iron grates had apparently been removed from the windows of these flats, but the tall shutterdoors and built-in blinds had been kept, obviously to keep the places cool and guard them to some extent against intruders. A great deal of activity seemed to take place behind each pair of blinds.

5

They stopped before one of the houses, decorated with a rim of blue tiles; Ciro's uncle rapped on the blind and they were let in.

It was cool and dark inside. After a while, Ciro could make out a large room, poorly furnished, with a few heavy rocking chairs placed around a table. A gramophone was playing in one corner of the room. Two round vases of painted earthenware, filled with dusty wax flowers, stood on the table. A large framed lithograph of the Sacred Heart hung from the wall, and a leaf of holy palm had been nailed to the wooden frame.

Ciro saw three girls in the room. Two stood behind the slatted doors, peering through the blinds, and the other, a blond thin girl, was doing her hair with the help of a Negro boy who sat on the arm of her chair. The girls wore slacks, with small linen or cotton blouses covering their chests.

There was a huge ice-box in a small alcove next to the room, and a little old woman busied herself arranging bottles of beer in its compartments. The visitors were greeted warmly by the Negro boy and the young girls, who nevertheless remained seated and went calmly about their own business.

Ciro's uncle walked over to the old woman by the ice-box.

"Is she in?" he asked.

"She's in her room, I think; I'll call her. Shall I pour beer for you?"

She poured from a bottle and then looked at Ciro, without a word.

"No, thanks," he said, but at a gesture from Zenón she poured some in another glass and handed it to him.

A tall pretty woman arrived presently, having entered the room from a small court lined with painted buckets and pails seemingly intended for growing plants. She was big-boned, and walked with a pitching movement on a pair of tiny slippers, waving her arms to help herself forward. She had beautiful black hair, which she tied at the back of her head in a very tight *chignon,* and she was wearing a dressing gown. The black mass of hair pulling from her eyelids seemed on the point of snapping from her forehead.

"It is you, Zenón," she said smiling. "Ah, the son of a devil. He has forgotten us!"

6

"How could you say such a thing?" protested Zenón. They embraced affectionately, patting each other's back with noisy slaps.

"Have you had a drink?" she asked, and then turning to the old woman, "*Vieja*, are you keeping Zenón cool?"

"Do not worry, we are fine," Zenón assured her.

"Did you see my new acquisition? It wasn't here when you last came around," pointing to the big ice-box, its nickel moldings shining in the half-light of the room.

The gramophone was blaring very loud now. "Dago," the woman shouted to the Negro boy, "shut that thing. It's driving me mad."

The boy got up from the arm of the chair and walked to the machine. He was muscular and big and there was something comical in the way he wiggled his hips and in the thin stream of voice coming from the huge dark frame. He had been looking at Ciro all the time, grinning occasionally.

"And who is the young fellow?" the tall woman asked now, noticing Ciro for the first time.

"My nephew," Ciro's uncle announced.

"The one you used to tell me about? But he's big, a real big man now. He favors you, Zenón. *Vieja*," she addressed the old woman again, "pour some more for this one here." She moved and spoke calmly, peering deliberately into Ciro's face with all-surveying eyes which often gave off a faint scintillation of amusement. She carried a hand-bag under one arm, which gave the impression, puzzling enough when it came to the rest of her attire, that she was about to leave. She shifted the bag and took a lit cigarette the old woman handed her.

"It's been a hellish day," she said.

"Yes, it's been warm and oppressive all day long," confirmed Zenón.

"On such a day one should remain under cold water."

"You are right," Zenón agreed, "one should."

She pondered a while and then walked to the gramophone and played the same record again, very loud. The heat seemed unbearable in the room now. Ciro sat on one of the chairs, near the rustic bar built by the ice-box. The blond thin girl whom he had seen doing her hair when they arrived walked over to him after a while.

"Let's dance," she said. Ciro got up, took her by the waist, and started to dance with short clumsy steps. Nobody paid any attention to them and that made Ciro happier than he had been for quite some time.

"Your hands are damp," she said.

"Yes, they are," Ciro agreed.

They walked to the machine when the music stopped, and from the corner of his eye Ciro saw the other boy starting after them.

"Let me do it," the boy said, kneeling in front of the gramophone and fumbling with the tiny disks.

"Lay off, Dago!" the tall woman shouted from her place, turning her head, "lay off!" The boy left them, giggling, though visibly annoyed. He lifted his arms above his head as he walked away and broke unexpectedly into loud laughter.

"Dago is a little crazy," the girl explained as they danced again. Ciro said nothing. They danced for a while and then stopped to drink the beer the old woman poured. Ciro could hear his uncle and the tall woman chatting in a low voice.

She turned to consider them now from her chair. "Show him the place," she called to the girl, without addressing her by any name. "Take him around the house."

The girl grabbed Ciro's hand. "Let's go out back," she said. They left the room and crossed the tiny court with the painted buckets. Four small rooms overlooked the yard. There was a charcoal stove built into the rear wall, and protected with a zinc cover. Dago and one of the girls whom Ciro had seen standing behind the blinds were talking, sitting on the steps to one of the rooms.

They walked to the end of the little yard. "This is my room," the girl said. "It's cooler inside than out here." They went in and she closed the door behind her. A low wooden partition separated her room from the others, and they could hear Dago and the girl chat on the other side. "Sit down," the girl said.

Ciro looked around. There was a single chair with a porcelain basin and a jar sitting on it. Two or three slices of soap were on the floor around the chair. There was also a large iron bed with long posts rising almost to the ceiling; these were connected by rods, and a mosquito-net was strung across the top of the square frame.

A crucifix hung from the wall over an unpainted night-table, and two small religious lithographs had been pasted to the wall on both sides of the crucifix. A small bouquet of red and yellow roses stood in a glass filled with water. A few dresses hung from a string nailed to the wall, opposite the bed.

Ciro sat down on the edge of the bed. The girl started to re-arrange the flowers, emptied the glass in the basin and refilled it from the jar.

"I must keep them contented," she said, carefully placing the glass on the table again. "My saints, I mean. They are very good to me."

"Yes," Ciro agreed.

"Are you religious?" She took his hand now. "You must be." Ciro smiled again and said nothing.

"Your hands are still cold," she said.

"It's warm here, though," Ciro said.

"Yes, but it will be cooler in a few minutes. It's getting dark now."

"Yes, it's getting dark," Ciro agreed again.

She took a little handkerchief from one of the pockets in her slacks and began wiping the small crucifix and the lithographs on the wall.

"I was very sick last year, in this very room. And I prayed for a long time that they would save my life, and they did. I keep fresh flowers here, ever since. Do you go to mass?"

Ciro looked at her and gave no reply.

"Do you?" she insisted.

"On Sundays," he said.

"You do better than I. I rarely go, but I pray here."

Dago and the other girl were having a violent argument now, on the other side of the partition. Ciro could hear the torrent of words, uttered in the boy's high-pitched voice. "Dago is jealous," the girl said. She was sitting on the bed now. "He acts like that whenever he gets jealous."

"Like my new dress?" She pointed to a hook on the wall. Ciro looked up, lifting his eyes for the first time since they had started to talk.

"This one," she said, rising from the bed and taking down a

green frock which looked too small for her. She was thin and fairly well built, except for an ugly brown burn on her left arm, which she didn't try to conceal.

"Like it? I love a new dress. Here, smell the material. Doesn't it smell good and clean? It makes you feel good."

"Yes, it is true," Ciro said, "it makes you feel good."

"I used to have an evening dress. That was some time ago, though. I had a picture taken. Here."

She opened the night-table drawer and took out a leather wallet from a batch of odd papers, curling tongs, and worn out puffs. She looked through the wallet and finally took out a small photograph. She was wearing a long gown in the picture and looked prettier and much younger. The ugly burn was showing on her arm. Ciro looked at her again, realizing that she was not very young any longer.

"It was taken at a big party, in Traganza."

"I know the place," Ciro said.

"There is a small pond and a stand where people dance, and they sell drinks near the stand."

"I know," Ciro was delighted at the girl's description of the familiar places he had inspected with morbid curiosity from the road.

"How come? I bet your mother doesn't know that." She was laughing now.

"I've seen it from the road, when we go diving to Dueñas."

"It's nice in Traganza."

"Yes," Ciro said, "but it is cooler in Dueñas."

"Oh no, it couldn't be nicer than it is in Traganza."

"No," Ciro insisted again, "it is much nicer in Dueñas. You may rest assured."

"You win." She was amused.

"That day in Traganza," she went on, "a friend of mine announced that I could sing, and they made me climb up on the stand."

Ciro had a sensation of extreme well-being now. The beer had delivered him into a soft mellowness, from which he had no desire to emerge. Dago had quieted down, though Ciro could still hear him walking past the door, presumably on little errands from the zinc cover to the room in front. A rooster crowed now and then in a nearby yard. Through an opening at the top of the door Ciro could see a piece of sky.

The girl was lying near him, on her back. Propped on one elbow Ciro watched her.

"Sing," Ciro said.

She began to sing in a low voice, looking up at the wood-panelled ceiling. Her hands crossed behind her head she sang absently, or rather hummed to herself. Ciro wondered once whether she was aware of his presence at all. She went on singing for a long while, and then stopped. She untied her hair slowly and wove it back into a single loose braid on her shoulder.

It was getting dark in the room. Ciro thought of his uncle, but didn't make any movement. Finally the girl rose to her feet. "It's late now," she said. "Your uncle must be getting impatient out there."

"Yes, I must go," he said.

She got up, took a hairpin from the night-table drawer, pried it open with the aid of her front teeth and plunged it into her braid. The hair was smooth and very blond on the nape of her neck. She walked unhurriedly to the door and opened it. They went out into the little yard again, and retraced their steps back to the room in front. The doors to the other rooms were now shut. She put her arm around Ciro's waist and they walked very slowly as they came through the narrow hallway.

There was only one girl in the front room; she was peering into the street. The old woman stood by her ice-box. Zenón and the tall pretty woman were still chatting in a subdued voice, but they got up from their chairs when they saw Ciro.

"We must get ready to go now," Zenón said, "it's late." He walked to the old woman and handed her a few coins. She tipped her head to one side and then to the other, as though a little abashed. "Buy yourself cigarettes," he said, "and take good care of your ice-box. It's a very good ice-box, so spacious and shiny." He nodded to the tall woman. "Very fine," he added, "it is really very fine, you may have my assurance." She gave a pleased smile and proceeded to show her visitors to the door.

"You come more often to see us, Zenón," she said as they stepped out into the street; and then looking at Ciro: "You take care of this one too."

Ciro and his uncle walked back again through the old section of town and turned into the street leading to their house. It was really dark now, but from a distance Ciro could make out his aunts leaning against the balcony rail, their arms resting on the brocade cushions. A few minutes more and they were home. They went up the stairs and were let in.

"You are late for supper, you two," Felipa said. Ciro sat at the table and helped himself to a piece of the Sunday roast.

The other members of the family took their places around the table and started to eat.

"It was rather pleasant out," Ciro's uncle said.

"Was the square very crowded?" Felipa wanted to know. "Being Sunday it must have been." Ciro was aware of a vague deference in her bearing.

"There was quite a crowd," Ciro replied; and then frowning, "the usual one, they are always the same."

When dinner was over, Ciro sat on his stool at the far end of the front balcony. The street was empty now, except for the breeze rustling gently about him. He looked up at the summer sky and then, for a long time, he looked down in wonder at the street, where no noise could be heard.

In San Isidro

Nobody comes to this part of Havana. San Isidro stinks too much of stale commercial coitus. Along with the smell deposited here by countless armpits of slaves, brought from Guinea in the foul holds of ships and cast onto the Machina Pier or Luz Pier, there's the sickening smell of the first Chinese tricked into the six-month voyage from the Yangtse, the fresh basil smell of the first kept women, the smell of the cologne worn by the French and Cuban pimps, the smell of onions rotting in the warehouses, the smell of useless disinfectants and used condoms, the greasy smell of Jewish kitchens. And all these smells have combined into a great smell of rotten mangoes, ancient prostitutes, age-old bladder infections, white flowers, and death. And this is the splendid smell that rises from the whole neighborhood. It must have started at the old Paula Pier. It's the smell of infamy, pus, and vomit. If you haven't smelled it you don't know the full measure of the uselessness of human suffering. Three centuries of suffering, almost four.

About this time it starts to seep up from the gutters. Those who live here don't notice it, they're immune to smells. Spend a month in San Isidro and you can sleep the rest of your life on a battlefield two days after the battle, when they haven't finished burying the dead, or in an elephant graveyard. What pours out over the street are the fumes of three centuries of futility; they drive away even the animals. The sad remaining brothels lock their doors, where hardly anyone knocks. Shutters close with a muffled sound. An icy liquid oozes from the deadened streets.

Now the smell is enough to paralyze you, to drive you mad. Not a soul goes by, not a breath of air stirs, not a sound is heard. It smells of the blood of many layers of humanity, of millions of arms drained of life, of festering slime, of incurable tumors. The district is three centuries old, but those are really three long ages of weariness. If this is

*the New World, the rest of the globe must be immensely old. No one
leaves here but for the great morgues, built before anyone thought of
air conditioning. Here, a madhouse seems a cheerful place bathed in
golden sunlight, a hospital is really a luxury hotel where no one suf-
fers, a prison is a model school.*

*You can't walk any more; the smell has overrun everything, para-
lyzed everything, petrified everything. It smells like the breath of some
carrion eater at the end of his feast. You can't shout. Your shouts go un-
heard, there's no echo in this heavy sticky air, in this suicidal stench.
The empty circus must have smelled like this after the banquets; and
the smell must have remained hidden in some unknown subterranean
conduit in Rome, only to surface here and now.*

*It's really nothing but a marvelous smell of blood, orgasm, dust,
and human sweat, but so concentrated and distilled that our sense of
smell no longer recognizes it, and it produces madness.*

AT 3 A.M.

*They're really just exaggerations, stories people tell, people from back
in 1910, from when the great pimp Yarini got killed, people who don't
have anything else to talk about and get bored. These visions are the
ectoplasm of legend, which once it starts creates its own world and its
emanations and its white foam. If you look carefully you don't see what
you thought you saw. Just ask this old Jewish madam who spends her
life spitting uncontrollably and at an incredible speed, sixty times a
minute, until they take her away, exhausted, still spitting, drained by
the ulceration in her mouth that's been making her spit ever since she
got off the boat that brought her from Rumania a million years ago.
Or ask this perpetually queasy peasant who's been pregnant for twenty
years, with the same disturbing belly that never changes size. Both of
them, how horribly indifferent they are to everything! Sad creatures
who dance a terrifying danzón, so exasperatingly slow that the spectators cry out in desperation. Sitting there in a huge chair, a fat woman,
the mother of all fat women, presides, smiling steadily with an expression of infinite pleasure and with her eyes closed, as though smiling at a
vision seen only by her. She sits there naked and barefoot; her gigantic
breasts are so white they dazzle you. Head and visage are dwarfed by*

14

this huge body, but thanks to the smile the face abides and dominates the street. All look at it with an air of deep-seated affection.

This public consists entirely of men of a sickly white color. They stand there ruminating in their grotesque underwear with their socks held up by garters.

The street is now empty and clean, without a speck of dust. Everything is so clean it's disgusting; the absence of dust produces a trembling; it's an insane emptiness that no one has contaminated or spat into. The air's been sucked out, and the heat is stifling. The walls are nearing the point of combustion. The sides of your arms split open, with burns that immediately begin to discharge pus. Nothing is moving, everything is baking. Although it seems that nothing is happening, everything is frying, bubbles of boiling fat burst through the skin and disappear quickly in the oxygenless air. The peepholes in the shutters are burning quietly and reach those extreme high temperatures at which heat becomes icy. You have to walk down the middle of the street so as not to disappear, stuck on these livid walls that dry the skin. You can hear the heat, and it's amazing that everything doesn't burst into flames. Next to the walls it's frightfully cold. The walls burn with their cold, and to irritate the wounds instantly, they exude a sticky fluid like that of some plants.

The walls swell, contract, tremble with their immobility. Nothing can burst in this exasperating vacuum. The hands become inflamed, you have to grope your way forward with your eyes closed so your eyeballs won't melt. The wax boils thickly inside your ears. Balconies throb with shudders that agitate the void and strike your eardrums. It's become impossible to find your way; not even Christopher Columbus's compass would work in this place, and the admiral would wet his pants in fear. Only the ancient stenches remain firmly in control; in this forest of glaring lime they soothe the soul and lead it down the consoling pathways of hope.

AT 4 A.M.

Your street corners secrete horror, they open wounds. At night you can hear them weep with fear as the ghosts of whores and headless pimps walk by, drowning in their blood as punishment for their cruelty.

Your sewers haven't worked for thirty years; they're choked with the mournful semen of twenty despairing generations.

Rock me in your arms, rock me, O tender, rheumy-eyed great mother! I want to join those despairing ranks, take part in the great banal sorrow of your suicides, smell the first spurt of blood from the slit throats, hear the last moan of the hanged. Rock me in your great leprous arms, pus-smeared lover; feed me from the great raw pustules of your breasts; nourish me with the fluids of your body, with your blood, your sweat; quicken me with your foul acrid breath; pour the putrid blood of your arteries into the putrid blood of mine. Let me have a share in your pain and infamy, let me have a share in your ulcerated wounds, father San Isidro! Make me clean, compassionate old whore, with the pus of your monstrous wrinkled thighs, purify me with your secretions, wash me in the downpour of your urine. Don't exclude me from your pain, don't exclude me from your sorrow. Save me, save me, putrefy me, you alone can save me! In you alone will I find rest and love. Impregnate me, mother, with your smell of aromatic oils and cesspool, of patchouli and vomit. You alone, mother, can purify me, your suffering alone can redeem me. At my last hour, mother, father San Isidro, sublime toothless faggot, plunge my swollen, rotten body into the waters they've assigned you in the old bay, there long to lick the pus of your ancient flank, along with the debris and the dead fish.

Homecoming

"Mais essayez, essayez toujours . . ."

J.-P. SARTRE, *Les Jeux sont faits* (final scene)

I

What was the right term for those things? Freudian slips? Alienation of the self? He had trouble translating the fashionable psychological concepts, which he'd read in English, only half understanding them, mainly to impress others.

But which, which of the many actions he was taking and had taken, were truly authentic acts and not just effects of the last hasty reading of some book whose pages he had barely begun to cut with the precious paper knife with its fantastic handle, or of some half-followed conversation, or of the influence of his most recent acquaintance, or of the last movie he'd seen?

Within the spectrum of all the acts possible, he had sampled an enormous variety in the forty years of his life; but none seemed to have the least consistency. All had been as though written on the sandy bed of some meandering stream, and all retained the barren taste of sand.

It was as though a vacuum intervened between him and each of the episodes in his life, between him and the people he knew and who seemed to be more or less fond of him, so that he viewed all of it from far off, as distant objects congealed within seconds of their birth, while he was unable to cross the terrible barrier and touch them.

And after every episode—that's what you had to call them— of traveling, loving, hating, working, talking, he was left inert, indestructible in a way, as though whole and untouched, not consumed, not used, ready once more to be filled with possibilities, like a stubborn virgin whose virginity could be miraculously restored at the end of each night of love, the top of his head shining through the thinning hair, temples a little gray, but his face still young, strangely boyish beneath the scattered lifeless tufts.

His hands betrayed his real age. They were the hands of an old man, a bit gnarled, as though battered by a thousand lifeless and bloodless acts, a thousand caresses haphazardly bestowed for lack of something better to do.

"But how long are you going to keep that boyish look!" his women friends would say, interesting women with a certain tired elegance and lovers even tireder, and envious of the perpetual rosiness of his cheeks.

His imagination was extraordinarily potent. And it was, as he told himself with painful lucidity, the only life he had, his only true and authentic life.

Walking along the street, at the dinner table, in the bathtub, on first waking up, reading for hours with his eyes fixed on a single letter, talking to people without talking to them, looking at them without looking at them, at the theater during half-heard plays, listening to music without following it, working without working: always he would imagine.

He would imagine that he could speak to all human beings, from whom he felt separated by that strange impassable vacuum. He made up for the vacuum by imagining that he was talking and being listened to most attentively and then quoted by everyone and invited everywhere. He imagined that everyone was looking at him, that youths fell under his charm, that he was admired and desired by all. He imagined an endless conversation, brilliant, caustic, and profound, in which only he took part, talking, talking at top speed, intelligently, pouring forth brilliant ideas about the currently fashionable philosophy, poet, or novel.

His amatory ventures were almost all, if not imaginary, at least highly imaginative. He spoke passionately to the objects of his adoration, who were almost always too busy to see him; he wrote them endless letters, which he never mailed; he imagined great scenes of amorous ecstasy, of physical pleasure, of spiritual communion, which were never translated into realities. As he burst into imaginary places he surprised his darling of the moment and meted out punishment with a clever phrase, and pardon with an understanding smile.

Furthermore, he was obsessed with thinking of himself as the man of destiny who solved the most delicate problems, reconciling conflicting views, preventing possible wars, rescuing whole countries from disaster. His old age would be bathed in a glorious golden glow, as generations of the high and mighty would come to his peaceful retreat in search of his wisdom. His greatest fear was of those deadly Saturdays of the immense city of New York where he lived and which had drawn millions of others like him, and of the empty Sundays with their terrible taste of ashes.

This sensation became most acute during the periods of his most intense infatuation with his successive new darlings. Then only they and their words were real. Everything else took on an undefined color, became blurred, and surrounded him with a world of sorrow in which he dragged himself along painfully, barely able to perform life's most indispensable acts and utter the most essential phrases, pressing his hands against his stomach in a nervous gesture habitual to him, until the current darling reappeared and spoke; and then for a few hours his universe grew calm and regained its reality.

Each new incumbent had the power of demolishing a whole world of ideas, genuine or borrowed, and of attitudes. When Alejandro came upon the scene, so deliciously ignorant of everything, so marvelously contented and at peace in his ignorance — and then, so balanced, so confident, so impassive and free of all problems — he began to feel deeply ashamed of his years of reading. Ah, to be like Alejandro, to *be* Alejandro!

From the calm depths of his eyes Alejandro would sometimes look at him curiously, wondering who this strange being might be who showered presents on him and avoided his presence, who wrote him very odd letters not devoid of a certain melancholy elegance of style, and spoke to him of premonitions and intuition, assuring him that he could sense him from any distance.

This talk of premonitions was a residue from another passion, a gruff and irritable Argentinean, an exiled member of some obscure group in Buenos Aires, who, along with a spurious *porteño* accent, left him with a great love for spiritualistic writers he never found time to read. The Hindu resignation he had borrowed from the Argentinean went very well with an elegantly cynical tone that he thought was in vogue in Santiago and had enthusiastically adopted from a Chilean mistress.

He could not stop himself from faithfully imitating each one of them, copying gestures, speech, good or bad habits, and never resting until he'd turned himself into an exact facsimile of his beloved, trying at the same time to keep up the first impression that he thought he had made, of the great seducer, the unattainable yet desirable lover. In exchange for one kind word he overwhelmed them with absurd gifts, promised them a life of perpetual ease at his expense; and more than one, of parasitic inclinations, had taken him at his word.

He had a few friends, mostly young married couples, in whom he sensed a certain tenderness and whose life he envied, ascribing to it a degree of happiness that was far from corresponding to reality. They would show him little courtesies, and he would in turn perform services for them with no awareness of their true value and in the same sleepwalking manner in which he went to work every morning. These friends, who no doubt appreciated him, were somewhat intrigued by the elusive mysterious life of that man who turned up when least expected, after a long absence, and in whom the only sign of each new crisis, each new passion, was the exacerbation of his violent stutter.

Because, to top it all off, he stuttered. This was his greatest humiliation, the painful vestige of some dark unknown tragedy of his childhood. In agony he would await the inevitable moment when people would turn away to stare at an apparently fascinating spot on the floor so as not to see the convulsions of his face, contorted by the word that stubbornly refused to let itself be pronounced. Once the crisis had passed, he would simultaneously blush and grow pale; and to prove that his defect was purely imaginary, that it had never, never existed, he would launch into a rapid and pointless harangue, peppered with brilliant phrases, jokes, and bursts of inopportune laughter, until he would stumble on another odious word that would produce new convulsions. Blushing with embarrassment and shame, he would seek refuge in his apartment, shut

the windows tight, and light the gas flame of his heater, sorrow-
fully asking himself whether it might not be better to let the gas
escape unlit.

And then he would tell himself that the world of his imagination was the only one worth living in, would gather the audience for his great moments and imagine the usual earth-shaking
crises; and as he charmed the one and resolved the others, his life
gained new meaning, his heart grew calm, and, as he heard the ap-
plause and received the thrilled handshakes, he felt the tears stream
down his cheeks and he embraced all of humanity in one immense
embrace, fervid and compassionate. Ah, humanity, poor, sad, ill-
starred humanity!

Like millions of others in the enormous city, he lived completely alone in an old apartment that had to be heated with gas
or coal (there was no central heating) and that was freezing cold
every morning. The building was one of many thousands built
for working-class families during the last century. As successive
generations prospered and moved away in search of more modern housing, these dilapidated, half-ruined buildings came to be
inhabited by ancient ladies, widows who survived on the provi-
dential welfare check, old men who worked as night watchmen in
some factory while they waited for death, pianists without a piano,
violinists without a violin, singers without a voice on whose walls
a forgotten recital survived in a yellowed snapshot, actors out of
work, actresses with no role, and by the enormous mass of people
that poured into the city from the hinterland, endowed with some
little talent that had led them to break out of the comfortable ruts
of life in their home town and condemned them to die of loneliness
in cramped rooms, dashing every morning from an empty bed (or
one temporarily shared with some kind but fleeting guest) to light
the gas heater and drive off the cold.

Because of the general housing shortage, it had become the fash-
ion among artists, pseudoartists, and people with more originality
than means to rent these small places and decorate them capri-
ciously until they became a strange mixture of extreme poverty and
useless eccentricity. The decoration varied with the tastes or aspira-
tions, hidden or avowed, of the inhabitants. From a filthy corridor

you would come into a little living room adorned with exquisite gold-framed mirrors. From a leaking ceiling a surrealistic eye contemplated the frantic lives of the current tenants. Bright prints of French castles proclaimed that their owners had been to Europe and had most decidedly seen and done it all. A smell of incense flooding the dirty hallways revealed the inclinations of those who spent the nights squatting next to their ancient ever-cold stoves, meditating.

A whole world of folk whose chief aim in life was to make it clear they'd seen it all, living next door to a world of folk left over from the last century, who'd never seen anything. Time passed quietly, with loneliness as the sole unifying element; and the old ladies, as they panted up the stairs carrying pieces of firewood to burn in their old stoves, saw little difference between the pale faces of the first generation of tenants and the pale faces of the generation following.

His next-door neighbor had come from Central Europe as a young woman in the long-gone days of the Emperor Franz Joseph. Her children had been born here, and here they had left her. She had received him warmly when a young couple had decided they were philosophically incompatible and he had taken over the tiny rooms they called an apartment, appearing there in the full flowering of his Japanese period, with splendid kimonos of perfumed yellow silk that dazzled the good lady, and fragile screens of bamboo and rice paper with which you could in an instant create or dismantle even tinier cubicles. His neighbor, barefoot just as she had been when working in the summers of her far-off village and with her perpetual kerchief over her head, helped him to clean up the debris left behind by the none too neat young couple. She opened boxes; she was frightened by the hideous masks of Japanese theater; she marveled as she opened the fans that went on to decorate the walls; she unrolled, before he could stop her, the just-imported mat of aromatic straw; then, under the expert direction of the pale tenant, she hung the large Japanese lantern that was to decorate the kitchen, set up the wind chimes by an inside window to fill the room with the fragile music of glass as they quivered in the breeze, helped him to store the luxurious pure wool serapes from an earlier period, and, almost with tears of gratitude, accepted the aromatic green tea that could only be bought in very special shops in remote corners of the city.

When the first admiring connoisseurs arrived, the kind neighbor discreetly withdrew.

She and an ancient Irishwoman enveloped in many a layer of time and dirt, always on the lookout for the mailman, sometimes the bearer of good tidings and on some mornings the source of her newspaper, would be the only elements of continuity in the series of mutations that he and the few square feet of his habitation were to undergo.

II

One day, his terrible consciousness of each of his acts shed its light on the sum total of all the acts of his life, and he was stunned. He pushed the idea aside; but it burst in on him again, ever more frequently. Ceaselessly he would go over and over the years of his life, the days of his years, the hours of his days; and the idea never left him for a moment, but tormented him and eventually brought on nausea. For a long time he lived in a kind of stupor, walking down the streets only half conscious, his thoughts frozen into a fixed image that he could not escape. He grew paler, he stuttered more, he avoided his old friends, he pressed his hands against his stomach more frequently with that nervous gesture of his; and when, on rare occasions, he did find himself in the company of others, he sat there absent-minded, taciturn, with nothing to say, not at all the witty fellow everyone found so charming.

News from afar of a death in his family reminded him of its existence, to which he had been giving little thought, and brought him out of his silence. He had to go to Cuba, to his country, in which he hadn't set foot for years, dismissing it with a vague gesture as something incorrigible and hopeless. He had been born there, of foreign parents; but his way of acting, of talking, and of being had nothing in common with that of his countrymen. Meeting any of them always made him extremely uneasy; he would become more nervous than ever and make endless desperate but useless efforts to prove to them that he was one of them. But he didn't dare to go there. In a vague way he was afraid he'd end up by feeling like a stranger in his own country, and so he put off the trip indefinitely with a gesture of annoyance: "I love it from a distance."

When the tragedy struck his family he suddenly felt obliged to put in an appearance, though he could not have explained even to himself why he felt this sudden loyalty to his far-off relatives; and so, after acquiring an abundant supply of tranquilizers, barbiturates, apathy-producing roots imported from India, and outlandish clothes that in case of need would always help him to set himself off from the natives, he embarked on his voyage.

He was agreeably surprised. These people, whom he had feared for reasons as unknown as those for his violent stutter, received him in the most natural way, even affectionately, smiled at his fits of nerves, let him dress as strangely as he wished, with an artless tolerance for everything foreign that he found quite disarming. "He's lived abroad so long . . ." was the justification they found for him.

His relatives discreetly allowed him the freedom he had feared losing within the narrow limits of that small country; and the old friends of the family paid a good deal of attention to him, treating him to delicious and indigestible lunches during which they covertly gazed at him with innocent admiration. What a change from New York, that immense city where nothing and no one had the least importance!

He observed the life of these people through the prism of his rosy stereotypes. They seemed to be happy, infinitely happier than the inhabitants of the harsh city where he lived. Their faces were relaxed; their manner, calm; their bodies, well fed and at peace. Ordinary and everyday things were no cause for embarrassment here, as they were in that other world where he lived. These people were at home in their world. He repeated the phrase several times — they were at home in their world, to be at home in one's world — delighted with his brilliant discovery. Up there in the frozen north he'd lost the old art of being at home in his world (even translating the phrase could be a problem!), and now he'd have to learn it all over again, patiently and lovingly.

Moved by his discovery, a vague smile on his lips, he wiped the tears from his cheek, knowing that the driver of the car taking him from his relatives' house to downtown Havana was watching him.

And then the sun, that marvelous, ubiquitous January sun that comforted him and gently warmed his back, shining down from a clear sky, making him forget the depressing northern winters and the violent shivering that grated on his sickly nerves, and bringing back old memories of childhood: tea under the roof of some delightful, and imaginary, garden house; vacations spent on some never-glimpsed farm.

In the personal relations of those around him he sensed, and envied, a spontaneously sensual intimacy fostered by the splendid climate, the noontime breeze, the bright sunshine.

Ah, the things he'd lost, the things he'd forgotten in his long voyages in other lands! If only he could *recapture* it all, he kept repeating to himself, aware of the Anglicism he was using, but considering it appropriate.

On his arrival, more to impress his sedate relatives (who, anyhow, were not impressed) than because he really wanted to, he sought out a young artist who had stirred up a certain amount of critical commotion and whose name had been mentioned to him by one of the couples he used to visit. He was hard to find, and getting his attention was harder still. Although everyone was very friendly, it took a long time for an outsider in Cuba to enter people's lives, which revolved around small but apparently satisfying concerns. Finally he saw the painter, who introduced him to his friends. The rest was easy. Even though they considered him rather odd and were a bit disconcerted by his stuttering, they soon accepted him, for all his strangeness.

They found his vaguely foreign accent attractive, as well as the contrast between his different ways and unpronounceable name and his pathetic efforts to sound like a native. Since he was a great reader of the dust jackets of books, he knew how and when to quote and was very skillful at it, stopping in midsentence, suggesting ideas for others to complete, covering up his ignorance of a topic with the flood of his frantic chatter. He moved quickly from Kirilov and the absurd act to the notion of the gratuitous and then leapt to the New Criticism and Being-towards-death; and although his new friends soon saw through his pretense and amused themselves by imitating him, he never knew it.

When he got back to New York, loaded with books that reflected every artistic and literary movement in his recovered fatherland, books that he felt himself obliged to read and never did, he was horrified by what he saw around him. He fell back into a profound listlessness from which he emerged only to talk nonstop about his trip, his regained fatherland, the emerald-green countryside, the sun, the sun, the sun.

The decor of his small apartment quickly changed. Gone were the Oriental screens so that the air, what there was of it, could circulate freely, as on the balconies and verandas of his quaint and far-off country. Abstract paintings gave way to simple palm groves presented almost photographically, if not to crude lithographs that faithfully depicted Cuban landscapes. His neighbor's apartment was suddenly enriched with a splendid ottoman, its place taken by two large rocking chairs, dug up in a secondhand shop and hastily repaired. The jazz records and the mournful dances of the Yemenite Jews fell silent; and the dingy rooms were flooded with *criollas* and boleros whose never-changing lyrics sang of dubious love, love in bad taste, and with the notes of some old Cuban dance, endlessly and blissfully repeated.

One Sunday afternoon, more deadly than all the rest, he finally asked himself: What if he were to go home? My God, go home to his own people, to love them all, to be one of them, to live there even if it were among the poorest of the poor, among those who in spite of their poverty seemed so peaceful and content, so *sosegados*. How he loved that word! *Sosegados*—at peace! Wouldn't they find room for him? Wouldn't they be moved by his sincerity?

No sooner did the idea surface than his imagination took care of all the rest. The dreamt-of hours of tenderness, the imaginary afternoons of love, the grand nights, all were quickly shifted aside and replaced with scenes of the reclaimed fatherland. And what if he started a movement, a homecoming? His country's prodigal sons . . . The Prodigal Sons—it sounded so wonderful! Soon everyone would love him. Why, all he wanted was love, just love, the same love that all of poor humanity was really looking for.

He felt more alive than ever, more vital, as he put it; he stopped talking to his former darlings, turned down all invitations, surrounded himself with books and clothes from his distant homeland

and pushed aside or threw out, with a little embarrassment, the books and clothes from all his previous adopted homelands.

The decision had been taken. All that remained to be done was to dispose of the jumble of his furnishings, quit his tedious job, and leave. Leave!

He wasn't worried by what he read in the papers about revolutionary movements in Cuba and the resulting countermeasures; it even made him smile mysteriously to himself. Who knows — with his knowledge of foreign languages, his new books, his prudence, his unusual personality, couldn't he become a messenger of harmony and tolerance among his countrymen? After all, they were all brothers, they understood each other in the great unspoken ancestral language in which men of one and the same land understand each other . . .

III

And so he left. More generous than ever, he distributed his possessions among his few friends, gave away the warm clothes he'd never need in that wonderful climate that was waiting for him and that he'd never, never leave. Out went the books: books of naturalistic philosophy; books on Hinduism, on yoga, on spiritualism, books on socialism, his collection of obscene books, his collection on primitive art. He forced his aged neighbors to accept his motley furniture, and they received it with shouts of shock, delight, and terror.

He would make himself over from the bottom up; soon he would be wholly and exclusively himself, moving into *his* culture, *his* environment, where nothing had to be explained, where everything had always just *been*. And besides, he'd be welcomed into the world of the *intelligentsia*, at whose golden threshold his young friends were waiting for him with their delicious biting humor, their lively imaginative chitchat, so high-strung, all of them, and so happy.

When he got there, one morning, he found the city a little changed. It was hard to say what the change was, exactly. As always, people seemed cheerful and carefree; but there was a kind of uneasiness in the air that at first he couldn't quite put his finger on.

What did immediately strike him was the sight of countless uniforms. On every street corner and at all hours you would see groups of soldiers and police with large-caliber modern automatic weapons. He was struck by seeing that when they were off duty the soldiers walked around heavily armed, holding their girlfriends with one hand and their formidable automatics with the other.

Small military vehicles patrolled along the streets of the old city every few minutes with monotonous regularity, invariably manned by two soldiers and two sailors who rode backward to cover an escape in case of attack.

To immerse himself more fully in the atmosphere of the place he rented a room in a hotel in the old part of town where distinguished visitors used to stay in colonial times; and he smiled, trying not to see them, at the pale young women who came back to their rooms at daybreak, with a weary look and smeared makeup. From his hotel he tried to get in contact with his friends, whom he could not find, no doubt because they were busy just at that moment.

He didn't like the look of the elegant clothes he hadn't been able to get rid of—they seemed too foreign—and so he went out to look for something simpler, something with more of a local flavor to it. He came back exhausted, as though his new surroundings required a great effort for every little act, and happy, with an elegant Irish linen shirt decorated with countless pleats, enough to wear out the eyes of whole generations of seamstresses: a *guayabera*, that neat and cool peasant garment that had overrun all of Cuba in a few years, driving out European attire. He gazed at himself in the mirror for some time, pleased with his appearance. He was still young, not wholly bad-looking in spite of having turned quite bald and of the glasses that corrected his extreme nearsightedness. Here he could start life over again, give it some meaning. Why not? Hadn't he adopted and then discarded, rapidly and with the greatest of ease, countries, religions, cultures, postures, ideas? Now he was going to adopt his own culture, his country, his very own, which, maybe, might just need him.

He stretched out on the cool bed in his room facing the harbor; and as he abandoned himself to minutely detailed visions of his future life in his regained ancestral home, he slipped from rosy wakefulness into happy sleep, like a child, without noticing it.

The second day of his new life, he decided, he would spend at the seashore to gain strength from that fiery air that was going to heal the wounds of his body and his spirit.

Quickly walking along the broad old verandas with a greeting to the ancient faded figures reading their papers next to the windows, he went out on the street, hopped into a taxi, and asked the driver to take him to the beach, any beach. To his surprise, the driver answered him in English; and when he insisted on speaking Spanish, the man insulted him by saying he sounded like a foreigner.

At the beach he was vexed at finding himself surrounded by tourists, and even more vexed when he noticed that, just like them, he was rubbing oil into his skin to protect it from the sun. He laughed at himself for a moment, ordered a drink, and stretched out in the sun.

Hour followed hour pleasantly enough, moved along by the native liquor that sweetly penetrated the senses until it had destroyed the sense of time. (The sense of time: that was what was so different here, that was at the root of this country's, these people's, profound knowledge.)

It was almost night when he left the beach. He was on the edge of town; and although the streets were not well lit and almost empty, he decided to walk toward the city to enjoy the gentle sea breeze, refreshing after the heat of the day. He'd let his thoughts wander aimlessly, wherever the breeze might want to carry them. He felt happy, a little lonely; but that didn't matter now. His new life would begin tomorrow.

He had walked a short way down the avenue flanked by pine trees when a brutal light struck his face, blinding him and making the whiteness of his peasant shirt of Irish linen shine against the darkness. The light came from a car from whose quickly opening doors several uniformed men emerged, pointing weapons toward him.

"Get in!" said one of them; and before he could offer any resistance or ask any questions they dragged him into the car, which immediately drove off.

Inside, with the car going at top speed accompanied by the

piercing scream of its siren, he thought he was having a nightmare. He felt his wrists being gripped, and then immediately brutal blows began to strike his face and ribs. The blows took his breath away; he couldn't cry out; and his captors maintained a stubborn silence, as though they knew him, and methodically continued their work. He lost all sense of time; his mental activity was reduced to waiting for each new blow to fall.

The car continued on its way for a long time, ignoring the traffic lights and scattering the pedestrians. It crossed part of the city and then stopped in front of a modern building. They violently dragged him, handcuffed, up a broad, almost luxurious, marble staircase, at the end of which they pushed him into a room lit with fluorescent lights and hermetically shut.

Leaning against a wall he felt the coolness of the granite against his aching cheek and the sharp draft of air coming from an electric fan on the opposite wall, drying his sweat. He had closed his eyes to see better, to think, or not to think; and when he opened them he saw he was surrounded by the men who had brought him and by some others, all looking very much alike. It occurred to him that perhaps they looked alike because they were all in uniform.

The interrogation lasted exactly twenty-four hours.

At first he tried to ask what was going on, but he could barely bring out a single word. He stuttered grotesquely, his head and neck shaking violently. One of them joked, "Spit out the gum, buddy!" and they all laughed uproariously.

Although he decided not to say anything, they asked him his name and he had to make the effort to pronounce it. A violent blow from a stick knocked him to the floor. When they lifted him up, half stunned, he heard the man who seemed to be in charge warn him not to invent foreign names, because they knew exactly who he was. Against his will he began to weep, and with the cuff of his *guayabera* he wiped the blood from his lips and the tears from his blackened cheeks.

Without any violence, almost delicately, a herculean man took him by the arm and asked him to look into his eyes. When he had him facing him and so close that he could feel his breath, he looked at him for a moment. Then, raising his formidable knee with a lightning movement, he buried it in his groin. He fell to the floor moaning and twisting in pain. "Bulls-eye, Fillo! That's sure-fire," he heard one of the men say.

In order to confirm the declaration that it had been a "bull's-eye," Fillo lifted him up again, with the same gentleness as before, and the formidable knee was raised anew. This time he lost consciousness as he fell.

When he came to he found himself lying on a very soft couch. He tried to move his legs, and a brutal pain in his groin clouded his vision. He was drenched in sweat. He opened his eyes and saw the men sitting at the foot of the couch. They were talking and smoking in a relaxed way. He remembered that they hadn't asked him anything more; ever since they'd made him get into the car, they'd gone about their work like someone doing a job naturally, methodically, and without interruption, as though they expected that the mere fact of their doing it would infallibly produce results.

They were talking about an attack that had seemingly taken place the day before. He could sense the huge building around him all abuzz. He heard doors being opened and shut with a bang, amid constant footsteps and voices. Several times someone suddenly burst into the room and then, on seeing it was occupied, slammed the door. People had been killed, among them two high government officials. But he still couldn't understand what he was being accused of, because they weren't really accusing him of anything. If they'd let him speak, call his young friends, he'd explain everything to them and the horrible mistake would be cleared up. Some terrifying words gave him a partial clue to what was going on: "If he's not the guy, it's all the same . . ."

He looked around him. At the other end of the room, two young men were sitting on the floor up against the wall, staring at him. He realized that their hands were tied, because one of them scratched his chin against his shoulder. Their eyes revealed no thought whatsoever, as though they were lifeless. Now and then the younger one blinked.

He realized that he was tied down on the couch. He looked to one side and saw that a wire ran from his right arm to a switch on the wall. Another wire ran to his left arm from some place that he couldn't see. He closed his eyes.

The first shock had the great virtue of making him once again lose consciousness. When he awoke from the second, he screamed with pain. His left arm was enormously swollen. He felt a terrible thirst. He noticed that his mouth was full of clotted blood that was choking him. When he tried to speak to ask for water, he realized he'd bitten off the tip of his tongue. It occurred to him that never again would he stutter. He felt himself smile.

He came to once more when they pulled him out of the car and the breeze struck his face. The sound of the waves crashing hard against the shore told him he was very close to the sea. They left him standing by himself on the rocks, very close to the road. He heard a voice: "Let him be, Fillo, he's finished."

The car doors closed again. He saw the dark shape move away behind the beams of the headlights. He managed to take a few steps, spreading his legs to keep them from rubbing against his testicles. He opened his mouth to let in the cool night breeze.

A few minutes before he died he lost the terrible lucidity that had shed an unbearable light over his last months. Before madness set in, he remembered isolated and insignificant details of his life: the elaborate monogram on a handkerchief, the shape of his fingernails, the most annoying outbursts of the Argentinean, the delicate humid palms of Alejandro's hands.

Then he started to walk, high-pitched screams coming from his wide-open mouth, as he sang, tried to talk, howled, his body rocking back and forth on his spread-out legs, balancing himself, amazingly enough, on the narrow ledge of rocks.

The first place where the horde of crabs sank their claws were his nearsighted eyes. Then between his delicate lips.

Potosí

It looked like rain that morning, just the way I wanted it. When the dock workers started making a racket I jumped out of bed, opened the balcony shutter a little, and looked up at the sky, which was just lovely, low and lead-colored. It was drizzling a bit, so the stevedores had to work with their capes on. What a relief, a day like that, what with this constant sun here in Cuba! They say the dead bring rain on All Souls' Day and cry because they've had to leave the earth, but that's got to be just a story. There've been years when I've had to go out when the sun was so hot the stones were cracking, and I took an umbrella so I could stay all day in the cemetery. After a whole day traipsing around that maze I've come home with a splitting headache and had to call her, and the last thing I want is having to call her. It's worst in Colón. Colón is huge. And then the sun goes down early in November and I've had to run so I could read the inscriptions, with my eyes right up against the marble and no time to wash a tombstone here and there or have a look at the crosses of the poor folks. The Chinese Cemetery is different. You can get through the Chinese Cemetery in a jiffy, and the year I go there it doesn't take me any time at all and doesn't give me any headache even if the sun's shining because since I can't read the inscriptions in Chinese, I'm done right away. Now with the Polacks it's different. They go in for writing the names and dates in Spanish and stuff about David and psalms and six-pointed stars above it all, and I've really got to hustle if I want to read all the inscriptions with the sun blazing down on the Jewish Cemetery of Guanabacoa. If they were like the Chinese and wrote their inscriptions in Polish I wouldn't have to strain to read them all.

And the bay looked just lovely that morning, almost raining but not quite, just drizzling now and then. I put on my suit, because I save it for times like this when it clouds over a little, and I got my umbrella in case it started to rain harder. I crossed the square and looked back at the balcony.

She'd gone out already. I can tell when she goes out because she closes the inside shutters and you can see they're closed through the side windows, and she fastens the hurricane bar from back in the Spanish times, she's so damn scared somebody'll break in and steal her jewelry and money I'm up to here with it, I mean, a ring or two and a couple of pesos! I can tell when she's home, too, because then the shutter's open; she leaves it open so she can look through the window just in case she catches sight of me. Some days I get so fed up with her being there that I won't even look over toward that balcony. And that's when she's not waiting for me down by the street door so she can see me go in or out and be sure I haven't left. I've wanted to move for a long time, but there's no way and I've got to stay here in this place, knowing that if something happens to me the manager will go tell her so she can come before anybody else, just like she's told the elevator guy that if anything happens to her he's to rush right off to tell me. God knows how often I've prayed for the elevator to get stuck and break down for good, so she can't go out; but the damned elevator, that cage kind from back in the Spanish times, the first one, no, not the first one, the second one in all of Havana, it won't break down, and if it does the Polack sends for a repairman, and he's as ancient as she is, and he fixes it right away.

I had a good look when I left the building; she wasn't in the coffee shop having coffee, and when I went around the corner that waitress who always catches a cold in October and doesn't get rid of it till June told me she'd caught an early bus. So I calmed down; I crossed the street slowly and caught the boat to Regla. She must have gone to Colón or Calvario; she likes to go to Calvario Cemetery on All Souls' because it's really small and she can explore it all. That's the only day she doesn't worry about staying out of the rain and complain and say she's gotten old. That's the day she forgets all about her horrible old age and feels young again.

I didn't need to worry because anyhow she'd never dream I might decide to go to Potosí, which she's only seen once, I think, because she says she doesn't like it. If she'd known that was the morning I was going to pay the man for the open book in marble with my name on it and Auntie's, because the man told me he'd

34

set it up for me that morning! It's all right with me if they bury Auntie there. Poor woman, she's sent in all her installments and so the vault's all paid for, and she's had to skip meals plenty of times, because Auntie knows what that one's like and she doesn't want to be buried with her in Colón either, because she says she wouldn't have any peace. And I told Auntie I'd bring her here if anything happened to her and that she'd bring me if anything happened to me so as nobody'd know and she'd never find out where I was and couldn't watch me anymore. And when Auntie says something she does it because when they took my sister away and she came back with the baby, a week old, Auntie was the only one who knew who the father was, but she'd promised my sister not to tell anybody and so she didn't, and when they said she was crazy and locked her up in Mazorra and took away her baby, even then she didn't tell anybody who the father was. And although that one wants to know everything and went to see my sister in Mazorra every visiting day even though she knew every visit made her feel worse and she promised her she wouldn't go see her anymore if she told her who the father was, she couldn't find out and Merci died without saying a thing, not a thing, about who the father was. And she says she'll never forgive my sister as long as she lives for dying without telling her who the father was, because maybe we could at least get money for the baby's doctor's bill out of him and for all those expensive medicines that we had to buy and that are still sitting there, and I know she's keeping them so she won't have to spend any money in case she can use one of them someday. Now burying the baby, no, that she didn't have to worry about, because I paid for burying him myself back when I was working in the office because the baby died before they kicked me out and since I had money and Merci asked me before she went crazy to pay for a first-class burial for the baby, I paid for it and spent a pile of money on a lovely burial and I sure showed her, with her grumbling about spending so much money on the kid.

And Potosí was so lovely that morning! The chapel smells a little of humidity and of mice when they open it on All Souls' Day, because they only open it once a year; but after it's aired out a little it's nice to sit there between the doors on either side. Off through one you see the country, which I really like, just as lovely as can be; and on the other side you see Guanabacoa. And there's some huge trees by the old road. Since the vault is next to the wall I asked the man to plant me a laurel tree, they make such a nice shade, or rather not a laurel because a laurel would jack up the vault that's cost us so much money because the man told me he wanted to do a first-class job even if we paid him a little at a time. Well anyhow, it doesn't matter what he plants as long as he plants something. Besides, since she's never going to come here, whatever he plants, she won't have it cut down, with her crazy talk about how she hates trees and bushes because they breed mosquitoes. But there's no danger of that because she's going to go first although she hopes she won't and that I'll go first. But just in case, since she's so good at predicting things like when she said the baby wouldn't make it and he didn't make it, here I am with the vault all bought and paid for and the bushes the man told me he'd plant so we'd always have shade.

Well, I got sidetracked when I came in because I always like to look in at the bones because out at Potosí the deposit's open and from up above you can see the bones when the sun hits them, very white they are and I think that's why they keep the place open, so the bones will turn white because that way they look prettier, because they don't look pretty when they're dark from the humidity of all those years. Anyhow what I like best at Potosí is that the deposit is open and that doesn't happen at any other cemetery because they don't have the deposit open at any other cemetery.

And besides, what kept me even longer was that when I went in the chapel I copied down what that marble slab says, the one you have to walk over, I copied it again because I like it a lot. Every year I copy it all down and then I tear the paper up so if some day she comes to my room she won't find it and start asking questions, because there's no other slab like that in all of Havana and since she's got a way of finding out everything maybe she'll start asking questions and wind up seeing that I copied it at Potosí and discovering it all. But I'm never going to come back to Potosí and I don't care anymore if she finds the paper, that's why I didn't tear it up and why I've got it here.

And this year I found another slab because instead of going to the vault the way I always go, the chapel was open and they say mass on that day and so I went in and when it was over I went out on the right and I found another slab that I really liked a lot because it's got the strangest inscription and a deaf-mute wrote it for his son who was also a deaf-mute and I read it over and over and I copied it down on my basket. It's the strangest slab and you can hardly understand what it says, but what really gets me is how much it must have cost with all those flowers that make a border around the inscription, and although it started to drizzle again I managed to copy it down and now that I'm not going to Potosí anymore and hardly step out so I won't run into her I look at it all the time.

And what was most surprising about the slab, which was broken at one corner and you could see they hadn't buried anybody there since they'd buried the deaf-mute's son, was that there was an anthill there and the ants were crawling up and down, but then I figured they were probably going down among the deaf-mutes on their way into other graves.

Well I'd spent quite a while what with copying down the two slabs and the mass and a lady who asked me to help her push aside the stone over a family tomb, the kind where you go down and just spend a while sitting there and chatting because they're old tombs, the kind with niches, because all the men, what with its being All Souls' and everything so hectic, they were very busy and the man who always helped her move it wasn't there what with its being All Souls' and all that commotion with the flowers and the people whose conscience bothers them once a year and they go and clean up the graves and they can't even clean them themselves but have to call the man to do it for them and then all those kids that are all over the cemetery that day to pick up some change carrying cans of water for the vases and taking the money away from the poor man who if he can ever earn anything it's that day because sometimes they don't even have any food because he doesn't work for the cemetery and sometimes when I go there and don't see him I leave him candy on top of the graves for his children.

And then I found the man who was dripping sweat with all those people wanting to leave their flowers at the same time so they can get out of there fast and I asked him if he'd set the open marble book on the vault for me and he told me yes he had, he'd set it up the day before because he knew I'd come and he was going to have a lot to do that day and wouldn't be able to set it up for me and that made me feel really good because now I had my vault and after I paid him I asked if he'd seen my aunt because my aunt knows I've been coming here regular ever since we bought the vault and sometimes she comes too, poor woman, and the man said no, sitting over there on the vault, that's not your aunt, that's your *mamá*.

My Aunt Leocadia,
Love, and the Lower Paleolithic

FOR MUNDELE

The other afternoon I went into that enormous storehouse of useful and useless things that in Cuba we call "the Ten-Cen" and that the Americans built with the name "Woolworth" on its façade, a name no one could ever pronounce.

In that great club where we've all killed so many afternoons, young people meet and peek at each other furtively across the counters, and the more daring among them may arrange a romantic rendezvous in a dark movie house or at the little hotel on the Calle Rayo, only to stop loving each other afterwards and go back to peeking furtively across the same counter and trying to stay out of each other's aisle; there are well-dressed ladies who down enormous quantities of food in the midst of the tremendous racket while they tell each other about their ailments, their faces glowing with a hard determination to keep on living; and, among many other things, there are faded gentlemen who go there to let their hands stray among the females jammed against the showcases.

As I was mulling over the possibility of a *café con leche* it occurred to me that, alas, young people had the disadvantage of having no memories and not even knowing that not many years ago the Ten-Cen had stood at the corner of Amistad where now there was a shop, with two towers, run by two solidly middle-class Spaniards, and on the opposite corner there'd been a café with enormous mirrors where the fat politicians with their Panama hats would go to spend the afternoon and which had some private rooms facing Rayo that with their conspiratorial air represented for me the height of sinfulness. But then it seemed to me that very old people would probably think that, alas, in comparison with them I had no memories and didn't even know what you could get in the Ten-Cen before there was any building with two towers, and that in turn the dead were probably feeling sorry for them because they had no memories of when there were no sidewalks on that corner and the street wasn't paved and slaves crossed it on their daily errands, or peasants bringing provisions to the city from the nearby farms, and feeling greater pity or even greater envy for those who are yet to be born, who have no memories and who in turn, once they're old or dead, will pity or envy their descendants for the absence or the ever-renewed abundance of memories. And I thought of something I'd never thought of before while a very chubby and very beautiful waitress served me my *café con leche* as I sat by the entrance from San Miguel. I thought that the dead would always outnumber the living, that the sum of those who have died will always be vastly greater than the sum of those who at any given moment live on the earth, and that the number of the dead is swelling constantly; and in my mind I reread the obituaries in the morning paper and I understood that kind of satisfaction that I always feel when I read them, the satisfaction of a mathematician who sees his calculations confirmed with every passing day. I thought that we live surrounded by the dead, on top of the dead, vast numbers of the dead who are quietly waiting for us in the cemeteries of the world, at the bottom of the sea, in the countless layers of the earth that will never again see the sun; and perhaps, without our even noticing it, their ashes are in the cement with which we build our houses, or in the cup we raise to our lips every morning, ashes of faces and eyes and hands, which stay with us as long as we live and surround us and are by our side and beneath us and on top of us. I thought of the world's huge depositories of bones that turn into dust that the wind scatters and we breathe in, and I thought of the fourth of May 1894 and the twenty-eighth of August 1903 and a day in the year 328 B.C. and of all the millions of human beings who were alive at that moment and making love and deflowering virgins and sobbing and stabbing a brother and masturbating and eating and buying honey and thinking what I'm thinking right now and going to war and treating their sores, and of whose lives nothing remains, nothing, nothing at all, not the slightest memory, because the buildings that housed their lives have already turned to dust and the papers on which they wrote their names have disintegrated and their dust lies beneath many layers of earth that perhaps a bulldozer dug up yesterday morning and a man turned into cement with which another man built the wall on which our hands are resting at this very moment.

The day before, I'd been in the National Library, and carefully, because they were falling apart in my hands, I'd started to leaf through the 1910 issues of a magazine that came out on Saturdays and in which an artist illustrated the week's tragedies: "The Crime in El Guatao," "Her Throat Slit by Jealous Husband during Performance at the Payret," "A Brightly Lit Suicide," "Peasants Hanged Nude in La Luisa," "The Knifing of Tulipán," and so on; or the artist went to the morgue and drew profiles of the bodies lying ever so quietly on the zinc-topped autopsy tables with their crushed skull or the trench running across their neck from ear to ear and the sharp borders of the wound that let you see the beginning of the trachea, or with their head completely cut in two, lying there peacefully on the zinc tabletop, or with the dark furrow of the hanged and their dry mouth half open and the lids half closed over the eyes or one eyeball burst from its socket, or the head of the old black man who turned up dead on the Cerro and on whom they found a piece of paper that said, "I am 140 years old, I was born in the Congo and sold in Havana in 1787," and who knows who wrote it and stuck it in his pocket so that when he died they'd know he was over a hundred; and so the artist filled up his sheet with the profiles of the dead, and as I thought of them I asked myself whether nothing was left of them, whether no one would ever, ever remember them anymore, and the few who did remember them would soon be dead. And I asked myself whether nothing, nothing at all was left, then, of black Pablo Dupuy and the American they found in the bathtub at the Hotel Plaza and the Irish sailor Farrell whose skull was crushed on the Alameda de Paula and the girl I saw yesterday on the corner of Industria and the delicate blue veins of her breasts and the Chinaman Lon Fuy whom they burned on the Calle Soledad and white Esperanza Otero who hanged herself and the homeless mulatto who fell asleep at La Ciénaga and the train cut off his head while he was sleeping. Nothing left of our profiles, calm in death, and our dry mouths and our half-closed eyelids and our slit throats, our bodies mutilated or battered by sickness? And will there be no one to speak of us far off in the next millennium, several meters above us, and we several meters above all the unknown millions who preceded us?

I poured some sugar in my cup, and as I slowly stirred it I set to calculating the number of human beings who have died; but when I finished I realized I'd fallen short.

Feeling a little better, I looked around me. The crowd continued to churn, with those streaming in from San Miguel bumping into those coming from inside the great store. The place was brilliantly lit. In the midst of the throng, a man on a ladder was replacing a sign that said "Giant Raspberry Supercake" with one that said "Hot Dogs, 15 centavos."

The air conditioning, set very high, made me shiver a bit. I drank a sip of my *café con leche,* which was still warm, and then added a little more sugar. I looked down at the clean granite floor that a boy swept whenever the crowd thinned out a little. My imagination toyed with the fate of those few square meters of ground where perhaps only a century before, when this had been a poor district on the edge of town, had stood a wooden house with trees and maybe with a cow, and a century farther back an as-yet-undivided estate held under a royal grant, and two centuries farther back a forest of palms and *yagrumas,* and right there beneath the row of identical chairs where the ladies were chewing, maybe there was a path and a man ran down it fleeing from someone or just because he felt like running, and I reconstructed the forest, which had been dislodged to make way for countless forms of life and where only stealthy or peaceful men had walked, and before them, only frightened animals.

Gradually I came to realize that the very space where I was sitting, surrounded and buffeted by the clamoring crowd rushing to buy one last toothbrush before closing time, had been the patio of my aunt's house, where, in violation of every public health ordinance, she had planted a small ceiba tree in a large tub, and it had gotten too big for the tub and grown as high as the rooms of the upstairs apartment in search of sunlight, and she'd planted some basil and several rickety rosebushes; that the space occupied by the sinks and the shiny coffee urns and the advertisements for ice cream and milkshakes, right in front of me, had been her room, the front room of the huge house, the room with the high-legged wardrobe with the mirror, full of turn-of-the-century clothes and very sumptuous yellowed bed linens. A little farther on, where a noisy group of schoolboys on their way home from school was slurping up large dishes of ice cream, my great-grandmother had died, after spending her days in an armchair next to her bed, in the company of her cat, which slept all day on her lap and which disappeared when she died. From time to time one of her granddaughters would come and undertake the delicate operation of bathing the old woman.

For a moment I stopped hearing the constant noise of the Ten-Cen and remembered that the room opened onto the patio, that it smelled of dried flowers and earth and moldy leaves and damp towels and bedpans that needed emptying and floors washed with buckets of water. A door led out to the patio; the other door had a grill that reached up to the ceiling; every now and then a rooster would perch on the tub and crow; and seen from inside the room, through the grill, the patio had the melancholy intimacy of all the patios in Havana. Every room was a world apart, separated from the others by the doors of frosted glass crowned by a lacework of wooden roses; and when the sun reached the tubs in the patio the light streamed into every room and a swarm of insects blinded by the light rose from the rotting earth.

All of that had been reduced to the endless black counter and the chewing schoolboys and the tremendous din of the store and the background music seeping through the hubbub and the chill of the air conditioning.

I knew my Aunt Leocadia in her last years. In what had been the parlor of the old house on the Calle San Miguel, a showcase with cracked glass panes announced to the world that my aunt was a dressmaker skilled in pleating and embroidery. Everybody talked about my aunt's rich customers, but I never saw anyone come through the door that had been a window in the last century and whose grill was rusting away on the patio floor, behind the ceiba. Now and then the room would shake with the vibrations from complicated electric machines. That meant my aunt was making lace.

But my curiosity and the mysteries began in her room, which I could only glimpse when she opened the doors to take some money out of the huge wardrobe that no one but she ever opened. Gradually I came to know the room's secrets. There was a brass bed with a light switch resting on the pillow and connected to an ancient blue lightbulb hanging from the ceiling, and a dressing table with two purple lamps hand-decorated by my aunt and a powder box with gilded feet and two worm-eaten paintings, because my aunt had studied art at the Academy of San Alejandro. When I remembered that one of the paintings showed the pond in the Quinta de los Molinos, with the artificial island in the middle of the greenish water covered with *suche* leaves, I laughed to myself, and the beautiful chubby waitress stopped and gave me a somewhat hostile look. I avoided her eyes and recalled the time my aunt got sick and they let me go in to see her. She was lying on worn and not very clean sheets and scolding somebody for wanting to use the bed linens, embroidered years before, that she kept in the wardrobe and that no one, but no one, was allowed to touch.

I remembered that my aunt had been forced to sublet the back rooms and those of the upper story to tenants who never paid and who engaged in epic battles that frequently brought on the intervention of the police. A wall separated my aunt's rooms from these others; but one could keep track of her neighbors' private lives by the frequency of their fights, during which they shouted at the top of their lungs.

I suspect that my aunt protected herself against that hostile world by shutting her room off from the outside world. On more than one Sunday I found her completely alone in her vast apartment, going over her out-of-fashion dresses and her linen and batiste bedclothes. I supposed that only the chosen of her heart would be admitted into her sexagenarian virgin's room. Later I found out that the frosted glass doors had been opened several times with ever-fresh faith, only to be closed again, leaving the room's inhabitant ever alone.

Over the years I'd always heard the stories they told in the family about my aunt and in fact often asked to hear them. Once, on the beach in Matanzas, shortly after independence, she'd saved a reckless bather from death, swimming an enormous distance with her in tow. When my aunt emerged from the waves pulling the rash but rescued woman by the hair, the crowd applauded, stirred less by the rescuer's deed than by her splendid figure. I laughed again, out loud this time, partially covering my face with my right hand. Two clerks stared at me and whispered to each other.

My aunt's first suitor had died a tragic death. Someone had shot him during the violent early years of the century. She mourned him deeply and never spoke of him again. If the topic came up in her presence she fell silent.

My aunt's next disappointment in love inflicted deeper wounds that clouded her judgment, never very clear, for a whole long and painful year. Contemporary rumor, which was fond of linking pathology and black magic, attributed her derangement to some powders dropped into a cup of coffee. The fact is that as a result of her unfortunate experience my Aunt Leocadia fell into a stupor that lasted exactly a year. The doctors saw no hope for her; and the family had to be constantly on guard to keep my aunt, who refused to put on any clothes except such underwear as was indispensable for covering her nakedness, from going out into the street to the delight and amusement of the irreverent young folk of the Calle San Miguel and the great anxiety of all the neighbors. Her recovery was as strange and unexpected as her illness. The industrious women of the family had undertaken to embroider a gala cape for a traveling bullfighter, but the work could not proceed beyond a certain point. There was a flaw in the design that destroyed the symmetry of the figures. Suddenly my aunt emerged from her stupor, stood up, and, as she pointed out the mistakes made in embroidering, shook off the deranging influence for good, and the matador could continue on his tour. This episode, too, my aunt never again mentioned; and when I asked her something about it one day, I was met with an icy silence.

I don't know how long after that it was (my aunt had become quite prosperous) that a man came to the house whom she introduced as her partner and who proceeded to settle in the patio, far beyond the tub and the iron washstands. I tried to remember whether this guest had come to the house as one more tenant and the partnership had developed later, or whether the agreement had come first and the partner had then settled by the headquarters of the business. My aunt, over forty now, was still beautiful. She no longer went to the Quinta de los Molinos on Sunday afternoons to paint. With the optimism of those boom days of the twenties, she now believed in the virtues of money and, as always, in the possibility of love. She bought stock in banks that would soon fail and take all her savings down with them. I never heard anyone speak well of her guest, whose arrival no one in the family has ever been able to explain and who was much younger than she. I know my aunt adored him. Her collection of embroidered robes and her less yellowed laces stem from this period.

But the man had bad habits, a passion for the fruit of other people's labor, deep admiration for his own good looks, and a somewhat excessive love of the good life. Once I caught my aunt looking at an old portrait. It was of him. When his real aims became clear and the profits from the business began to go astray before reaching their sanctuary in the front room, my aunt let him take his handsome profile and his questionable habits elsewhere. The breakup must have been a painful one. On rare occasions, when everybody had already forgotten about him, she would suddenly mention him, like someone who wants to get over an unpleasant memory by talking about it.

One day somebody solemnly announced to the family, "Aunt Leocadia's touched her trigeminal."

They all started to get their trigeminals touched and of course that eventually produced a sneeze. My aunt did not recover her youth, nor did anyone else; and the Spanish doctor who guaranteed that touching that small nerve at the base of the nose would not only restore youth but cure every ailment ended his visit to Havana a little richer than when he'd come.

At that time a widower used to visit my aunt. I remember that on Sundays she began to take her faded gowns and other garments out of the wardrobe and dress herself up to receive him. My aunt's new suitor was a heavy, boisterous man clad entirely in white and starched even to his tie. He sported ivory-handled canes, a watch chain and fob, showy tie pins, and a heavy gold watch. He lived off the ill-gotten opulence of the most recent conservative cabinet and spoke of it as Milton does of Paradise lost, but unlike Milton he counted on returning to Eden. My aunt listened to him with fascination. The man talked constantly about an invisible princely past, and the family came to be enraptured with his collection of canes.

At that point I realized I ought to leave. I felt the curiosity of my neighbors at the counter as they kept close watch on me; but I couldn't do anything but stir what was left of my coffee with a stubborn movement of my hand and the spoon, my eyes glued to my empty glass, while the noise continued to swell.

After a while family rumor had it that the widower had moved in with my aunt. I could see him clearly. He was coarse and common; time and events only accentuated these qualities. He slept surrounded by photos of his dear departed. What my aunt came to know were the dregs of a happy but ever more remote past. The years rolled on and his friends did not return to power; and so the thick watch and its chain soon disappeared, to be rescued from the pawnshop by my aunt every year for the widower's saint's day, and the tie pins and the famous cane collection disappeared, along with the remaining suits stiff with starch, and in their place appeared his children, abandoned for years in public institutions of charity. Gradually they followed their father and moved in, claiming to have jobs that never quite materialized; and my aunt saw her family increased by three huge awkward teenagers somehow bestial in their appearance and habits who wolfed down everything, and by their sister, a lively but clumsy creature who talked constantly and at the top of her lungs about the convent home for indigent girls that she had just left, dwelling morbidly on all the attempted rapes and abductions that had occurred in that holy place, and who reacted violently to any suggestion that she be still.

The family, happy to be reunited, aired its differences by brutally screaming at each other in battles that drove my terrified aunt to seek refuge in her room.

These new inhabitants of the house, along with the depressed economy, drove away my aunt's family and her clientele; and she was left alone, with only the widower to defend her from the attacks of the frightful menagerie.

The noise in the store had become unbearable. It was near closing time, and the voices of the customers on their way out swelled to a deafening pitch as the human wave slowly moved toward the San Miguel exit. For a moment a woman rested her whole weight against my back, almost crushing me against the counter. I tried to pay and get out of there fast, but the chubby waitress didn't hear me. While I kept calling her, trying to make myself heard over the deafening noise, I thought of the years of poverty and hunger and recalled my aunt fixing a meal of soup for the famished ward heelers of the neighborhood and participating enthusiastically in their campaigns, believing, as did they, in a possible return to the feast they had lost forever, and eventually politicking herself, hoping only that the widower might be able to work again after all those years of enforced idleness. I remembered that during one fleeting interval of relative prosperity she acquired a massive dining room set that she immediately proceeded to hide under slipcovers, in preparation for a wedding that could not be far off. I took part in these preparations as enthusiastically as did she; but the wedding never took place, as my aunt, with her strange stubbornness, kept putting it off until she'd completed what she called her outfitting. I recalled the many scenes during which the widower threw his children out of the house, while the whole neighborhood would gather out in front and the rest of the family would shrink in humiliation.

And I recalled another occasion when they brought my aunt from a first aid station with her face battered from a fall. By that time she was having a hard time walking. Weeping indignantly, she complained there was no respect in the world anymore. As they'd helped her out of the car that had taken her to be treated, a voice, more solicitous than the rest, had risen from among that crowd of children that always turns up to watch any incident and had recommended, "Hey, hold her head down or she'll crack her old skull!"

Exasperated as I was by my vain efforts to make myself heard through the ever-swelling racket, I must have made a sudden movement, because the woman on my right drew away with a start. With all my heart I wished I could be left alone in that enormous place, as my aunt had been left alone when they made her move out of her home. When the owners of the old house, yielding to an offer from the Ten-Cen, sold the property, my aunt fell gravely ill at the prospect of an eviction. Slowly the rooms were emptied and their contents transferred elsewhere. Most of the lace-making machines were auctioned off because nobody made lace anymore; and away they went, along with the dining room set, the mint and basil in their flowerpots, the stored-away furniture, the widower's trunk, the photos of the dear departed, the moldy roses, and the rusty washstands.

All that was left in the huge empty house was the ceiba and the rosebushes that nobody had pruned in years, and my aunt in her room with its mirrored wardrobe, to which she alone had the key, its purple lamps, and its worm-eaten paintings. As soon as my aunt got well, the wreckers' pickaxe would come to demolish the house.

But my aunt never got well. The widower's children must have sensed she wouldn't, because suddenly they made their peace with their father and set themselves up as best they could in the half-empty house to defend his rights—or so they declared at the top of their lungs. My aunt was a long time dying. Outside, the pickaxe grew impatient while her illness and her dying slowly took their course. Those of us who were closest to her took up positions near her, taking turns at her bedside day and night in a kind of silent battle against the bestial tribe that was shouting outside, pounding on the walls and slamming the doors. As the end drew near and the intruders nearer still, we all felt a sense of duty and put aside our usual occupations to watch solicitously over my aunt's final moments, tacitly united in our determination to beat them to the key to the wardrobe.

The ruckus in the store reached an unbearable level and then suddenly ebbed as the mass of the customers spilled out onto the street.

One day when I came to relieve another relative in the sickroom, my aunt, paralyzed and unable to speak, looked at me with an expression of terror in her eyes, which had once been very beautiful and which over time had come to bulge. The widower entered the room; and when he left, the eyes focused on him and followed him till his shadow disappeared behind the glass door, and then turned again to me, almost bursting from their sockets to guide my attention to the wardrobe, which was closed. Then they looked at me again, and the head moved sideways. I shuddered. I looked at the wardrobe. It stood where it always stood, in the corner; but between one side of it and the wall there was a little gap. The eyes kept looking at me insistently. I went up to the wardrobe and I could see that at its back, barely concealed, one of the boards was resting on the floor. I pulled the wardrobe a little farther from the wall and then I saw that all the boards in back had been moved and that the inside was almost empty. The pieces of lace, the embroidered sheets, the great shawls smelling of camphor, were all gone. Only the old dresses were still hanging from their perches. With a violent effort I looked back at the face that was watching me from the pillow. One of the lamps was casting a pale glow onto the terrified and lightless eyes. My aunt was dead.

It was very late. The Ten-Cen was empty. The chubby waitress had left. A boy was washing the last cups of the afternoon, almost exactly on the same spot where her iron bedstead had stood. A little beyond where the ceiba had grown, two clerks were checking the day's receipts with an adding machine.

I felt the hard polished granite under my feet. I drank the rest of my cold coffee, paid, and left.

The Sun

Two hours and fifteen minutes before the fall of the first hydrogen bomb and before its cobalt sheathing made contact with the eaves of a house by the harbor, generating heat equivalent to ten thousand times the thermal energy of the sun's nucleus and scattering billions of particles of strontium over a radius of a hundred kilometers, to remain suspended in the air for more than five, though not quite six, decades, eliminating all possibility of plant or animal life, the old man recounted the small sum of money on hand for his needs. A little more than a minute earlier (he never did keep track of time) a clock had struck two.

Once more he spread his few banknotes out on his bed, and with them the silver coins and the nickel and copper small change. He lifted the newspaper off the pillow and set it on the chest of drawers by the door, placing it near enough so that he could later put it on the table without having to get up. He avoided all sudden movement ever since he had first gone to see a doctor twenty-four years earlier, and he scrupulously obeyed the order to be careful with stairs. He had set himself a maximum of sixty-eight steps, the sum of the number of steps leading to the apartment of a friend who lived across town and whom he used to visit, plus the number of steps he had to climb as he returned home. The few other times that he left home in the course of the year he always tried to choose a route free of stairs; and if this proved impossible, he either gave up the proposed visit or, if he proceeded with it after long soul-searching, returned home annoyed, because he always had to count with the twenty-nine steps he would be forced to climb in order to regain his apartment.

Being excessively impressionable, the old man had given up his employment twenty years before, when he was still young, because of the fear and torment occasioned by the sixty-eight steps he had to climb every day to reach his workplace (this must be the true basis of his limit of steps allowable, which might at first glance seem arbitrary). As a result, his income diminished. But he was convinced that strict obedience to his doctor's recommendations had prolonged his life, and he felt a certain smugness when he remembered that the physician had died some years before. He had been found dead on the third landing of a staircase leading to the home of a patient.

He finished counting his coins and, without leaving his armchair, stacked them carefully at one end of the chest of drawers in piles of ten, twenty, and thirty, according to a detailed list of budgeted expenses that he kept on a sheet of paper lying permanently on his night table. He enjoyed perfect health, but he always took good care of himself and was convinced that his good health was due to the rigid plan according to which he had organized his life. His younger neighbors felt sorry for him, thinking he felt lonely, and would come to chat with him; but after a while they always bothered and tired him, because they talked nonstop and in loud voices and paid no attention to the topic of illnesses, about which he could have such far-ranging discussions with his second cousin. After a few minutes' conversation he would send them on their way, alleging his need to rest.

During the previous week he had exceeded his limit of steps because of an unexpected complication, the death of a former colleague whose means were too slender to allow for his being laid out in a modern funeral home with an elevator. He ended his week with depressing speculations about how many of his surviving friends would be able to afford a funeral home with an elevator, because, like him, they were all too poor and would have to be laid out in a poor funeral home without elevator or at home, meaning, in most cases, on one of the upper stories of a building or even in an attic, where the rent was lowest. His Sunday was made bearable by his remembering that his oldest friend lived on a ground floor in the old part of the city.

But this week's numbers were better than he had dared to hope. He added up the steps he had climbed and found, to his immense satisfaction, that they did not exceed sixty-two, including, of course, the front-door steps, which, although he clearly understood that they could not properly be considered steps because they were only the means of access to a building, rising very little and easy to climb, he had at last, after a drawn-out debate during which he could not bring himself to consider them genuine steps, been including as such in his weekly accounts. This was the best result he had obtained in some time, and the figures were clear: fifty-eight steps in the week's two round trips, plus the four at the front door, made his sum of sixty-two. There you had it, all very clear, because numbers don't lie. With a slight sigh of satisfaction he wrote down his results, put the small notebook reserved for this purpose back in the night-table drawer, and rubbed his forehead as though he were tired. Then he rose from the armchair, bolted the door, and slowly moved toward the bed. A few seconds later he was sound asleep.

Quickly, but step by step because his legs were still very short, he left the building, juggling a briefcase in which he seemed to be carrying books too large for him. In his left hand he carried a paper bag with his snack. He passed by the legs of two men coming up the stairs. When he reached the street he looked up to a window on the fourth floor of the building. Someone was waving to him. Setting down his briefcase, he waved back and acknowledged the urgent warning to be careful crossing the street. Then he went on his way. The first bell was going to ring any minute, and he'd always won the prize for punctuality.

His deep black hair was carefully combed and his face carefully washed. As soon as they'd bathed him he'd sprinkled himself with talcum powder, but so quickly and inexpertly that as the powder came into contact with the damp skin it had formed large white blotches on his neck and ears. His whole body gave off an air of great cleanliness and neatness. He had lovely black eyes and long lashes, and a skin lightly toasted by the summer sun. The small figure turned the corner and disappeared.

With the unconscious brusqueness of a sleeper she put her hand to her chest and tugged impatiently at her nightgown. As the lace tore ever so slightly, the single button popped off and then disappeared between the sheet and the pillows; and the gown, as it fell open, displayed her breasts and part of her belly. The man sleeping by her side woke up. He had been dreaming that he saw her completely naked, as he liked to see her while she protested weakly, unable to resist his demands, begging him, with sudden inexplicable modesty, to close the shutters, and finally covering her eyes to hide her nakedness. With his awakening his dream came to a sudden end; but contrary to what always happens, he found that reality was even more beautiful. He smiled. At that moment he was, miraculously, able either to continue his dream or hold on to reality, that is, change dreams. He felt he was master of endless possibilities; but this time he did not feel that these possibilities pressed on him or exasperated him, driving him to action, as they did at those moments of violent sexual arousal. He could stretch out his hand and rest it lightly on the naked skin. Or he could go on gazing at her without touching her. Or he could go back to sleep, knowing that when he awoke, the exquisite shape would be there, the color of its delicate blue veins changing ever so slightly beneath the skin as the whim of the clouds made it glow more or less brightly in the noonday light. The range of possibilities sent a shudder through him.

But he did not touch her. He only looked at her. He had fallen asleep totally naked so as to relieve the terrible midday heat. His body was not touching hers, but he could feel the heat given off by her skin, along with a smell of fresh and vaguely perfumed sweat. He drew in the odor of the body sleeping by his side, trying not to make even the slightest sound that might awaken it and not to move a single muscle of his own body. She seemed immune to the heat that rose from the asphalt of the street and came in through the half-open window. He was sure that if he brushed against her, her skin would give him a sensation of fragrant coolness, as though of water. Seeing her like that, separated from her body, drained, sunk in languorous sleep that imparted a deep rhythm to the rise and fall of her breasts, he thought that she belonged neither to him nor to anyone else, that she could float in space indefinitely by herself, exquisitely free and pure, giving off that air of well-being that during their most passionate embraces made him close his eyes with a feeling of profound tranquility. A sense of anguish suddenly came over him as he thought that one day his body might no longer lie next to hers, but her nearness quickly made him forget his fears.

His eyes rested on her leisurely, embracing her with his gaze. He feared he would again feel the stifling pang that the mere idea

of not being with her produced in him, but this time the vision before his eyes and the breathtaking details of her sleeping body were
more powerful than his pain. He felt the blood flow toward his
thighs, slowly at first and then with an unmistakable throb. But he
took delight in putting off the moment when he would touch her,
soothed as he was by the comforting sense of eternity that comes
with the first surge of sexual passion, and feeling that he had all the
time in the world.

With a tired gesture she put out another cigarette. She felt especially nervous and impatient. These crises were not unusual for her;
they were no doubt temporary, but they had become too frequent
of late. She tried to delay as much as possible having to recur to
sedatives to get through these trying hours. The doctor's exasperating face had something to do with it all. Fifteen minutes earlier
he had checked on the patients; and passing by her bed he had
asked her the same routine question that she knew meant nothing,
just as she knew that even as he asked it he was thinking of the answers of the previous patient or the condition of the next. One day
she tested him and didn't answer, and he muttered the same ritual
words with which he always concluded his fleeting visits, without
noticing that the patient had not replied.

   She felt a dull rage, which the conviction that doctors also have
their troubles could not soothe. She was on the verge of ringing to
ask for the sedative that she was authorized to take, but she managed to overcome the temptation. She was sure that if she gave in
to her need for sedatives all the exasperation she had accumulated
in the last two years would suddenly burst forth and that then she
would have no choice but to use them constantly till she could get
out of there.

   With an effort she changed her position, shifting the heavy plas-
ter shell that had once been white and that time and soot were
turning an unpleasant grayish color. By this means she was able to
reach a cooler area of the sheets, a few inches farther over; and this
gave her a pleasant, though fleeting, sense of relief. Her breathing
became more relaxed.

   But with the sensation of coolness came the usual shudder that
ever more often ran down her spine as the moment drew closer—

inevitable but still a few weeks off—when the stout man who seemed to devote himself exclusively to these tasks would come, armed with hammer and chisel, to free her from the casing that held her motionless, so that the doctor's thick hands could again prod into her body to determine whether one of the femurs, which had been dislocated months before, had settled properly into its socket, while perhaps tugging lightly and cautiously to check the firmness of the transplant, which, still tender and pink, was only now beginning to set within her, taking care not to damage the ligaments that were to hold the two structures together and support the weight of the body once nerves, tendons, and muscles set about the task of movement, clumsy at the outset and doomed never to be perfect.

At what point, during all these months that had become years, had the man hindered the formation of even the slightest clot so that the periosteum that enveloped the alien fragment he had just inserted into her body forever might join with that of the two ends of bone exposed to the light for the first time? To distract her mind she used to think about that new resident within her body, one that had perhaps been brought from the far side of town and fixed within her as soon as the drill had finished its patient rasping work. From what other body might it have come? Where and when had it been removed and carefully preserved to prevent the death of its cells?

She often played with this idea to block the arrival of what she truly feared: the first wave of hatred, to be followed by the second and the third and the fourth and all the rest, which could only be checked by complete exhaustion. The same hatred that sealed her mouth during all those visits by parents to whom in theory she should have been grateful for her life and whom she actually credited only with the infinite capacity for violence that was unable to come to the surface and therefore churned inside and devoured her. Ought she really to be thankful to them for her life? After all, had they consulted her concerning the questionable honor of bestowing it on her?

She looked about her, taking in the all-too-familiar landscape of the huge room and of the world that surrounded her and to which she was so tightly linked that it seemed to her impossible ever to break away from it. What she saw was its own best antidote. It was the time of day when that whole world came to a halt under the weight of noon and the effort to rebuild one's life seemed thwarted by the oppressive heat that seeped in from outside. The body was overcome by drowsiness, but if it could make it through this hour it would draw ever so slightly nearer to the point at which its decay would cease and its recovery begin. The same process was repeated in each of the beds lined up against the two walls. She had devoted whole afternoons to observing how the sleeping face of every patient there reflected the journey toward death and then the return.

At the far end of the ward there were faces whose eyes remained shut or stared out at the emptiness of many afternoons just like this one. From her point of observation she examined the bodies lying in the absurd positions by means of which the most extraordinary balancing acts had briefly succeeded in banishing pain, while an equally extraordinary and delicate balancing act had managed to hold death in check. A fly invaded the nearly perfect sterility and silence of the room, but without provoking from its inhabitants, furiously and instinctively busy with just living, more than an occasional moan (which need not be interpreted as the result of pain) or a sudden and almost imperceptible contraction of a nerve.

Her happiness was three weeks and four days old, the precise amount of time that had elapsed since that morning, wonderful for her, when the head librarian of the daytime shift had bent over the stamp pad and died. When they raised his head to see why he wasn't moving, she saw — because she had come over in response to the cries of two readers sitting near him — that the left part of his forehead and part of the temple, which was resting on the pad, were covered with a large humid stain of reddish violet, and that what at first had seemed to be bruises produced by the rupture of the surface blood vessels soon proved to be ink from the stamp pad that had marked him with the same reddish violet color with which he had marked mountains of papers.

The feeling of freedom and joy exceeded all her expectations. She could hardly get used to it, and every morning she entered the enormous room with a sprightliness that was unusual for her age and that the passage of time and the repetition of her euphoria did not diminish in the slightest.

The sudden collapse of the shoulders and the ink stain on the forehead had had the virtue of reversing the causes of pain and pleasure for her. That other incident, which she had tried, patiently and in vain, to forget had now become something that she recalled, trying to reconstruct lost details that had escaped her memory and, failing that, inventing new imaginary details that would enrich the long-past terrible scene whose more precise outlines the passage of time had inopportunely blurred, much to her annoyance. Unable to remember the traits of all the faces that had looked up from their books, pale and shaken by the sudden violence that forced them instantly to stop reading, she reconstructed them by choosing at her will from among the long line of faces that had passed before her, whispering set phrases intended to ask a question or give thanks, and by then placing them among the startled audience, which, at those times when the memory of the scene beat upon her consciousness most fiercely, she imagined stretching out even beyond the rather isolated newspaper room.

Again she reconstructed the agitated scene, taking no small delight in exaggerating the role played by the now dead librarian, which she had tried childishly to make light of throughout the years that followed the event, but had inflated beyond the dictates of prudence during the last three weeks.

Had one been able to question the second assistant (the ranking that he had established rested on simple seniority) about the precise meaning of the commotion, the good woman would have declared that the late librarian, in a violent outburst quite unexpected in so sweet-tempered a person, had screamed in the most dreadful way at the first assistant because of a mistake that if the matter had been taken to the director would almost certainly have been considered trivial. But the second assistant had changed shifts shortly after the incident, had subsequently married, and now lived in a far-off town where she was preparing to greet the arrival of her second grandchild. At any rate, her account would not have explained why the third assistant was given to frequent bursts of tears or why the daytime staff so often requested a change of shift. And so how could one get to the bottom of the matter, when the second assistant lived so far off and the third assistant had requested and been granted retirement?

The street was now crowded with people who pressed together to let the traffic through and who walked rapidly along the sidewalk, going in and out of the shops but paying not the slightest attention to the narrow entrance marked by an arrow, a hand with a very long pointing finger, and a sign that said: "TODAY! MATINEE! TODAY!"

Standing at one end of the stairway that led up to the auditorium, the man was watching the passing crowd, which was impervious to the efforts of the sign painter, who that morning had insisted on draping a great banner with the title of the play in huge letters over the façade of the building, hanging it from the roof at considerable risk to his life, and impervious likewise to the two or three advertisements that he himself had strategically placed in the newspapers. He kept the small vestibule dark, waiting for the first patron to arrive; but in the dimness he could see that the ticket seller, her elbows resting on the table that served as a box office, was dozing away.

Again he fixed his eyes on the door, waiting for the moment when one foot of the first theatergoer would step over the threshold and, once that foot was firmly placed inside the building, the other would begin to climb the stairs.

But no one came. He couldn't shake free of the idea that luck had forsaken him. The week before, he'd had to cancel two evening performances and undergo the humiliation of having to return their money to the two lone patrons. In a few minutes he'd have to open the door that led to the dressing rooms and tell the actors that the second matinee of the week had been canceled. That was what was most humiliating, and that was why he was putting off the moment in which he would push open the door and make his painful way to the dressing rooms. He glanced into the totally dark auditorium to make sure that no one had sneaked in while he wasn't looking, something that had happened more than once in the past. Then he thought of the nights when the theater was full and he had to help the ticket seller, who couldn't keep up with the demand. And if the public was not only good-sized but also responded favorably to what was happening on stage, a mysterious chain of reactions came to link it with the actors.

He took about two minutes to complete his evocation of the great nights and then imagined the expression that would appear on the face of the leading lady — that was no doubt already there, waiting for him — when he started to tell her the matinee was canceled. He looked at his watch. Four o'clock.

He gave up and slowly headed for the door to the dressing rooms. He was startled by a noise that grew quickly louder and that at first he was unable to identify. He looked down the steps, and once he identified it, his right arm stretched out to the switch and with a slightly convulsive movement turned on the light in the small vestibule. Many feet, countless feet, were charging up the stairs. Their sudden movement succeeded in rousing the ticket seller, who was wide awake by the time the first banknote was pushed at her with a demand for the first ticket.

After that, all was commotion, joy, delight. He barely had time to think that the sign painter was right and that the public, furthermore, was a strange and capricious monster. All he could do was smile, smile at each new patron who entered the auditorium, which was rapidly filling up and for which he turned on the full illumination. During a moment when the stream of patrons stopped, only to start again, he pushed hard on the warning bell for the actors, which would no doubt pry the leading lady loose from the novel that she used to bring just to offend him. Shortly after this he closed the door of the auditorium, shutting it off from the noise of the street. He looked again at his watch. It was four fifteen. He remembered that his watch gained a minute a day. He cast one last glance into the packed house and walked rapidly down the stairs to get a little fresh air, filled with a deep and wonderful feeling of gratitude and bliss.

The approximate weight of the bomb is estimated at eight tons. After reaching the apex of its trajectory, the ballistic missile, under optimal conditions, requires 9 minutes and 50 seconds to reach its point of impact.

If fission occurs at various locations a few hours after dusk, the dark side of the Earth will be illuminated to such an extent that a hypothetical observer would be under the illusion that a new solar system had been born.

A Little Romance

Last night I spent a long time sitting in Philosophers' Park. Nobody knows that that park where Luz Caballero sits meditating as he faces the Avenida del Puerto, his elbow resting on his knee, with a bust of Saco on one side and one of Padre Varela on the other, is Philosophers' Park. Just as nobody knows that the name of the park with the amphitheater is, or ought to be, Greek Park, because it has paths where you can meditate and statues. One fell over, or they took it away, because it's gone. Just the empty pedestal is left, but I like it that way. Nobody knows that, because when you get right down to it nobody knows anything. Just as nobody knows, either, that behind the park there used to be a promenade called Cortina de Valdés, or that a hundred years ago the house with the Gothic arches used to be a monastery. But of course nobody knows it, because as I said, nobody knows anything.

I was out of breath when I got to the park. I'd been walking all over the old part of Havana. All the benches were taken by young couples. I rested for a bit on some free space on one of the benches and then went over to the carnival they've set up across the street. Something unexpected and very enjoyable happened to me there. By chance I got into a conversation with two girls. They were neither pretty nor ugly, but they were nice. They were having a heated argument about the shortest way to Casablanca. I explained it to them, but so as not to lose their company I convinced them there was nothing there. That left them not knowing what to do; and since I had nothing more to say to them, or, it seemed, they to me, I invited them for a ride on the Ferris wheel. I hardly ever do such things; but I suddenly thought that's the way really good times begin, with an invitation to ride on the Ferris wheel. Afterwards they let me treat them to an ice cone, because that's all you can get there. Then we went for a ride in those little electric cars that bump into each other to scare you and make you laugh, although nobody's scared. The three of us wouldn't fit, so they started to argue about who'd go with whom till I stepped in once more, took the chubbier one by the waist, and made her get into one of the cars. Right away she started to bump and scream and forget all about the argument. Since the seat was very narrow, I put my arm around her shoulders, and she didn't say a thing. The other one, who was much slimmer, was riding by herself in another car and seemed to be having a good time. I realized I should have picked her; but it was too late for that, and all I could do was look at her from my car while she laughed to herself, showing her small teeth, whenever she crashed into another car. With one such jolt a strand of her long hair got into her mouth, and that seemed to make her choke with laughter. A boy tried to climb into her car; but she pushed him away rather violently, suddenly turning serious. That's when I saw, before she drove off again, that she was prettier than she'd seemed at first glance.

I get seasick easily, so I didn't ride on the flying saucers when they took it into their heads to go; and I stood there watching them while they whirled through the air, screaming with fright, holding down their skirts, clutching the chain so as not to fall off. A boy started to scare them by violently rocking back and forth against the chain while it was whirling at top speed, and it looked as though his seat would come loose and throw him into the bay.

Everything was going just fine; but when I invited them to come sit in the park, in the dark part, they said they had to go. I insisted it was still early and that we ought to rest a while in the park, but all I could get from them was a promise they'd come back tonight.

After they left, so as not to go straight home, I sat down on a low stone wall behind Padre Varela. The benches were full of lovers frantically fondling each other. I heard the sound of scissors behind me. An old woman surrounded by bags and wrapping paper was cutting up bread and throwing it to a dog. They seemed to be all set to spend the night. I tried to get a good look at the old woman. It was very hard to do in the dark. She was sitting with her back to the carnival. When the pieces of bread stopped coming, the dog lay down among the bundles. The old woman looked inside the bag closest to her but couldn't quite make up her mind to take anything out. She spent a long time like that. Then she wrapped herself in a burlap sack, clutched her legs, and rested her head on her knees. It occurred to me I ought to give her some money so she could get something to eat. I toyed with the idea for a while but I couldn't make up my mind to do anything.

Tonight I'll have to get to the park early.

What luck! The girl came, the slimmer one. Very late, but she did come. Another one came with her, not as young and not as pretty either. I'd waited a long time, walking up and down in front of the carnival. I tried to remember whether I'd said I'd meet them over there or in the park or at the wall by the Avenida del Puerto. When it seemed they weren't going to come anymore I sat down on the dark side, where the lovers sit. It was Monday, so hardly anybody was there. I'd come very early. Behind me, in the same place as the night before last, I saw the old woman from Sunday, but without the dog. She was slowly eating something greasy and wrapped in newspaper that she pulled out with her dirty fingers. It took her forever to swallow each mouthful. I had to look away. I noticed that her hair isn't white but yellow, maybe from the soil of the park.

After a bit Ester and her friend arrived. I thought we could go on all the carnival rides since they were empty and there was nobody to bother us. Ester said no, that we should sit down on a bench on the other sidewalk, the one that's lit, and anyhow she had to leave in a minute. I paid no attention. Women always say they've got to leave as soon as they show up for a date. Over where we sat down, a street light shone right in my face, while she was partly hidden in the shadows. And I wanted so badly to see her in the light and close up! (This morning, for example, I couldn't form any clear mental picture of her.) The light bothered my eyes but I didn't want to suggest moving. That might have got her telling me again that she had to go. Pretty soon her friend said she wanted to look at the ships on the bay and left.

Then I could see that Ester isn't pretty in a straightforward and ordinary sense, but in some vague, almost subtle, way. There's a touch of mockery in her eyes, but I suppose that's because I started right in to tell her, without stopping, everything that was going through my head. Whenever I did pause to let her say something, she just kept quiet. She's given to watching people and laughing with a show of her teeth. I asked her to meet me again, there or any-place she wanted, in her house if she liked. She doesn't seem like the kind of girl that hangs out in a park, even though she's come to meet me like this, without knowing me and so late at night. All this time I couldn't take my eyes off her. Her skin is so delicate. I think of all her skin, tight and delicate under the dress that hugs her thighs and forces her to walk with short little steps.

WEDNESDAY

Last night she didn't come. Maybe because it was drizzling. It would drizzle and clear up and then about nine it turned to a steady drizzle. By then I knew she wasn't coming, but just the same I kept dragging myself around the park getting wet. The carnival was closed. I walked up and down the streets that run into the avenue. I went down Cuarteles, as always, and then up Peña Pobre, hoping to run into her, though I avoid going there since they tore down almost the whole block to build one of those awful "parking facili-ties." I didn't see her. I was tired and went back to the park and sat down on the wall where I was sitting Sunday, the day we met. I don't know why I felt so worn out and still feel that way today. I haven't been able to do a thing. As though I'd walked all over Havana.

THURSDAY

It's a good thing Ester came last night. She showed up alone. Actu-ally I didn't want her to come. You start attaching importance to these things, and they get blown up out of all proportion.

That's what I told her last night, laughing, when we met. As always she kept looking at me and seemed to be having a good time. We had to talk about *something*. I talk to her constantly just so she won't leave right away. She laughs and looks at me. What might she be thinking about when she's looking at me? We were sitting on the bench she always insists on, under the street light. After a little argument that she always wins, I go along with her, although the light bothers my eyes. Today, for example, I've had to wash with *vicaria* water just to write these lines in my notebook. I don't believe in these things, but my cleaning woman is always singing the praises of *vicaria* and sets a bowl of the water out for me overnight so I'll wash with it before starting to write. And so as not to argue with her I wash myself, because I know she's watching me.

Ester didn't stay long. I suspect somebody doesn't want her to come. That's the only explanation for her being so reserved.

FRIDAY

God, how pretty she is! Last night I could really see her in the coffee shop. She finally let me buy her a cup of coffee. I was coming through the park and saw her waiting for me on the corner. Maybe she wasn't waiting for me and had just come for a little fresh air; but for some reason it seemed to me that, yes, she was waiting for me. Everybody was looking at her and I couldn't help showing my annoyance, because after all she was with me. Her hands are small. She chews her nails and hides her hands from me so I won't notice, and I pretend I don't. Last night I told her she has very pretty hands, and right away she hid them against the seat, under her thighs. The skin of her arm is very delicate. The light shone on the brown hair that rises in waves from her forehead and that she's constantly patting down. How I'd like to run my fingers through her hair! Last night I noticed something in her that I hadn't noticed before, something extraordinary. She has some delicate little moles on her forehead; the smallest one is on her temple, almost hidden by her hair. She really has a beautiful forehead. Now I'm recalling her lips, always half open with a little mocking expression. Last night, maybe because of the heat, she was wearing a dress cut low under the arms that showed a bit of her breasts.

66

I'm trying to remember what we talked about last night, and I can't. I was relieved she was there. I'd been so afraid she wouldn't come. A few minutes before she got up to leave, I put my hand on her shoulder. She quickly drew back. All I told her when we said good night was that I'd be there waiting for her. I can't say how long we talked.

On my way home I saw the old woman with the dog, sleeping on the sidewalk. It was very late. It had started to drizzle. The drizzle must have awakened her. She came over toward where I was, under the tree, and threw a blanket over her head. She gave off a sickening stench. Other shapes that had been sleeping on the grass and that I hadn't seen also got up. I saw them looking for shelter under pieces of newspaper or bags. The headlights of a bus hit the old woman. Her skin is blackish and wrinkled. Her body is a mass of bones covered with burlap sacks and rags. I've never seen such an old face. The dirt on her face has hardened as the sweat and the rain have dried, and her wrinkles have grown rigid. It's depressing to see a sort of homeless shelter like that, hidden among the trees.

Last night I didn't see Ester. But the worst of it is that maybe she was close by and I couldn't see her. Though come to think of it, even if I didn't see her, she was bound to see me. In the afternoon I decided to buy some dark glasses. I never go out in the afternoon because it's so hot, and I spend the time reading or writing; but I realized I had to wear dark glasses so the irritation of my eyes wouldn't be so obvious. In the mirror I could see the glasses looked good on me. Maybe Ester will like the change. But it was so dark that now I'm not sure whether she came, because I had trouble making things out. I ran after two women who I thought looked like her but weren't. I decided to wait for her without leaving my spot.

The old woman was in the park again, in her usual place. As I watched her, and just to pass the time, I started to wonder what dirty miserable people like that might live off. When she's with others, they never talk to each other. The others laugh or talk to themselves as she does, or dig through their bundles in search of something. While I was watching her she spread a newspaper on the grass and lay down to sleep.

TUESDAY

I saw Ester last night. I wish I'd never seen her! Sunday night she didn't come. I waited two hours in the usual place. The old woman picked that time to hang her clothes on the trees because it had rained and everything was soaked. She came over to me to ask for a cigarette and I quickly changed places to avoid her, but I didn't go far. I thought Ester might be looking for me from a way off and if she didn't see me she might leave. But it seems she didn't come. I stayed in the park very late. I'm sure, positive, that she didn't come.

Last night I left home early because I thought I might have to spend a long time looking for her. I kept walking around, in hopes of seeing her come out of some place. I went down Cuarteles, exhausted, and I saw her. She was with her friend from the first night, who didn't recognize me. They were heading for the park, though not by themselves but with two boys. The younger one had his arm around Ester's waist. Ester was wearing the same tight dress as on the first day, the one that clings to her thighs.

THURSDAY

Last night I got ready to go out; but at the last minute, when I was all set, I decided to stay home. The weather isn't good; and besides, I've been going out too much recently. I don't feel quite well.

SATURDAY

I stayed away from the park Thursday, and last night, too. The weather was still bad. It's gotten to where it's raining every night, and it's so humid it's not healthy for anybody. Yesterday afternoon I felt better and eventually went out, because I was tired of staying home. I realized I ought to go to the barber. That always makes me feel better. That barber's always trying to push some product or other, some brilliantine, some hair dye; and this time he wound up making a sale. I'm in no mood for arguing these days. He didn't just sell me something, he demonstrated it for me. By the time I realized what was going on he'd dyed my hair — with a patented German product, he says, and because the dark hair goes better with the dark glasses. If I don't like it, it wears off in a few days. Maybe he's right. At least you get to change the same old way you look. And while he was at it, he went on to sell me an eyebrow pencil, according to him so the eyebrows won't clash with the glasses or the dark hair. I wound up buying it all, I was getting that eager to get out of there.

Before going to bed I went out again. I dropped by the park, quickly, without looking much, because I was sure Ester wouldn't come and I didn't want to build up any false hopes. I stopped a moment in the coffee shop and had a cup of coffee. Just to buy something more I bought a pack of cigarettes, which is something I never do because I don't smoke. After I bought it I wondered what I'd do with it. Suddenly I thought I could give it to the old woman, who'd asked me for a cigarette the other night. I crossed the street and saw her in her usual spot. I came up without her seeing me. She was sleeping. I sat down near her for a bit to see what she was doing. Sitting on the grass so I could see her better, I spent a long time observing her carefully. I shouted to see whether she'd wake up. Gradually she came to. When she saw the cigarettes she grabbed for the package. There was something so sordid about her that I decided not to let her have it. I put it in my pocket and went home. Sordid, that's the right word for it, sordid.

SUNDAY

Something terrible has happened. I wish I'd never met Ester. Last night I saw her again in the park. I think it was the worst night of my life. I haven't been able to sleep. I sent away the cleaning woman because I don't want her to see me like this. Besides, she pokes her nose into everything. Ester and I were together a little over half an hour. When I got to the park she was sitting there; and she greeted me as though nothing had happened, as though we'd seen each other the night before. I couldn't think of what to say. I sat down next to her. It was very noisy because they'd started up the carnival, and those loudspeakers make a dreadful racket. I had to repeat and shout what I was saying. At one point she brought her ear closer to me so as to hear. She was laughing because it seems I was blowing in her ear as I talked and that made her laugh. Her ear brushed against my mouth. Her ear is covered with an almost invisible down. The music stopped but I was telling her something and although there wasn't any music anymore I kept on talking into her ear. All I remember is that I kissed her on the neck and under her arm and that what happened afterward was awful. I think Ester stood up suddenly, because I fell to the ground. People started to gather around us, those people who are everyplace and don't have anything to do. I heard her screaming and saying terrible things to me, but I can't remember what they were. All I know is that last night was the most horrible night of my whole life.

MONDAY

Last night I sat in the usual place. I wasn't expecting anything, but since that's better than staying home I wound up going to the same old place. Very late, it was almost morning, I walked along the streets, stopping in front of many houses. It was so quiet you could hear the breathing of people sleeping next to the windows. Maybe Ester sleeps next to the window. It's so hot. Maybe she sleeps naked to take advantage of every little breeze. I looked in a window and tried to pierce the darkness. Maybe she sleeps next to the window. Maybe she sleeps naked. I am very tired.

My most serious mistake was not to give her my address. If I'd given her my address maybe she'd try to see me, but I didn't. That was my worst mistake. What if somebody knocked at the door in the middle of all this silence . . . She didn't come last night, either. Though I knew she wouldn't come, because there was a heavy drizzle, I sat for a while in the usual spot, covering myself with newspapers.

I think the old woman is sick. Last night I sat near her a long time. She didn't budge. She was sitting propped up against a tree, with her eyes closed and her head leaning back against the trunk of the tree, which isn't her usual position. I've noticed that when she dozes off her chin always sinks onto her chest, with the body leaning forward, and her head comes down to rest on her knees. Last night spit was dribbling from her mouth. Maybe she's dying or close to it. But then, when you reach that state you're no good to anybody. I was there almost through the early morning hours. Anyhow, it's hard for me to be at home.

Something extraordinary happened to me this morning. I woke up in the park. All night long, in my mind I was going over every moment of my life. I must have fallen asleep. There are a lot of hours in a night, and I can't have spent them all thinking. The trees started to turn blue and then green. It got lighter. At that point I know I fell asleep. When I opened my eyes the sun was shining on my face. All night long I'd been hungry. When I woke up I'd got over it. I came home because the sun was beating down on me and went to bed without breakfast.

Ester and I bathed naked in the waters of a spring. Since it was night, the mad perfume of the ilang-ilang tree rose from the depths of the forest.

Ester hasn't come, but I'm sure she will. The trouble would be if she came looking for me and didn't find me. Or if she came very late one night. I'm so hungry I can't think straight. The old woman gave me something to eat and some newspapers with which to cover myself. I fell asleep in spite of all that racket that comes from the carnival and all those crowds of people. Tonight I'll have to bring something to eat.

The Visitors

While Clara was getting ready to leave, something new suddenly dawned on me, something over and beyond her lies. I'd been suspecting it for a long time, and this new revelation was just one more piece of evidence that would keep me awake till morning, relishing my discovery. But that Franco should also be lying, that he, too, should know . . .

Seeing my suspicion confirmed plunged me into a state of total confusion, shaken and unable to speak, too upset, for the time being, to draw any logical conclusion. I tried to calm down. My first impulse was to conjure up every kind of excuse for her, to look for the most convincing reasons in the world—to think, think!

At the risk of being punished for leaving home without permission, I'd gone as far as her house, telling myself on the way that the last thing I'd do would be to spy on her. But maybe it hadn't been her. It could very well have been somebody else who'd been coming out of the pawnshop that morning just as I was nearing her door. How could I swear to it if, instinctively concealing myself, I'd held back and only seen her from behind, the mass of her body surging like a vast tide. Hundreds of women might walk like her and even dress like her.

"I've got a feeling we'll find out something tomorrow," she said as she got up. "I'll come early. Make sure you have everything. It's crazy not to have everything always in stock. Nobody knows who might come or where from. I've told you that a million times."

My mother smiled her nervous smile, apologetically.

"First thing in the morning I'll send Tomasa to buy some of everything. Don't you worry, don't bring a thing."

Clara headed for the door. Her great body shifted in complicated movements; it moved and advanced slowly, while the folds of her dress, very clean but nearly falling apart with age, fanned the air. The iron prison of all the corsets she had used throughout her life had, by pushing her immense rolls of fat upward, turned her hips into right angles that shook and trembled with every shift of the enormous body. The tide moved forward and disappeared. Yes, it had been Clara.

It was perfectly natural for Clara to have lied. I detested her so much that I almost wanted to catch her in this act of treachery and dreamt of the chance to unmask her in front of them all. But how could it not have occurred to me that any evidence of falseness against her would necessarily apply to Franco, too?

And it wasn't this conclusion that exasperated me. After all, Franco *could* lie. There was nothing extraordinary in that. He might even lie just to pass the time. It was perfectly natural for him, as he dropped in here and there and talked his head off to make people laugh, to tell the little white lies we all tell. He talked a lot; and anybody who talks a lot is going to lie sometimes, without even realizing it, to fill a void in the conversation. So of course it was perfectly natural for him to lie. But to lie to us like this, so systematically and about such a subject . . . Why, good Heavens? Why?

Right from the start Franco had wanted the matter to be cleared up. He knew that my mother had been deeply upset that night when, at bedtime, she'd noticed that her wedding ring was missing, a gold ring with small diamonds that I'd always seen on her left ring finger.

We'd had countless visitors that evening; and we were all on edge, afraid that at any moment the door might open to let in my Uncle Tono, who lived with us and was opposed to those visits and raised a tremendous fuss whenever the strong smell of tobacco revealed that we'd held one of our little gatherings. That evening a lot of people had dropped by to say hello and had left right away, driven off by the pervasive edginess, only to be replaced by new visitors who (and this always surprised me) had felt the urgent need to talk to us just at that same time. In spite of all the years that have gone by, I remember that there was a lot of confusion and a lot of smoke; and I think that Tomasa, who never did have a sense of moderation, served a lot of rum, which somewhat raised the volume of the voices.

At the start of the evening Tomasa had been her usual solemn self, giving strict orders that were quickly obeyed because my mother was delighted to see her take a personal interest in keeping up the good name and prestige of the household.

The first to arrive was the German doctor, who, as always, talked his head off, though since none of us spoke German, nobody understood a thing. He laughed a lot and then left. Next came Nelly. She spoke a little Spanish and told us she'd lived in Cuba some time ago and how happy she was to be able to return. Now that she'd come back she'd always be near us. She said she was an American, though my very rudimentary knowledge of the language never allowed me to identify any English word in what she said. But I never dared to say anything, because once, when Aunt Eva brought in one of her boyfriends, to impress him and because she was treating him for a kidney problem, the man had been so rash as to declare that he knew a little German and that what the doctor was saying was nothing like it. When that happened, Tomasa reacted the way she always did when something deeply disturbed her: she raised her hand and brought it down with a smack on the boyfriend's face, to teach him respect. The man left, his face showing the imprint of Tomasa's fingers. For a little while Aunt Eva was unhappy about it; but then she said that if that was the way he was going to behave in the future, it was a good thing he'd left.

Right after that, Madariaga appeared. He seemed upset, but now that I think of it he always seemed upset by one thing or another and used to have very little to say. When he left, Toni came, bringing along her mother and her fiancé. Almost immediately after that the three soldiers came, one after the other in rapid succession.

There was no end to it. It was always the same, especially when time was short and we were afraid my uncle would come home, as though they'd agreed to come all at once; and when I think of those days now, I imagine them impatiently waiting for the chance to come talk with us, only to have to leave right away, driven off by our deep uneasiness.

Besides my mother, Tomasa, and me, Aunt Eva had come that evening with her sister-in-law Concepción. They always helped Tomasa in the preparations. Clara had dropped by, too, showing up as she always did when everybody came, as though, way off in the tenement where she lived, she had some way of knowing everything that was going to happen. When the evening was about to end and they were all leaving, I saw her holding up Mamá by one of her hands, while she was talking to Franco, during a moment of great confusion. Just before going to bed, Mamá said she'd lost her ring. So there wasn't the slightest doubt: Clara had slipped it off her finger; and I was sure, yes, absolutely sure, that sooner or later everything would become clear.

I remember that Nelly was there right at that moment; but no, come to think of it, I don't think she saw anything because she was talking to Aunt Eva, and poor Nelly was such a scatterbrain. But Franco did, yes, Franco saw it, Franco for sure. And how it hurts me to have to admit that!

At first I thought he'd play one of his usual tricks, just for fun, and wait a little. Maybe he wouldn't even be very hard on her. With everybody there, he'd deplore Clara's low behavior; but he had tact and a certain delicacy, and without any unnecessary disturbance in the flow of our lives, which was so pleasant just then, my mother would get back her ring, which had so often helped us survive periods of crisis. In time, I'm sure, Clara would once more have been welcomed in our home.

As I said before, at first Franco had insisted on clearing it all up thoroughly and right away. He seemed worried by the loss of the ring, and he asked when we'd last seen it and whether there was any chance that Mamá didn't remember where she'd put it. But during his next visit, Franco had been very tight-lipped and even acted a bit offended. I started to think he wanted to avoid the subject. Maybe he was thinking about it. Clara wasn't there, and a lady who lived with her had come to say she wasn't feeling well. But during the next visit, Clara had been there; and while Franco seemed afraid to talk and had very little to say, she kept on repeating that the ring would show up, because things didn't just disappear like that, into the air. Finally Franco spoke. Although the ring was very valuable and he knew how much Mamá was affected by losing it, we had to maintain the peace and quiet of our home at any cost; most likely it had slipped off her finger, and there was no point in all that fuss about what was, after all, a trifle.

My mother was less upset than I expected by this assessment, and Aunt Eva also seemed to accept it. But Tomasa rejected it with a brusque and unequivocal gesture. She opened the windows to air out the room, swept up the ashes from the floor, and withdrew into her kitchen without saying a word. I've thought a lot about it, all through these years. It's never seemed to me that at that moment she knew what was going on right before our eyes, but I can say that she knew Franco very well — what's more, it was she, Tomasa, who had first brought him when he needed us so much — and that her keen insight told her that Franco was holding back more than he needed to.

And now here was Clara, with her smug hypocritical smile and her little eyes shining underneath the lashes darkened with charcoal, demanding that we get together the next day to establish the facts. As she left, while she was bending down to give me a kiss, I felt the hard bristles on her upper lip, which she carefully bleached with peroxide, rub against my cheek.

It was all perfectly natural, coming from her. But having Franco side with her was more than I could stand. What made him behave like that toward my mother, who'd shown him nothing but kindness? I could remember the first time he'd come. After the necessary arrangements, he'd arrived one evening, very late, when almost everybody had left. He couldn't speak. He wasn't Franco, but just a sound like an animal groaning and struggling to breathe — the broken remains of a human will. Finally he managed to stammer out his name, in a strange, twisted voice. Mamá fell ill from the enormous physical effort that a visit from somebody like that demanded of her; but she begged him to come again, ignoring Tomasa's stern warnings.

At the close of his second visit, my mother handed me a piece of paper on which Franco, with endless difficulties, had spent a long time writing something. "Thank her for me," was what was on the paper. I felt deeply moved, even though back then there were so many things I couldn't understand. Without thinking of herself, and even putting herself in danger — yes, I must declare it here in spite of how much I've loved him — putting herself in danger and neglecting the others, who needed so badly to speak with us, my mother always asked him to come back and devoted a lot of time to him. "He's the one who needs us most," she used to say.

Almost all his life had been spent working in the tobacco fields; and it had been a restless one, as he moved from one place to another every year, always involved in some amorous adventure on the plantations. He loved to tell about them, as though he really believed he might repeat them some day, in a tone that often bordered on the obscene and that put my Aunt Eva, ever mindful of propriety, on guard. He'd been coming to the house for a long time, maybe two years or more. Every now and then he'd say it was time for him to leave us; but he'd put off his departure on one pretext or another, and we all knew it was hard for him to go away. For me he was an unfailing ally, always ready to back me up in every whim, no matter how outlandish, and to ask and obtain forgiveness for me. There was a secret bond of comradeship and affection between us, which I like to think went unnoticed by anyone else.

But there was another part of my mind that I didn't dare to reveal even to myself. For days on end, by some automatic mechanism of its own, my brain fought off a thought that was too distressing but that at last sank silently into my consciousness: Casio had been there, too. Casio, whom everyone listened to with such profound respect, who for so long had watched over our home and protected us from so many dangers. He, too, had been there. The idea throbbed in my brain for many days before I could accept it: if Casio had been there, he must have witnessed the theft. And yet he kept quiet.

No doubt the others had also seen it all, but the others were different. There was a kind of seniority tacitly respected by all. Compared to Casio and Franco, nearly all of them were newcomers. And besides, in one way or another they'd all become Clara's protégés, though she was always indifferent or hostile when someone came for the first time. Later she became friendly with them — more with some, less with others — choosing them according to her tastes and always managing to be useful to them, as though the point were to make them feel grateful to her.

But Casio deferred to no one. When appropriate, he was even strict with me. He was extremely respectful toward my mother and showed a special benevolence toward Clara, as though she needed it more than anyone else. Sometimes he spoke to her in a particularly considerate way that I secretly resented. I remember him being in our home ever since I can remember anything. He'd arrived the same year that Tomasa had come as our cook, the same year that I was born. If, for some reason that he never explained, he was absent, the conversation lagged, in spite of Franco's efforts and the German doctor's bursts of laughter. Still, Casio never talked much, but rather listened, and from time to time made some casual commentary, always cautious and prudent.

There had to be some other reason, something I didn't understand, something inexplicable beyond my comprehension, since Clara couldn't possibly have power over Casio, too. I kept on repeating this to myself, and two days after his last visit I asked Tomasa. Maybe she'd know.

"Don't think," she told me. "It's better not to think. Tomorrow is Friday, people will come, and maybe we'll understand it all."

Her wrinkled black face showed signs of worry.

Friday came. Waiting for the usual time, I watched Tono, my uncle, eat with maddening slowness and then sit there at the table for another endless half hour after his coffee. At moments like that a disturbing thought always ran through my mind: What if all of a sudden he decided not to go out? But he finally left; and without a word we speeded up our preparations, since the unexpected delay had shortened the time between his departure and his return. Clara had not come early, as she always did, even though she could tell from his surly silence how much Tono disliked seeing her in the house. They loathed each other, they never talked to each other, and when they absolutely had to, they pretended to be talking to my mother and carried on their arguments as though they were arguing with her.

Aunt Eva and her sister-in-law had come a little after Tono had left, and the front windows had been closed after him so that unexpected relatives and neighbors would think there was nobody home. My mother took her place at Tomasa's right, next to the door that led to the patio, which Tomasa used in her frequent trips to the kitchen. Tomasa had served the first glass of rum. Aunt Eva lit a cigarette. An hour went by and none of the usual visitors gave any sign of life.

It was very strange, almost incredible. Nothing like it had ever happened to us before. Never had I seen my mother so flustered. Three hours went by, during which we tried, but failed, to keep up a conversation. The dining-room clock struck twelve.

"Perhaps they felt uncomfortable the last time they were here," said my mother. "Maybe we're making too much out of losing a piece of jewelry that after all wasn't worth a great deal."

My mother seemed very dejected.

"Maybe," said Tomasa. "But I've always said that with these folks you never know where you stand."

I realized she was trying to feel offended, but in fact she felt lost and confused. For the first time in all the years she'd been with us she had absolutely nothing to say.

"We'd better quit now," my mother said after a bit. "It's late, and Tono's going to come any minute." And, turning to me, "Get ready for bed while I go with your aunts to their room."

But to our further dismay Aunt Eva and her sister-in-law announced that they didn't plan to spend the night, as they did every time they came if it got late. They said this in a confused manner while Aunt Eva stammered in search of some excuse that she finally found and nobody heard. We knew they were lying; but we lied, too, by the suspicious haste with which we pretended to accept their excuse. The four women stood there looking at each other for a moment, not knowing what to say; and that made everyone feel even more uncomfortable. Finally Aunt Eva and her sister-in-law left, almost without any goodbye. In her hurry Aunt Eva forgot her purse; a few seconds later she came back for it without saying a word.

"Why didn't anybody come?" I asked my mother.

She didn't answer. Only many days later would anyone give me an answer.

What had happened was as unexpected as it was absurd. Till then, Tomasa's putting out the word was all it had taken to bring numerous visitors, happy at the prospect of talking with us. Sometimes we were so exhausted we had to stop, against the wishes of my mother, who would have received them all. But today no one had come. We were crushed.

How strange, how unexpected, how terribly depressing it all was! As I lay in bed, unable to sleep, I thought of the brazenness with which Clara had announced her visit three days before, and of her inexplicable absence that evening. How could she act like that and risk coming under suspicion? And above all, what did the others have to do with all of this? Up to a point I could find an explanation for Franco's silence and even fool myself saying I understood it; but the strange behavior of the others, the unexpected mass desertion . . .

During the following days, only our daily routine kept up the appearance of life in our home. Conversation was limited to the absolutely necessary. My mother withdrew into a world of her own whose confusion she could not hide but tried to clear by means of deep sighs. Sometimes she made me sit near her and caressed me, but she didn't mention what had happened. Tomasa's bad mood had turned into a kind of constant and almost uncontrollable clumsiness. Once, when my uncle scolded her for spilling water on the table twice in a row and only succeeded in getting her to spill it a third time, she went off crying and threatened to leave us if we kept on tormenting her. But I knew she wouldn't leave, at least not till we'd got through the crisis. Neither she nor my mother ever stepped outside the house, and I knew that was because they were afraid some unexpected visitors might come when we weren't there to receive them. I was forbidden to go out for any longer stretch of time; and I had to stand at the window and look at the world through the grill or, at most, play on the sidewalk and stay close to the front door. I missed my long walks with Tomasa, but I didn't complain.

The days went by and nobody came. One day Aunt Eva dropped in after lunch, I think just to make a show of acting as though everything were normal. She tried to explain her staying away by talking about how the heat affected her; and she went on running this topic into the ground, without ever mentioning what had occurred. When Tomasa came into the room with the coffee, she greeted her as though nothing had happened.

Aunt Eva was just starting to drink her coffee when the front door flew open and I saw Clara standing on one of the steps. She hesitated a moment, as if trying to decide whether she should go ahead. Finally she came into the room, as though driven by something stronger than she, and stopped in front of my mother, breathing heavily. She seemed to have walked a long way under the pitiless noonday sun. Her hair was down, and her sweat made it stick to her cheeks and forehead. Her clothes, always so clean though very plain, seemed shabby and dirty.

"What's been keeping you?" My mother had stood up. "Why haven't you been coming?"

She offered Clara her cheek, as always, but Clara didn't seem to notice.

"Here I am," she said in a hoarse and somewhat muffled voice.

"We were really worried when you didn't come. Sit down, rest a little. You're sweating; you must have walked over. And in this heat!"

Clara stood still for a moment, and then, in the same tone of voice, quivering with emotion, she almost shouted, "I've been ordered to come here. I don't know what they want of me, but you'd better get ready. There are people out there who want to talk."

We'd never seen Clara like that. Her attitude was defiant, an attitude of wounded dignity. There was no trace of her former somewhat haughty composure, which could instantly slip into unbearable unctuousness, or of the self-assured familiarity that so annoyed me. Her movements were brusque and clumsy, as though she'd suddenly lost control of her arms and body and had to fight for every breath of the hot air in the room.

Tomasa was talking to herself as she set the cups on the table. Suddenly, and in an aggressive tone, she told Clara, "Her brother's sleeping back in the bedroom. We can't have any visitors now. Have you gone crazy?"

"Do as you're told! That's what people like you are for," Clara shouted at her.

Tomasa started to head for the patio, along with Aunt Eva, whose first bewilderment on seeing Clara had turned to indignation at her offensive behavior toward Tomasa. Just then Tono appeared at the patio door. The angry voices had awakened him, and he'd jumped out of bed barefoot and in his undershorts.

"What's all this racket? What's going on?"

He was obviously annoyed by Clara's visit and, in keeping with his habit of not addressing her, he was speaking to me.

But Clara answered for me, speaking to Tono for the first time in many years, in the offended and dramatic tone that had replaced her usual smugness.

"I know there are people who hate me, right in this house and outside this house, too. They'll be glad to know I'm being accused of stealing. But it's a lie. I'll deny it to my dying day. It's a lie!"

"But nobody's accused you. How can you say such a thing?"

My mother was trying to calm her down.

"What's this? Stealing what?" asked Tono.

"It's a lie! It's a lie!" Clara kept shouting in a frenzy.

She was making wild gestures and talking directly to Tono. Her huge body moved from one side of the room to the other before our astonished eyes, threatening to crush us with its weight, yet strangely weak and helpless.

"Everybody hates me, everybody's been after me since the last time I was here and won't leave me in peace. I can't sleep. They're knocking at my door at night. And it's all a dirty lie!"

She began to sob uncontrollably with rage and humiliation.

My mother helped her into a chair and asked Tomasa to bring some cold water. But Tomasa put a hand on her shoulder and said in a low voice, so only my mother could hear it, "There's no time, they're already here. We've got to get ready to receive them."

My mother looked at her brother.

"They're already here," she said very calmly. "We can't turn our back on them. We've got to receive them. It's been very hard on us not to have them come."

"You know how I hate all this stuff," he said.

"Be quiet and do as you're told," said Tomasa, looking at him firmly. "I'm giving the orders now."

"All right," said Tono.

Tomasa had brought the box of cigars and the bottle of rum from the kitchen; and with a movement of her head she ordered us to follow her to the spare room on the other side of the patio, next to the kitchen, a room that was never used except for these occasions.

Clara turned around abruptly and pushed ahead of everyone to her place at one end of a cot that stood along one of the walls. My mother sat down in the big rocking chair, next to the patio door. Tomasa took her place on a low bench, facing my mother; in this position she could move freely. Tono sat down on a chair and rested his feet on one of its crosspieces to keep them off the cold floor. Aunt Eva took a small easy chair, next to the door that led to the other room, and taking me by the hand, set me on her lap. Although I was getting to be a big boy, I was reassured by the closeness of her calm strong body.

After a moment of silence, Tomasa spoke again.

"They're here," she said.

"Receive them," said my mother, bending down to pour herself some rum from the bottle that Tomasa had placed on the floor. But suddenly she jumped forward and was thrown down violently onto her knees. She had turned very pale and her breathing was labored, and she rested her hands on the floor to keep from falling over. Tono rushed to help her, but Tomasa stopped him with a gesture and he returned to his place.

"They're coming from very far away, after many days of silence and sadness, and they want to talk to us," Tomasa continued. She was sitting bolt upright, looking directly at the wall.

"Tell them we were waiting for this moment," Aunt Eva replied.

"They're thirsty and need to rest."

"Tell them we've kept the glasses filled."

"Don't anybody cross your arms or legs. Hands on your sides, palms up," Tomasa said. She took the bottle and poured some rum into the glass, drank a little, filled the glass again, and, without making any effort to help her, held it out to my mother, who was still kneeling on the floor.

"Crossed legs or folded arms mean secrecy and hidden thoughts," Tomasa declared for the second time.

My mother didn't see the glass Tomasa was offering her. She raised herself a little and tried to sit down, but again she was thrown to the floor. As she fell she overturned the rocking chair and jarred the small center table. The bottle fell over, and a little liquid spilled before Tomasa could pick it up. Tomasa opened the box of cigars that stood on the floor next to her, slowly lit one, and offered it to my mother. But my mother remained oblivious to everything. Her eyes wandered around the room, no longer able to recognize us.

Her breathing grew more labored, and I saw that drops of sweat were running down her temples. Although I'd witnessed the scene many times, it always affected me powerfully. I felt my heart beating hard.

I looked at Clara sitting on the bed, by the wall. She no longer seemed agitated and she sat there quietly, looking almost indifferent. Only when my mother's eyes wandered in her direction did she change her position uneasily.

I turned to Aunt Eva and asked her to let me sit on the floor, but she gestured to me to be quiet. My mother wanted to speak. Opening her mouth wide and breathing heavily, with her eyes now fixed on Clara, she moved her head as though trying to say something, and then began to rock her body back and forth. For a long time no sound other than her faltering breathing came from her mouth. She tried to form some words, and we heard a choking sound. She closed her mouth and then let out a long, intermittent, high-pitched hiss, penetrating and painful.

I felt my heart beat so violently I could hardly breathe, and sweat drenched my body. Aunt Eva's arm tightened around my chest. The sound grew louder, and when it stopped for a moment, Clara cried out. I looked at her. She was trembling and sobbing convulsively, and pointing toward my mother's eyes. She waved her arms as though struggling for air. She screamed again, got up from the bed, and ran toward the door; but Tomasa, standing up quickly, pushed her back to the bed with an iron arm. The huge body collapsed under the look in my mother's eyes, which I didn't dare glance at, while the hiss continued to come from her mouth. I started to tremble. I held on to Aunt Eva's hands, which were dripping with sweat and trembling.

I knew it was he. A long, long time had passed since the day we first heard the terrible sound, saw the poor wandering eyes, the twisted mouth trying to speak the impossible. Yes, it was Franco, who was coming from the dark to speak to us again through my mother's mouth. But a Franco who had fallen back toward darkness, grief, and punishment. The Franco of the first day, the creature without will, without speech. It was as though time had stood still and we were reliving the terrible scene of that first day, when he first came to our house. Or worse, a thousand times worse, because now he was not only deprived of speech, but his efforts to express himself were reduced to a terrifying subhuman sound.

Beneath that gaze, Clara's sobs turned into screams of panic; but her body refused to move when she tried again to reach the door. Her arms hung down helplessly; she sobbed and issued sharp cries of terror.

Tomasa knelt down by my mother and washed her face with rum, while in a low voice she rapidly recited a prayer, in which Aunt Eva joined. Only once did I dare to look at the eyes, the terrible eyes I was trying not to see. They betrayed the anguish and fear that lay behind the painful efforts to make themselves understood, the fear of darkness, banishment, silence, and oblivion.

Leaning toward my mother, but without touching her, something that she took great care to avoid, Tomasa placed her ear next to my mother's mouth, trying to decipher the words struggling to take form; but after one last supreme effort of her mouth, all expression began slowly to fade from my mother's eyes. But they were still fixed on Clara, as though they wanted her to be the last thing they saw, the precious vision of paradise they could not give up. The light continued to diminish until it was wholly extinguished. My mother closed her eyes, and the tension of her body began slowly to relax. Finally she was able to get up from the floor. With Tomasa's help, she managed to return to the rocking chair and sat down, motionless at last.

Clara, completely undone and helpless, began to cry, hiding her face in her hands.

I noticed that the pressure of the arm with which my Aunt Eva was holding me had begun to relax. I slipped to the floor; and Aunt Eva sighed deeply, leaned toward Tono, and began to talk to him in a low voice. My uncle shifted uneasily on his chair and laughed rather nervously, at a loss for what to say. Then Aunt Eva turned toward the others and began to speak in a foreign language that I couldn't make out, murmuring in a voice at once tender and ardent.

"It must be Nelly," said Tomasa, while she sprinkled Aunt Eva's face with drops of the rum spilled on the floor.

"Yes, it's Nelly," I said.

Years and years later, I remember the voice so clearly that it seems to me I can hear it right next to me. After a bit, it died down, and we were all still.

I looked toward my mother. She was rocking slowly, with her hands resting on the arms of the rocking chair and her head leaning against its high back. Although I couldn't tell just when it had occurred, her face had taken on a slightly somber expression of deep calm. Her black hair shone in the afternoon light. She was smoking a cigar; and the smoke, slowly rising toward the ceiling, intensified the serenity that enveloped her. I felt a deep peace after all that terror, and a feeling much like gratitude came over me.

Nobody was surprised by the calm we all felt. Casio had arrived, and the same beneficent influence always radiated from him. There was something in the air that signaled his presence among us; I was aware of it long before he began to speak. Suddenly we could all breathe more easily.

Clara was crying again, quietly, without the fear that had shaken her before, and so dejectedly that I was touched.

"God bless us all." Casio spoke, his voice shaking with barely controlled emotion. "These have been days of confusion and sadness for all of us, but very soon we'll see the light again."

He stopped and took a deep breath.

The sun no longer fell on the patio, and it was dark in the room. Tomasa struck a match, lit a candle, and set it on the floor, keeping it upright with some wax that she allowed to drip.

"Now, do what you've been told," he said to Clara.

Clara slowly raised her head, without taking her eyes off the floor; her hand groped under the front of her dress, drew from her bosom a small package wrapped in wrinkled newspaper, and placed it on the table in front of her. Tomasa opened the package, and we saw my mother's gold ring shine brightly on the table, reflecting the rays of candlelight.

"This woman has paid for what she did," Casio announced. "But she must not come back here."

He was quiet for a moment and then went on, "But it will be a long time before the others have atoned for their guilt." His voice rose, impelled by sudden wrath. "Franco has been banished from this house forever. I brought him here long ago. He lived all his life in the midst of violence, and when he came here he was in deepest darkness. You helped him with your friendship, and he achieved the peace he so badly needed."

"You've punished him enough," said Clara in a very low, almost expressionless voice. Her eyes were looking beyond the door, into the empty patio.

"He betrayed our trust out of desire for this woman, and his desire made him hide her misdeed. He couldn't believe it."

Again his voice shook. He was silent, while thick clouds of smoke slowly filled the room.

"He chose darkness over his own liberation." And then, after a somewhat longer pause, "He must return to the darkness from which he came."

I trembled when Casio pronounced the sentence. Although I was too young to understand Franco's motives and the nature of love and desire, I couldn't help thinking that the severity of the punishment was greater than his guilt, and for a moment I rebelled against the conclusiveness of that judgment.

We sat there in silence, overwhelmed by what we had just heard. There was to be no help for Franco. He had fallen from grace. But there was nothing — and this must be clearly understood — nothing we could do to alter the decision. The fate of the house was not in our hands. Casio gave, and Casio took away. Casio knew. His will was not only his own; it was also the will of others whom we would never know.

Evening had begun to fall, and the breeze began to blow. The flame of the candle flickered. Tomasa stretched out her arm and extinguished it with her fingers.

"Now we shall have peace," Casio declared. "I'm leaving."

After Casio had left, and Clara had gone without saying a word, never to return, and my mother and Aunt Eva had sat down once more by the patio door, no doubt to talk about what had happened; while Tono was shaving and singing in his room, and Tomasa lighting the stove for dinner, I sat down on the front-door steps to see the afternoon crowd go by. They all seemed exhausted by the heat of the day. The first evening breeze was starting to cool their tired bodies. Someone laughed out loud, and I thought of Franco, whom we'd never hear again, and of how he used to enjoy telling his stories about all the women he'd known, and of his irresistibly contagious humor. I remember feeling very sad and crying for a long time, without making the slightest sound or drying my face, so nobody would hear me from inside the house or see me from the street.

Love: The River Almendares, Now Full-Grown, Is Twelve Million Years Old

All my rage, my pent-up anger at her and at myself, died down long before the bus reached the bridge where she was waiting for me, even long before the first buildings of Havana showed their monotonous outlines beneath that terrible sun we always have with us.

I don't remember exactly when the incident occurred. I wish it would occur again. I wish it would occur again many times. I saw the hard expression leave the faces of those few of us who witnessed the scene, saw the lethargy induced by a long ride turn into a troubled restiveness, a nervousness that made us look, shift about in our seats, smile uneasily, perhaps with a touch of shame.

From where I was riding, balancing on the platform of the bus, I heard voices, I looked, and I saw the old woman, shaking with sobs, kissing and caressing the hand of a man who was offering her a cigarette. I couldn't tell whether the man offered her the cigarette to calm her down, or whether she'd asked him for the cigarette and then burst into convulsive stifled sobs, accompanied by great sighs as she grasped his hand and kissed it. The man didn't know where to look; he laughed nervously but at the same time you could see he was moved by what was happening. The old woman held the cigarette and wept silently over the man's wrist.

"You're so kind, so kind!" she repeated in a hoarse voice between bursts of her seemingly endless weeping.

The man touched her awkwardly on the shoulder.

"Calm down . . ."

He must have remembered that he had a lighter in his pocket, and he managed to pull it out and light it with the hand she left him free.

The old woman calmed down, put the cigarette to her lips, and lit it without letting go of the man's wrist. Her hand and shoulders were trembling. I saw that in spite of the lively breeze coming in through the windows, she very skillfully lit the cigarette, instinctively tilting her head forward until the tip was in front of the precarious flame and drawing deeply. In between little twitches of her shoulders she blew out a big mouthful of smoke before the wind extinguished the lighter.

With this she seemed to relax. She sobbed quietly one more time and then slowly let go of the man's wrist. Her hand slipped along his fingers as though caressing them. He patted her shoulder again and then straightened up, relieved.

The old woman was very neatly dressed. Her mouth was horribly sunken and toothless. She held the cigarette by pressing her lips together, and this shrank her face even more. She wiped away her remaining tears with a very wet, but very clean, handkerchief. A cheap ring sparkled weakly from one of her fingers. Everything about her — her starched blouse, her neatly ordered hair — gave off an air of cleanliness. She was rather on the heavy side. From time to time her dull eyes looked about her detachedly.

Again I wondered whether they knew each other and whether a conversation prior to my getting on the bus had brought on the repressed inconsolable weeping, or whether the man had offered her the cigarette to calm her after the onset of the crisis whose first moments I hadn't seen. Lost in my own obsession, I hadn't noticed a thing until I heard the first moans.

Some people got off at a stop, and I managed to get a seat a few rows in front of her, almost immediately behind the driver.

It was hard to know what effect the scene had had on the other passengers. The roar of the motor, the speed with which the bus was traveling, and perhaps the suffocating heat produced a strange withdrawn expression on every face. They were all looking out the window, as though they wanted to avoid looking at the other passengers or as though they were waiting for something.

I heard my own labored breathing, the short breaths of someone who's trying to hold back his tears, disturbed but strangely relieved. A somber determination had made me get on the bus and go to meet her. It has to be avoided at all costs. She's got to take something — I'd already told her that — find some means. There's got to be one. It's horrible to condemn someone to live, to cast someone into the world. Or else disappear where she'll never find me. Or kill ourselves. But there are ways, there've got to be ways, she's got to take something. She promised me she would. I keep thinking of the way a body hits the pavement, the confusion and the dirt, of a body that's hanging from the balcony—how odd, a gallows right in the middle of the city and in plain sight like a gallows in the middle of the countryside, a warning, as in old times.

But all of that suddenly faded. I managed to regain my composure. As the bus neared my stop, I saw her a little way from where we'd agreed to meet, almost at one end of the bridge. She looked incredibly fragile and ugly, with her long thin hair hanging in an abortive effort at a hairdo, her chewed nails, her drooping stockings, her dress, as always, tattered. I looked at her as though seeing her for the first time. There she stood, looking at the trees, with what was supposed to be a meditative expression. Beyond the trees ran the river, far below, reeking of fermentation by the time it reaches the bridge, dirty, topped by a green scum that rots in the sun and that, since it never rains, never dissolves. She'd told me to meet her there, which for her was the most romantic place imaginable. No doubt she was thinking of something appropriate to say when we met, something trite and affected that only she was capable of, something that I knew all too well and that stemmed from the greasy little novels pawed over by thousands of hands in the bookshops on the Calle de la Reina, something that at times could turn my stomach.

"There you are," she said.

I held her tight around the waist and she looked at me furtively. We started to cross the bridge. Beyond the park, among the trees, the river showed its black surface, barely moving, polluted, giving off its hot stench and humidity.

The heat was stifling. The stream of cars, buses, and trucks that were rushing toward the city or coming away from it as though driven by fury, created sudden blasts of hot air and covered us with dust. For a few moments we couldn't hear each other for the noise. From behind the clouds the sun was sending down a maddening glare.

We stopped halfway across the bridge. Below us lay the motionless green park. The trees blocked the view of the ground. It occurred to me that anyone falling from the bridge would be caught in the branches, groaning there who knows how many hours or days, like the men who died on the barbed wire entanglements of the First World War.

I put my arm around her shoulders and hugged her tight until I got her to turn toward me, but I didn't look at her. Somebody speeding by blew his horn and shouted at us.

"Everybody can see us."

"Let 'em."

The traffic on the bridge seemed twice as heavy as before. It was deafening now.

"Let the kid live."

She must not have heard me, because she made a gesture like someone who hasn't understood. I had to repeat what I'd said.

Suddenly she started to hit me with hysterical violence, first with her fists and then with her head and her purse, which flew open. Everything fell out on the ground. Her movements were so ridiculous I had to laugh while I struggled to pick up her things — a knotted handkerchief, a worn-out lipstick, torn stockings — and grab her by the wrists. I felt a hard blow from a shoe near my ear. I shut my eyes for a moment while everything went dark. Once I'd managed to pick up the purse I rushed at her to subdue her by putting my arms around her. I felt the wave of tenderness flow over me again. Perhaps if it was powerful enough it would drag us both into the river.

"Calm down, calm down!"

The gawkers were holding up traffic across the bridge. I heard a gale of horns and shouts. A man was looking at us from his car, smiling and advancing slowly like a satisfied animal. The traffic fleeing from the city rushed on, unstoppable, in the other lane.

But over by us it came to a complete halt. The car of the smiling man stalled. Unruffled, without taking his eyes off us, he tried to start it. I heard exclamations of astonishment and laughter. Several young men got out of a car that was still some way off and surrounded us with expressions of delight on their faces. One of them picked up a shoe and held on to it with a smile. She struggled out of my arms, and before I could get hold of her again I saw her toes protruding from a torn stocking.

The man succeeded in starting his car, and the whole line suddenly started to move. An old taxi, almost falling apart, came to a stop. A door opened. Still clutching her to me I dragged her by the wrists and pushed her into the car. I had to hit her on the mouth to make her get in. I saw that the driver was very black and very thin. Without looking behind him he checked with his hand to make sure the door was closed and then drove off.

"Some heat!"

While she struggled in my arms and bit my chest, driven by her fury and the first symptoms of her miscarriage, I began in a frenzy to kiss her sweat-soaked neck, her sad dirty hair, now hanging loose; and as I mixed my sobs with the dust, the memory of those sordid first afternoons of sweat and semen suddenly arose within me.

Before the car had left the bridge, I felt another gust of stifling air. As the old taxi shuddered along, the man's hands were shaking.

Happiness

Jorge had a hard time closing the last suitcase. The lock wouldn't snap shut. First he tried to close it with the normal pressure of his hand; then, once he saw to his consternation that the spring wouldn't give way for the latch, he tried to pry it aside, but in vain. Then he tried to force it. He noticed that his fingers were trembling slightly. It was hot, but he knew the real reason why the drops of cold sweat were running down one by one from his armpits to his waist. That always happened when he felt nervous.

He tried to hide his difficulties with the lock from Dalia, who was busy filling her purse with the final items for her trip — money, the ticket — but Dalia saw it all.

"Won't it close?"

"It's stuck. These things always happen at the last minute."

"Don't force it."

"Can't you see I'm not forcing it?" Jorge tried to control his irritation.

"Don't get impatient. Do it slowly and you'll see how it closes. The train doesn't leave till twelve."

Jorge faced the annoying possibility that the lock might not work in spite of all his efforts.

"If you have to, you can take it the way it is; the other lock is strong, it'll hold."

"No, if it won't lock I'm not going. I don't want to risk traveling with a half-closed suitcase. The way those trains go . . . We'll just take it to be fixed on Monday and I'll change my ticket to Tuesday."

Jorge felt another single icy drop run down his side.

"You're always making mountains out of molehills. If it won't lock, we'll tie it closed with a rope and that'll take care of it."

"You think I'd travel with a suitcase tied with a rope? Anyhow, what's the rush? Maybe this is an omen — I believe in those things. If I'm not there today, I'll be there Tuesday. It's all the same."

"And what will your family say? They'll think something's happened to you, or that I won't let you go. They already don't think much of me."

"The telegraph was invented many years ago."

It was that implacable logic of Dalia's which sometimes made Jorge feel he was suffocating. In moments of tenderness a feeling of gratitude would come over him and show itself in professions of love, of needing her and her affection, and in caresses where the line between gratitude and desire was hard to draw. But recently the moments of tenderness had become scarcer and the unpleasant suffocating feeling ever more frequent.

With a smile Dalia pointed to a key lying in plain view next to the suitcase on the floor, almost right under his eyes. Jorge inserted the little key in the lock, the spring gave way, the latch went in, and the suitcase was closed.

They had agreed that he wouldn't go to the station. Waiting rooms made him nervous, as did stations and above all airports—in a word, any place where his will was subjected to the will of others or to hidden mysterious forces. He was terrified of airports. That patient herd of travelers waiting for a harsh metallic voice to come out of a loudspeaker and order it to board a machine that might turn out to be a death trap! Poor people! Besides, he hated goodbyes, hated trains that after everything had been said and the last kisses exchanged, still didn't leave—those last-minute delays that made the whole sad hypocritical ceremony start all over again, till at last came the departure, to everyone's relief.

Once everything was ready, Jorge kissed her as they left the apartment. Before opening the door he felt an unexpected urge to touch her once more. He held her face and kissed her once, twice, three times, on the cheek. He almost told her, "Come back soon," but he contained himself. It wouldn't have been right. She let herself be kissed; but she squeezed his shoulder hard as she told him, speaking almost directly into his ear, "Take care of yourself, eat right. If the pain comes back, you know where the needle is. Boil it as soon as you feel anything and call the manager. She's a kind woman and she'll come right away. I've already talked to her about it."

She was wearing an absurdly small kerchief tied at the back of her neck; he liked to tell her it made her look like a Sicilian peasant, even though he'd never seen a Sicilian peasant. She called it her traveling kerchief, maybe because she pulled it out from the back of a closet every time she went to visit her family. She seemed pretty to him then. Might that be because she was leaving, which always aroused in him a strange feeling of tenderness and guilt, or because the little kerchief suited her so well, with her lipstick on and the perfume she saved for her trips and for the rare occasions when they went out together? No, he remembered he'd always liked seeing her with the little green kerchief that gave her a youthful air.

Letting her carry the toilet case and lock the door, he picked up the two suitcases, stepped into the hallway ahead of her, and went on down the stairs without stopping.

Fortunately a taxi was just dropping off a passenger in front of the building, and without any transition or tiresome wait he put the suitcases on the front seat. Dalia got in back, and the car drove off.

"Take care of yourself" was the last thing Jorge could hear.

Jorge climbed the stairs slowly, with a deep sense of relief but also of emptiness, as though the tension of those long two last hours, from the time they'd gotten up until the door of the taxi had slammed shut, had quite exhausted him.

On the stairs he met the manager, a thin, nervous woman with a piercing voice, pleasant enough in her way but a bit nosy. She was the only person in the pretentious ugly building who went beyond the cold greetings and the forced smiles they got from the other tenants — old couples, matrons swamped by children who kept up a constant din in the hallways — ever since the news that they were not married had apparently leaked out. A boy who was always sitting in the narrow lobby playing with toys for which he was too old looked at Jorge and Dalia every time they went into or out of the building as though they were something from a freak show.

"All by yourself now, eh?" the manager commented on the first landing.

"I'm afraid so."

"If there's anything you need, don't hesitate . . ."

"Thank you."

Jorge pictured the skinny woman dashing at him brandishing the needle and pitilessly plunging it into him, and he almost laughed with amusement as he made his slow way up the endless stairs. He loathed that building. Oh so respectable, and not one lousy elevator!

When he reached his apartment he decided to take a shower and straighten the place up a bit before having lunch. He looked at his watch. Eleven-thirty. He thought of the hours that would now creep by. Days, whole weeks of waiting were contained in those hours. They'd pass more quickly if he did a little housework.

But he did nothing. He felt intensely tired, and he hadn't figured on that. He lay down for a while on the still unmade bed and fell fast asleep.

He came to with a start. He checked his watch and saw he'd been sleeping for hours. There'd be no time for lunch. He tried to put his ideas in order as best he could. He calculated the time. He could still straighten up the apartment, air out the room, remake the bed with fresh sheets, change the towels. And his shower. The shower was indispensable. While the water heater in the kitchen did its job—he couldn't stand cold water, not even in summer—he'd get the other rooms into some semblance of order, or at least the room where he did his reading and sometimes tried to seclude himself.

While he was cleaning up he looked critically, as though seeing it for the first time, at the sparse furniture, the arabesques on the cretonne upholstery that matched the faded cretonne of the curtains. What was the sense of curtains in such a hot climate? And why no flowers? Why did Dalia loathe flowers? He loved them and sometimes bought them and brought them home, like in the movies. But he knew that even as Dalia accepted them she looked forward to throwing them out the moment they began to wilt. They attracted mosquitoes.

He ran a hasty last glance over the apartment, trying to take in even the most remote corner: all was in order. A little lifeless, as though sterile, dry, impersonal, but in order, or at least clean. (And why did what at other times seemed to him a little paradise of intimacy and comfort, especially on those afternoons when Dalia read to him, now strike him as lifeless?)

He dashed to the shower. The warm water ran all over his body, refreshing and calming him. He'd have time to lather up twice. The day was cool, but he'd worked up such a sweat with the suitcases.

He dried himself carefully, further refreshed his skin with cologne, and began to dress in front of the bedroom mirror.

Although he was waiting for it—only God knew how long he'd been waiting for it—his heart skipped a beat when he heard the sharp sound of the door knocker. "A firm knock, no hesitation there," he still had time to think while for the last time he smoothed down his hair. The knock sounded again, muffled but equally firm, as he was running toward the door. As he got there the thought of Dalia came most inopportunely and inexplicably into his mind: her little green kerchief, her recommendations to him. He threw the door wide open.

It was Laura.

His hand trembled on the doorknob. He was relieved to see there was no one in the hallway, that none of his disagreeable neighbors had seen her arrive. But his trembling and his observation were overwhelmed by the presence of Laura, by her quiet smile, by the deep serenity of her enormous eyes, by the exquisitely arranged hair, by the yellow of her linen dress, by the rich voice, calm and slightly ironic, that now broke in on his spellbound contemplation.

"May I?"

Laura, Laura! How long had he waited for the magic moment when he'd see her at his door, her figure silhouetted against the dim light of the hallway! How often had he imagined the scene: Laura smiling, Laura waiting, Laura repeating her knock on the door, vexed at not finding him in. And now, how he'd bungled it! He'd been planning to stand by a window that opened on the staircase and watch her without her noticing it as she waited in front of the door, waited for him to open it, waited for him, grew impatient—because she grew impatient easily—knocked on the door again, and then he'd run to her and embrace her passionately. But, bungler that he was, he'd forgotten his little plan, and so many other plans, dreams, schemes, all of them designed for the sole purpose of forever capturing that moment: Laura visiting him for the first time, Laura's voice sounding in the apartment and transforming it, Laura's dress rustling ever so slightly—but how silly he was! Dresses didn't rustle any more; that was before, in novels—but yes, Laura's dress would rustle slightly when she came in. That's the way he wanted it, and that's the way it would be.

Now there was nothing for it but to accept the presence of the quiet smile, the yellow linen dress that seemed to absorb all the light in the little living room (he'd half closed the shutters for this moment), and the small hand that reached up to the hair to make sure it was all in place—nothing but to ask her, with a clumsy gesture, to come in.

The initial seconds were strained. She set her handbag, a handbag that struck him as very large, on a piece of furniture and began to examine the room.

"So this is where you live."

Since he could think of nothing to say, absorbed as he was in contemplating her, she examined the room once more and repeated her words, which seemed to him to hold some profound truth. What broke the ice was their almost simultaneous realization that in his haste he'd forgotten to put on his shoes and had received her barefoot. They broke out into a loud burst of laughter—maybe too loud—and then he was able to embrace her.

At first he was deathly afraid she'd put up some absurd kind of resistance. Women were like that; just when they seemed ready for everything, some inexplicable fear, something like a defense against an invisible threat that loomed over the whole sex and only they could foresee, ruined it all. Though as a matter of fact, if anybody had put up resistance it had been he: resistance against meeting in dark movie houses that you left painfully frustrated, and then in sad little hotels with unpainted walls, which he felt would cheapen his love and eventually strangle it. No, no; they would wait until they could see each other free of the tyranny of time and place. And he, without explaining much, and she, without asking anything, waited patiently for the arrival of these days of supreme freedom, limited only by the return of a train that had just left.

But all his fears vanished with the first embrace, long, a bit tremulous, punctuated by sighs of relief.

She had come to give herself to him.

And all that afternoon, till well after sunset, Jorge felt that they were sinking into ever thicker and deeper layers of happiness, oblivious to everything: the passage of time, the spreading darkness, the sounds from outside, the insistent ringing of the telephone, a knock at the door, the voices of his neighbors, the eventual silence, the ticking of his watch that finally stopped, the world.

The light and his natural capacity for exaltation ebbed together, to be replaced by calm and silence. Jorge would have liked the silence to continue; but Laura did not let it last long and broke it, talking about things he didn't hear very well and really didn't want to understand. From her great handbag she began to draw things that confirmed Jorge's suspicions and made him smile: pajamas, brushes (why so many brushes?), a book, face powder, a powder puff, new and soft (like her skin, thought Jorge), underwear, those facial tissues without which women seem to find life impossible, strange metallic objects that (as Jorge found out later) were for her hair. But why would Laura talk while she was taking these things out of her bottomless bag and setting them up on the dresser? Was there any need for words?

Jorge began to prepare supper. For weeks he'd been planning an intimate little meal for this night. He'd meant to take a folding table that was never used and that he'd secretly repaired and set it up in the living room, near the balcony, with the doors closed to keep out indiscreet eyes, but with the shutters ajar to let in the cooling breeze. How often had he imagined Laura's hair stirred by the breeze, moving almost imperceptibly and bringing on her characteristic gesture of patting it down!

But brusquely he decided they'd eat in the dining room. That would make it all simpler. It had gotten too late, and once they'd had their supper they could take their time and chat.

They ate in silence. Everything Jorge had been planning all this time to tell her, or not to tell her, during this first night of real true intimacy — the well-turned phrases, the meaningful pauses charged with magic — gave way to ordinary observations.

"It's hard to believe, isn't it?"

"That's right."

"So, you see, everything comes in due time."

"You just have to wait."

"That's right."

"Some heat, eh?"

"Terrific."

That wasn't true. For some time now a benign, almost Edenic land breeze had been blowing on the city and cooling it.

Jorge thought intensely, very intensely, about his happiness. He cleared the table while Laura redid her makeup in the bathroom. Without meaning to he counted how often the faucets opened and closed.

From a drawer Jorge brought out a cigarette case he'd bought for this occasion. He prepared two glasses of liqueur, an ashtray, matches; and, just as he'd planned, he set it all on the living room floor, on top of a clean napkin. Laura would like these little touches. Then he turned out the light, opened the balcony doors, and lay down on the floor. Without a word Laura stretched out by his side and lightly kissed his shoulder. Jorge felt a certain sadness that he could not explain but that dissolved in the comfortable after-supper feeling.

But after a while the breeze became annoying and they decided to close the balcony doors. Within moments, the heat in the small room was stifling. Drowsiness, which Jorge could sense enveloping him with a mixed feeling of irritation and relief, eventually overcame them, and within a few minutes they were sleeping soundly. Jorge could not have said exactly when they left the hard floor and continued their sleep in the bedroom.

Just as he'd planned, Jorge got up very early, perhaps too early, went to the kitchen, and made coffee, strong coffee such as he knew Laura liked. When he returned to the bedroom with the steaming little cup, he gazed on her for a long time before deciding to awake her. It seemed to him that when we sleep we withdraw into a fiercely personal and remote world, sufficient unto itself, where everything (and everyone) becomes superfluous. Barely awake, she drank her coffee, smiled at him with blurry eyes, and her private world closed again behind her.

But the next time he came, Jorge realized that she was awake and pretending to be asleep.

Lying next to her, Jorge heard the sounds of the building, the voices of his neighbors exchanging greetings on the stairs, the motors of the first buses, a far-off voice shouting newspaper headlines, the drip of a faucet, Laura's breathing, irregular now, his own breathing. Then he heard Laura singing to herself, under her breath. Maybe she was staring at the ceiling.

He looked at his watch; he remembered it had stopped during the night. But he needed no watch to know it was very early, too early, and that the day, a very long day, had just begun. Closing his eyes tightly to keep out the sunlight, and to keep his tears from flowing, Jorge fervently wished for time to pass and not to pass.

The Execution

"And the trial starts all over again?" K. asked, almost incredulously.

"To be sure," said the painter. FRANZ KAFKA, *The Trial*, chapter 7

I

An hour before the arrest took place, the phone rang.

Mayer was in the bathroom, shaving. He had delicate skin, especially on his neck; and every time he shaved he inevitably bled a little.

He carefully dried the shaved half of his face and noticed that the lather covering the other half had dried a little. He stepped into the hallway but halted, perplexed, when he realized he'd left the faucet on.

For a few moments he hesitated.

The telephone sat on a low table, on a cushion that muffled the sound of the bell.

Mayer thought that if he went back to turn off the faucet, the phone might stop ringing. Retracing his steps, he turned it off; then he passed from the bathroom into the living room and picked up the receiver.

"Hello."

No one answered.

"Hello," Mayer repeated.

There was no answer.

"Hello, hello," he said again.

But still there was no answer. He waited a few moments, planning to hang up. But before he could do it, he heard someone quietly hanging up at the other end.

Annoyed, he went back to the bathroom. As he passed through the hallway he looked at the clock on the wall: six o'clock. He re-opened the faucet, moistened his face with his brush, and resumed shaving. His motions were precise, with just the right amount of pressure so the blade would cut the beard without scratching the skin.

Mayer concentrated his attention on his chin, where the stubble formed small, almost invisible, whirls that had to be shaved obliquely. Fortunately the skin was tougher here and so the razor could press harder. As the lather disappeared, he could see that he had worked skillfully and that his chin was sparkling clean.

The phone rang again. Mayer set the razor on the edge of the basin. He shut the faucet once more, reached the phone before the fourth ring, and answered tersely.

"Hello."

There was no answer.

"Hello."

Absolute silence at the other end of the line. A few seconds later, someone hung up, quietly, as before.

Mayer decided not to let it bother him. It wasn't the first time it had happened. The telephone intruded on him when he most needed his peace and quiet. At such times, especially in the middle of the night, he covered it with cushions, so arranged as almost to smother the sound of the bell.

He considered leaving it off the hook, but didn't.

He went back to the mirror, trusting that sooner or later the prankster would tire of the game and he'd be able to spend the evening as he'd planned, checking the works of his watch, which was running slow, and polishing and cleaning his lighter, whose cheap nickel finish tended to lose its shine. Much later on he'd fix his supper and eat. He wasn't planning to go out or expecting any visitors; the rest of the night would go by quietly as he read or, better yet, smoked in his small living room, as he often did, letting his mind drift aimlessly, in the darkness, with the windows open and all the lights out so the neighbors couldn't see him.

To make full use of those hours he had pasted dark paper over those windows where the outside light could seep in. During these soirées in the dark, he would smoke slowly till he'd used up his daily allowance of cigarettes.

He began to shave his neck, which was the area requiring the greatest care. Through the cushion he'd left on top of the phone, the bell sounded anew, patiently. Mayer decided to ignore it and finish shaving. The razor slid clumsily over the skin of his neck and he could see how the lather turned faintly red, first at one spot, then at another. He tossed the razor into the basin, rinsed his neck and face, saw in the mirror that the cuts were superficial, and decided to interrupt his shave. He found this disturbance of his daily routine deeply upsetting.

He went into the other room and looked for a moment at the table where the telephone, now covered, sat. Suddenly he uncovered it, picked up the receiver, and listened without saying anything.

No one said anything at the other end either. Mayer tried to identify some sound in the receiver. But there was absolute silence wherever the call was coming from. Mayer stood a long time with the receiver pressed to his ear, trying to pierce the silence.

He looked about the room. He thought he noticed that something in the objects around him, he couldn't say just what, had changed in some imperceptible way.

Several minutes went by without the persistent caller's interrupting the silence.

With infinite care, so as not to reveal his movements, Mayer set the receiver on the cushion and moved away. He looked at the phone for a moment. Then he slowly went into the room that faced the street. He couldn't help smiling when he noticed he was walking on tiptoe. As he passed his front door he lit a cigarette. He went on to the window and looked out onto the street. The light had begun to fade. He remembered that the days grew shorter in fall. After a few puffs that tasted flat he put out the cigarette. Then he went to his bedroom. He looked at the watch and the lighter he'd left on the bed as he came in. The metal reflected the pale light of an afternoon drawing to its close. Slowly he returned to the room with the phone. As he neared the door he again tried to walk without being heard.

He tiptoed over to the instrument and, kneeling down, held his ear against the receiver without picking it up. All he could hear was the same calm impenetrable silence. Obviously no one had hung up, because there was no dial tone. He got to his feet but thought he heard something in the receiver and quickly knelt down again. The silence continued, unchanged.

After a bit his muscles began to ache and he stretched out on the floor, resting his head on the cushion. Very carefully he moved the mouthpiece aside so that his breathing would not be heard. Then he realized that the noises from the street, car horns, people's voices, entered the mouthpiece freely and could be heard by those listening at the other end. Determined to deprive them of this small advantage, and straining to avoid any brusque movement that might betray his presence by the phone, he took out his handkerchief and very, very carefully placed it, still folded, over the mouthpiece. He listened anxiously to see whether his blocking the sounds had had any effect at the other end. But there was no noticeable change in the silence.

The afternoon was coming to an end and the small room was filling up with shadows. Every day the arrival of night brought a deep calm to Mayer. As the outlines of things became blurred, he felt something like a small daily victory. He preferred winter with its short hours of diffused, sometimes grey, light over the long days of summer when night was slow in coming.

But lying for some time now in a strained position on the floor, his body propped up on one arm and the muscles of his buttocks sore, pressing his handkerchief against the mouthpiece of the phone, Mayer felt, for the first time in many years, that the spreading shadows did not bring with them the usual sense of well-being and that his heart was beating wildly in his chest.

He was tempted to turn on the light, but he didn't dare. He realized that if he moved, his clothes would rub against each other and betray his movements, and his silent interlocutor would again penetrate that small private world that Mayer felt he had just lost. Perhaps forever, he thought, perhaps forever, pressing the handkerchief against the mouthpiece as a last line of defense.

His whole body was bathed in sweat that ran down from his sunken chest as far as his navel and then around his waist, soaking his back. He felt the sweat running from his thighs to behind his knees.

His eyes explored the darkness. Once again he was struck by the idea, fleeting and inexplicable, that everything was different, that each object, each book of his tiny library, each piece of his ugly, badly painted furniture, had undergone a profound change and, far from soothing him as before, was threatening him in some vague but dreadful way.

He felt that if he could manage to hold his uncomfortable position long enough, whoever was at the other end of the line would also grow tired and everything would return to normal.

Three short but firm knocks on the door startled him. Almost at the same time, he heard someone hang up at the other end of the line.

He got up from the floor; limping and almost hopping on one leg (he felt a ridiculous pain when he placed his weight on the one that had gone to sleep), he went down the hall to the front door, opened it, and found himself facing three heavily armed policemen. Afterward he remembered that one of them was very tall, blond, with the lovely face of an adolescent girl.

"Mr. Mayer?"

"That's right."

"You have to come with us."

Mayer said nothing. He raised one hand to the switch and turned on the light.

"May we come in?"

Mayer noted the polite tone of the oldest one.

"We have to search the premises before we leave."

"Come in." His voice was calm, Mayer could hear. "May I change my clothes?"

"That's not necessary," said the tall blond policeman, in the same polite tone used by the oldest one.

Tapping his numb foot against the floor, Mayer calmly waited for two of the policemen to finish their brief search while the third stood guard at the door. Suddenly he felt an enormous exhaustion come over him. His taps on the floor slowed down until they ceased completely, as the circulation returned to his numb leg.

He looked toward the window. It was almost night. Again he felt the familiar pleasure darkness brought him, and he was tempted to turn out the light while the search was going on. But he realized that such an action would be misinterpreted, and he waited.

Once the search was finished, one of the officers was carrying his jacket and some papers.

"Are these your papers?"

"Yes."

"Then let's go."

The youngest one turned out the light. Mayer cast a quick glance over the apartment. In the fading light, everything went back to its air of intimacy and repose.

With a sharp sound, the youngest officer closed the door.

11

The police station was extremely clean. You could have taken it for a hotel or a hospital. As in a luxury hotel, every now and then a little man in a dark uniform would come by with a gleaming dustpan — Mayer had never seen such a gleaming dustpan; it might have been made of highly polished copper — and a small broom, and with an almost imperceptible movement of the broom fed into the dustpan, whose mouth opened when it was set down, anything that might lessen the cleanliness of the place: cigarette butts, pieces of paper, dust. The place smelled of disinfectant.

From the door of the small office where they stopped on their arrival in order to verify his identification, Mayer could see two long corridors lined with doors on either side and illuminated by skylights in the daytime and, at night, by lamps fastened to the wall at intervals.

The booking officer offered Mayer a pen and with a precise gesture pointed to a line at the bottom of a sheet of paper he was passing him with his other hand.

"Read the statement and sign here."

"Where?"

"Here." And the man pointed to the specific line with his little finger.

Mayer quickly signed where he had been told.

"But you haven't read it," said the officer, looking at him fixedly.

Mayer did not answer.

The three officers who had arrested him and the booking officer looked at each other for a moment.

"Does this mean you agree to it?"

Since no answer was forthcoming, the officer placed the sheet in a folder, opened a metal filing case on his right, filed the document, closed the drawer, and turned toward him. After hesitating a moment, he spoke in a firm voice to a guard waiting by the door, "Take the prisoner away."

The guard, much older than the policemen and perhaps restricted by his age to working inside the building, led him down the corridor that began at the door of the booking office. They walked slowly. It was obvious that the effort of walking was a strain on the guard. At first he grasped Mayer by the arm; then, as his breathing became more labored, the pressure of his hand on Mayer's arm increased. As they advanced down the long corridor, the prisoner felt the man leaning on him more, struggling for breath.

"Would you like to stop a minute?" Mayer asked.

"Yes, please," the guard replied.

"Lean on me," Mayer suggested when they got under way again.

The man laid his hand on Mayer's shoulder, and Mayer could feel him resting all his weight on him. Since this position became very uncomfortable, Mayer grasped him by the arm and held him up firmly. That way they were able to proceed more easily.

After the first corridor they crossed a courtyard shut in by windows of opaque glass and lit by a single electric light, then a kind of vaulted vestibule that led to a slightly colder corridor that had metal doors with small barred peepholes.

With Mayer still holding him up, the guard opened a door at the end of the corridor, at some distance from the others.

"This is it," said the guard. "You're lucky. These cells face a courtyard. I'll come once a day to let you out there so you can get some fresh air."

"Thanks," said Mayer, trying to smile.

Busy with his breathing, the man said no more. He closed the door, bolted it, and then Mayer could hear him walk off.

Mayer inspected the cell. It probably wasn't much different from many others, though perhaps it was a bit cleaner. Floor and walls smelled of the same disinfectant as did the corridors in the whole building.

Mayer sat down on the bed of metal springs covered by a mattress and a sheet and screwed to the wall at one end. It didn't seem too uncomfortable. A pale light, probably coming from some lamp in what the guard had called a courtyard, illuminated the cell. Mayer took off his shirt, covered the narrow barred outside window as best he could until he achieved almost total darkness inside the cell, lay down, and fell sound asleep.

III

When another guard, younger and apparently healthy, brought him breakfast he announced to him that he would not be charged that day.

The almost complete absence of all sound in the outer corridor, which he noticed when the guard set down the tin tray on the cell's bench, leaving the door open several minutes, told Mayer that few of the cells were occupied. Otherwise, at this hour of the morning, he would have heard voices, the sound of falling objects, footsteps. All one could hear was a murmur coming from some cell impossible to identify but that must have come from one of them, since the section where he had been taken was completely cut off from the rest of the building.

When the guard had left, Mayer washed carefully in a small basin installed in one corner of the cell. Then, slowly, he ate breakfast. Once that was done, he washed his tray, set it on the floor in a position that would allow the water to drain off, and sat down on the bench.

Some time later (Mayer figured two hours) the old guard came and unlocked the metal door that opened onto what he called the courtyard, of whose dimensions and appearance Mayer knew nothing, since he had not troubled to remove his shirt from the bars or look out through the window.

"You're entitled to half an hour," said the guard, and left.

Mayer stepped outside and was pleasantly surprised by the size of the courtyard. It was quite spacious, perhaps four times the size of his cell. Other cells opened onto it, but their metal doors and peepholes were closed. They were obviously empty.

Mayer, who the night before had been under the impression

that the building had only one story, was astonished to see that the walls surrounding the courtyard rose to an enormous height. That part of the building had to be very tall, at least ten stories.

The light came down onto the open space as though shining on the bottom of a well. It seemed to Mayer that the sunshine would only touch the ground in summer, and then only for a few moments. It also occurred to him that as they struck the immense surface of the walls, painted white, the rays would produce an unpleasant glare.

He walked around the yard several times, first in one direction and then in another, until he had exhausted all possible directions. As he was beginning to grow tired, the old guard opened the inside door and, gesturing to him, said, "Time to come in."

As he returned to his cell Mayer felt tempted to ask him the cause of his respiratory difficulties, but he limited himself to thanking him and sat down once more on the bench. The outer door was again closed.

Two days later Mayer was taken to a room that seemed to him very far from the one in which he had signed the statement, though not really very different. This time it was not the old guard who came for him but a civilian official who read him the statement, showed him the signature he had placed on it three days earlier, and asked him to accompany him.

The interrogation room was at the far end of the building. When the official opened the glass door, silence fell over the room where three civilians and two men in uniform were speaking in a low voice, sitting behind a long table. The place was as scrupulously clean as the rest of the building; its light came from tall windows. Everything was modern and comfortable, even in good taste.

Mayer was invited to sit down on a chair facing the table but at some distance from it. He immediately noticed that a thick dossier had been set on the table in front of him.

After the usual questions about the prisoner's name, age, etc., had been got out of the way, the civilian in charge opened the dossier and addressed Mayer, "Do you recognize the signatures at the bottom of each of these documents?"

Mayer bent forward, because from where he was sitting he could not see the pages the official was pointing to. He stood up and started to approach the table.

"Allow me . . ."

"The accused must remain seated."

The official raised the dossier and set it upright on the table's edge so that Mayer could see it.

"Do you recognize the signatures?" he repeated.

As one page after another was displayed for him, Mayer could see his signature clearly affixed on the lower right corner of each one.

"I do."

The official looked at his colleagues again, and they nodded their assent.

"Do you remember the occasion on which these documents were signed?"

"I often signed documents like that."

"Do you know what they concern?"

Mayer did not answer.

"Do you know that an employee in a higher office, a suspected accomplice, has been found dead?"

Mayer remained silent.

The official repeated the question without obtaining any answer from Mayer.

After consulting his colleagues with a look, he continued, "They concern money that was never spent and that cannot be accounted for."

Mayer assumed that he was again speaking of the documents.

Silence fell over the room. The glare that came through the windows made Mayer blink. His days in the cell had heightened the sensitivity of his retina.

Those on the other side of the table put their heads together and held a brief conference that Mayer could not hear.

"Does the accused have anything to say?" the official asked.

"No," replied Mayer.

"Do you wish to sign a confession?"

"I do."

Once this procedure had been taken care of, the official who had brought him took Mayer back to his cell. The old guard was waiting for him by its door and turned the key in the lock. Mayer entered the cell.

The bright light in the other room had produced an acute burning in his eyes. He remembered reading a story about a long-term prisoner whose eyes had become irritated and who had treated them by pressing the palms of his hands against the humid floor and then immediately placing them over his closed eyelids. He tried this tactic and was surprised to feel some degree of relief.

Sitting on his bench he recollected insignificant details of the place where he'd just been, peculiarities that had attracted his attention in the faces, movements, and clothes of the officials. One of them was missing a finger on his right hand. When he felt Mayer watching him, he'd tried to conceal the lack of a finger by covering the mutilated hand with the other. Mayer asked himself whether he always covered his hand that way or whether he'd done it that morning when he saw himself being watched.

He recalled many other details of the scene that in one way or another had caught his attention, such as the face of one of the officials, which had struck him as infinitely placid.

The day went by without incidents. For some reason the old guard did not come to open the door leading into the courtyard, but Mayer didn't ascribe much importance to this fact. As he sat there on the bench, the hours slipped by, interrupted only by the sound of the door being opened for his midday and evening meals.

After supper, Mayer felt tired. Moments before falling asleep he thought of the signatures, crudely forged, that appeared at the foot of each sheet in the dossier. He tried to remember the face of some employee in the higher office, but he'd never seen any of them.

By the time he realized that Lens, who worked at the next desk, was the only one, apart from himself, who had access to the documents they'd shown him, he was almost asleep, and Lens's face blended with the jumble of distorted and tranquil images that is the usual prelude to sleep.

During the following days few significant or unexpected incidents interrupted the flow of prison life. The prisoner adjusted quickly to the daily routine. Occasionally the guard forgot to come and open the door to the yard; but Mayer didn't much miss those walks, during which the glare from the walls had sometimes become painful.

When he could get out he walked first in one direction and then in another around the small courtyard. Then he would stretch out on the ground, which was less humid than the floor of his cell, and on grey days would look up at the sky. He soon came to think of his cell as a temporary but by no means unpleasant lodging.

It seemed to him that, given the circumstances, things could have been worse; and he was thankful for little additional comforts, such as the use of the small courtyard, which, he was sure, was not granted to other prisoners. At one point he was filled with gratitude and had to wipe away the tears running down his face. When the old guard came to bring him his supper, he took a lively interest in the man. They chatted for a while, and the guard promised to buy certain medications that Mayer had recommended to him.

One day he felt a burning desire for it to rain. It was one of the few things he sometimes wished for. Mostly because he found rain soothing. He recalled having taken long walks under the cold rain of spring. The memory of those walks brought with it his first clear recollection — until now he'd only thought of her in a vague way — of Eva. But it was not a painful recollection, in spite of his intense desire to see her.

This recollection came to him often and distracted him during the long sessions of the trial, when Mayer, as a rule, remained silent.

The first time since his arrest that he saw Lens was during his second visit to the interrogation room. Throughout that session Lens avoided looking at him. The second time was at the session of the trial at which all the witnesses — there weren't many — testified, beginning with Lens as a witness for the prosecution. While another witness was testifying, Lens looked up for a moment and met Mayer's eyes. He tried to avert his glance; but time and again his eyes encountered Mayer's, as though they could not avoid it.

Lens became extremely agitated. He requested permission to step outside briefly. Since he had already testified, he was allowed to leave the courtroom. As he passed by Mayer, he looked up, as though driven to do so by an irresistible force. The usher who accompanied him had to hold on to him to keep him from falling to the floor. With the help of another usher he managed practically to drag him from the room. Mayer did not see him again until the last session. He'd aged greatly and appeared to be sick. He kept his eyes on the floor until the moment when, after sentencing, the presiding judge declared the case closed in scrupulous accord with every requirement of legal procedure.

But on that last morning of the trial, Mayer was far away from the spacious courtroom. It was raining, and Eva was by his side.

IV

During all the time that Mayer remained in the cell by the small courtyard it didn't rain.

On toward the second month, he heard the guard say he felt better, thanks perhaps to the prisoner's suggestions, though he couldn't be absolutely sure of this because of the many medications he was taking. For Mayer this was most gratifying news. He told the guard in turn that his health had also improved. He said this not to make him feel good, nor as a kind of thanks for the regularity with which he received his meals. His health really had improved markedly, an improvement he attributed especially to his now un-troubled sleep. When, occasionally, he awoke in the middle of the night he briefly enjoyed the silence that prevailed throughout the immense building and then once more fell sound asleep.

The morning when Mayer left his cell, flanked by the warden and an aide and followed by the chaplain, his wish was fulfilled. As the small procession advanced toward the great central courtyard through uncovered passageways Mayer had never seen before, he felt a few drops of rain fall on his forehead and his hands. Then the drops became more frequent, turning into a refreshing light rain he found most delightful. He looked at his manacled hands; and, as was always the case, he felt moved by the small drops of rain. When they reached the great central courtyard, the ground was soaked and glistening. The procession came to a halt.

Without understanding why, Mayer thought of Eva. By some association of ideas, he inwardly repeated to himself several times, ". . . my nard gave forth its fragrance." While he waited, images crowded into his mind, without disturbing him. Smiling, he thought that if he stayed there long in the rain with the memory of Eva, his incipient erection might become visible, which might disturb the chaplain.

But everything happened according to plan.

Seconds before the larger screw, turning at great speed and with enormous pressure, broke his second cervical vertebra, tearing through the spinal cord, its movement synchronized with that of the metal band that cut off the passage of air, Mayer, more clearly than ever before, had the sensation of being held, like a tiny defenseless creature, within the safe, immense, and fertile womb of iniquity, perfectly protected—forever! he told himself, forever!—from all possible iniquities.

The Master of Life and Death

I decided to change my work schedule so I could rest in the mornings. That way, I'd be more alert, less exhausted, after midnight.

But that morning I got up at dawn and immediately prepared to go out. I decided to leave breakfast for later.

My plan was to explore the building where I lived, and then the whole block; but then I thought it would be better to go a little farther off and start a few blocks away.

At first I felt discouraged, but soon I was surprised by how easy it was in spite of my being dressed normally. There's more good in people than we expect. I'd thought that I'd get better results wearing shabby clothes, but at the last minute I lost my nerve. Anyhow, it would have been unnecessary, because my results were rather satisfying, almost brilliant, at least at the outset.

At the first place where I rang, a young woman answered. She looked at me with the wary affability of someone opening a door.

"Good morning."

"Morning."

"Sorry to bother you this early."

"What can I do for you?"

"Do you have anything you don't need?"

"I'll see whether I have some change."

"No, not money; old clothes or shoes."

She seemed doubtful — whether about my intentions or about the possibility of giving me what I was asking for, I don't know.

"Just a minute . . ." And after a moment's hesitation she shut the door.

When she came back she was carrying several items of clothing, very worn but clean, and a newspaper.

"This is all I have. Have a look and see if it's what you want."

"I'll take anything."

I took the clothes and started to wrap them, afraid she might change her mind.

"Thank you ever so much."

"No, no, you're doing me a favor; I didn't know what to do with them. My husband wears things out so fast."

That made me curious and emboldened me to ask, "Is your husband all right?"

The question seemed to surprise her. She hesitated a moment and for some reason blushed and laughed.

"Yes, he's fine, but he wears out a lot of clothes."

I couldn't see what one statement had to do with the other; but I didn't want to go too far, and so I stopped asking questions.

"Thank you ever so much."

"Don't mention it."

For the first time she looked at me steadily, still smiling. She lowered her head, as though enjoying a private joke. For a moment I felt a rapport between us, but I didn't want to push.

I started to leave.

"Thanks a lot."

"Not at all."

She moved to close the door. I noticed that, a little late, she was making a connection between my appearance and my request. But the course of her thoughts must have shifted; she looked away, then closed the door, gazing down distractedly as she patted down her hair.

"Goodbye for now."

"Goodbye."

On the floor below—instinct told me to start with the upper stories and work my way down—no one was home in spite of its being so early. I took a mental note. I'd be back.

But the results on the second floor were even more surprising. An old woman opened the door. She seemed flustered and sweaty. Her unfriendly eyes looked me over from top to toe.

"What do you want?"

I made my request as best I could.

The woman went off without answering. Through the half-open door I could see part of the room, almost totally dark. Piles of newspapers tied with string blocked the way. The room smelled dank. On the wall that separated it from the rooms beyond, a picture was hanging askew. The light coming from the other side and reflected on the glass kept me from seeing the surface of the canvas. Carefully, I opened the door a little farther.

Next to the wall stood a piano with the keyboard cover open. More dusty newspapers and magazines were lying on the keys. From the feeble light in the place I deduced that it had a window. I stuck my head in and was able to confirm my deduction. The rest of the furniture consisted of a sofa, an armchair, a table without tablecloth but with the remnants of a meal. I withdrew to my original position before the woman, who was skittering back from inside, reached the door.

"Just now I can't find a thing."

"It doesn't matter. I can come back another day."

An insistent male voice sounded from one of the inside rooms, much to her annoyance, it seemed.

"Coming!"

"Really, I can come back some other time," I said again.

The voice from the inside room sounded again, with a kind of muffled violence. The woman made an angry gesture and once more left the door. When she came back, she seemed exhausted.

"I'm waiting for the pharmacy to open so I can go down to buy his medicine. I'm by myself, I don't have anybody to help me." In her voice I could sense fatigue and resentment.

I realized there was no time to be lost.

"They're already open. I saw one close by when I was coming in. I'll go buy it for you."

"No, that's out of the question."

"Don't leave him alone!"

She rushed off again. I heard her angry voice talking to someone, and she came back with a bottle and some money.

"Good Lord, how humiliating!"

I grabbed the money.

When I returned, the door stood open. I waited a few moments for the woman to come back. Not a sound came from inside the apartment. I stepped in.

I straightened the crooked picture. My first impression of the room was confirmed; but it seemed to me even narrower, with unpainted walls. Piles of newspapers lined its sides and spread as far as the table. I lifted some books from the piano keys, which did not spring up.

I looked toward the corridor that led to the inside rooms. Since I didn't see anyone, I knocked. There was no answer. I decided to go in. On one side of the corridor a walkway projected out over a courtyard; on the other side there were bedrooms. I passed by a closed door. I knocked again, to no avail. I decided the woman must be back at the far end of the apartment, and I called her. I moved on a little until I was in front of the second bedroom. A man was lying on an iron bed. The bed stood in the middle of the room, perhaps to take full advantage of the ventilation from the corridor. The man's eyes were fixed on me; his breathing was labored. I observed him a moment from the doorway.

"Your wife sent me for this medicine."

At first there was no answer. After a bit, the man directed me with his eyes to a night table, where there was a glass of water. I opened the bottle, poured some of the medicine into the glass, and held it out to him; but he didn't budge. I perched on the edge of the bed and helped him sit up. Then he slowly sipped from the glass.

While still propping him up against my chest with my free arm, I turned the pillows over, to cool them, and set them back in place; then I carefully let him down on them. For a moment he breathed easier, but in no time his chest was again heaving in spasms. The skin around his lips had turned dark.

Just then the woman came back. I felt the floor shake with the heavy tread of her feet, which were now bare.

"I've given him his medicine."

She laughed as though embarrassed.

"I'm fixing dinner, I don't have anybody to help out."

"Just relax, he'll get better, you'll see."

"What a lot of bother for you."

"We ought to give him an injection; he seems very restless."

"The spirit burner's over here. I'll boil the needle."

"Don't bother. I'm used to it," and I gently pushed her out of the room.

The burner was under the night table. Since the wick was dry, I held the burner upside down to make the fuel soak into it; then I set it back on the floor, but far from the sick man, lit it, and waited for the water to boil in a small pan encrusted with magnesia.

The sick man shifted his position again. Once more I helped him sit up on the bed. As I raised him, I felt him trying to hold on to my shoulders. I realized he'd grown weaker since I'd first heard him cry out. I moistened my handkerchief with alcohol and brought it up to his lips. Slowly he opened his eyes.

"I'm going to give you an injection. You'll breathe better in a minute."

There was no response.

When the water started to boil in the pan I poured it out, and almost burning my fingers I used the plunger of the syringe to draw up the contents of one of several ampules lying on the night table.

Standing next to the bed I saw that the breathing gradually grew quieter. The bare chest, covered by a tough parchment-like skin, stopped its restless movement.

I felt one of the sweaty hands. I noticed it gradually warming. With my handkerchief I dried the shiny bald head. The pale purplish ring that had appeared around the mouth grew lighter until it blended with the general yellowness of the skin. The nostrils slowly spread open, and the veins on the temples came back to life. The man seemed to have moved directly from asphyxia into sleep. I placed my ear over his heart. I heard a weak, labored sound that reminded me of a far-off old car that could stop at any moment because all its parts had broken down. I covered his legs with a sheet and opened the window and the doors to the rest of the apartment all the way. He was sound asleep. I watched him a while. A pursing of his mouth that I'd thought was permanent had disappeared.

I heard water running in the back; the woman was working in the kitchen. Beyond the room where the man was lying there was a bathroom, whose walls no one had washed for a long time. I tightened the faucets, which were leaking. In spite of my efforts, one kept on dripping. The floor was covered with illustrated Sunday papers. I figured they'd been put there to entertain the users of the toilet, or perhaps to avoid having to mop the floor.

In the next room a whole wall was taken up by a huge wardrobe with big mirrors. Bundles of clothes, apparently waiting to be washed, filled the rest of the room. I looked at myself in a mirror. My hair was tousled, and I combed it carefully in the weak light that managed to come through the dark paint that covered the panes of a window.

Looking into the last room of the apartment, I saw that the woman, still barefoot, was engrossed in cooking something, with her back toward me. I looked at her for a moment. Her brusque movements, and her whole body, gave off a kind of rough vitality.

As I passed by him again, I saw the man sleeping with his chest fully relaxed.

I opened the front door and rang the bell, as though I were coming for the first time. The woman answered the door with the same expression of curiosity as before.

"Your husband's asleep now."

"Bless you!"

"Isn't there anybody to give him an injection when he gets like that?"

"Some days my cousin comes."

"I could come now and then."

"But my cousin doesn't charge me."

"Neither will I. All I want is some old clothes you don't need."

"Wait a minute."

I left there feeling pleased and carrying the morning's donations. I went into the building across the street, which seemed more prosperous. As I stepped inside I thought that if I got the same results there I wouldn't be able to carry it all.

But contrary to all my expectations, luck was not with me. In some of the places where I knocked, the people were still asleep. At others they slammed the door on me, angrily. In still others nobody was home. I received a tie from a half-dressed man; a boy sitting in a hallway gave me a doll that was almost in pieces but that he seemed to be especially fond of. A lady handed me an empty tin can.

"At least you'll have something to hold whatever people give you."

I realized she hadn't understood what I was after.

I got back to my place exhausted. I looked over what I'd collected: two old shirts, a towel, the tie, the doll, some torn but clean stockings, a sheet, the can, a glass.

I turned on the radio and lay down for a while. When I woke up with a start I realized I'd slept almost an hour. But after eating something, I decided that in what time I had left before going to work I'd be able to go over the results of my efforts.

III

A little after midnight the alarm jolted me out of my sleep. It took me a while to get up. I was very tired from the morning's expedition and the pressure of the day's work at the office.

With my hand on the "off" button of the alarm I fell back asleep. I had some vague dreams and a nightmare. I woke up several times, startled and afraid I'd drop off again and not wake up till morning. Every time I looked at it after long complicated dreams, the big hand had barely advanced by half a minute. Through sheer willpower I managed to tear myself out of bed.

When I reached the square with the few things I'd been able to collect, some of them were already there.

The father and son were sleeping in their usual spot. Under the arch nearest the dock, Joaquín's wife was talking to him quietly. Joaquín's eyes, intense and sullen, were fixed on space.

I came close to them. I offered them the things I'd collected, making it clear they could take what they wanted.

Joaquín kept on staring into space with the same expression. His wife raised her head and glanced at me dully for a moment. She looked indifferently over what I was offering and took the best items. Then she tightened her kerchief under her chin, crossed her arms, and rested her back against the wall.

I sat down on the ground near them. After a while, the woman leaned over, took a bottle out of a bag, poured something that looked like soup into a can and handed it to Joaquín, who drank it slowly, without looking at us. Then she refilled the can and handed it to me. I felt hungry and drank all she'd served me, after which a deep sense of well-being came over me. I went over to the father and son and left the other things near them.

By the sidewalk I saw a piece of cardboard with some caked mud on it. I cleaned it thoroughly, placed it near Joaquín and his wife, and sat down. I was incredibly tired, far beyond mere sleepiness.

The square was empty. Not a breath of air stirred in the sticky heat. The flare of the refinery on the other side of the bay was burning more brightly than usual. The columns of the high arcade were tinged with a yellow that grew more intense when a slight breeze fanned the flame. In that humid heat, everything seemed saturated with grease. A fire truck returned silently to the firehouse. I imagined that the attendant at the first-aid station would have nothing to do tonight and would be reading by his lamp. I stretched out on the ground.

When I woke up for a few moments, the dogs of the old woman who comes there very late to sleep, all of them very clean and recently washed with perfumed soap, were sniffing at me and pressing up against me to spend the night. Joaquín's wife had disappeared. Joaquín was sitting up, smoking. He offered me a cigarette, which I accepted with the nonchalance I've learned so well.

I looked toward where the young black man usually lies, under the high arcade, but he hadn't come. Maybe he'd found another place to sleep, though I know he doesn't have much strength left. This worried me. He's the one I have to keep my eye on. My whole day's activities are just preparation for him, for being as close to him as possible every night.

IV

Now that it's all over, my thoughts often drift back to that square, and I see it in every slightest detail. I could name its every last stone.

The first to arrive — although I've lost them and it's all receding into the past, I prefer to speak in the present tense; I'm sure they're still alive — are the young man and the older one. They always come from the direction of the city. They cross the square slowly, loaded down with bundles; the older one pokes around in the big garbage cans and from time to time hands part of what he finds to the younger one, who wolfs it down without a word.

Their usual place is the doorway of an always-closed shop. They carefully set down their bundles of newspapers, wrapping paper, pieces of clothing, a shoe, a bag, and they rest, perhaps waiting for the square to empty out completely. Then, with long pauses between one movement and another, they take off their shoes and move over to the edge of the sidewalk, where there is a spigot.

The older one applies a little pressure to the valve of the spigot, which drips day and night; and they both wash in the puny stream.

I've never heard them talk. I've learned they are father and son. They look strong and, in spite of the old man's bandages, relatively healthy. There's not much to be hoped for from them.

The rest come a little later. Joaquín, the white-haired drunkard, always arrives by himself. He goes directly to his usual spot, where the lower arcade forms a very sheltered corner, lies down on a doorstep, and goes to sleep. Last night the woman came and laid papers over him.

The thin young black man shouts a while before falling asleep. He's very sick. I don't know where he gets the strength to shout like that.

Long before he gets there I can hear him coming from the direction of the harbor. He likes to argue out loud. He always settles down under the higher arcade, by the door of an apartment house — sometimes in the vestibule, but the last resident to come home throws him out of there. I think the north wind must make it hard for him in winter, because the arches, so tall there, give him no protection.

Resting on his things, with one arm propped up on his raised knee, he argues a little. As soon as someone tells him to be quiet he lies down and goes to sleep.

The last to arrive is the old woman. She comes when the others have already fallen asleep. She comes with three dogs, all very clean and with colored ribbons tied to their necks. She moves laboriously with a great bundle under her arm. Her skin is tough and very wrinkled, like a stone; and the gnarled fists that hold the bundle or threaten the dogs never open. The animals drink from the faucet, and then she drinks too.

Some nights still others come, almost always men, not very young, who sleep at various spots throughout the city and go to the nearest one when they feel drowsy. Some of them discover the arcades of this square and take a liking to them, only to leave them later for other places, disappearing for a long time or never coming back at all. There are busy nights when as I go off to bed I see the arcades full of sleeping bodies.

The only ones I can really depend on are the father and son, the black man, Joaquín, his wife, the old woman, and the animals. If they haven't come by the time I go home, I know they'll come soon. On hot nights I go out to enjoy a breath of air, which no sooner blows than it dies down.

I walk slowly along the higher arcade. Soon they'll come. It's after midnight. They can't be long.

Far off I hear the voice of the thin young black man arguing out loud. Some group of late-night revellers imitate him, and this riles him no end. It'll take him a long time to fall asleep. Joaquín comes, brought along by the woman. She stays a while talking to him in a low voice and then leaves.

After the casual visitors, who arrive earlier, come the dogs with their owner. Later, much later, the father and son.

Hidden behind the column farthest from the lamppost in the middle of the square, making sure they don't notice me, I see them as one by one they arrive and then fall asleep.

V

These days the thin young black man sleeps almost all the time and hardly eats. He no longer leaves his sheltered spot. Sometimes when I go to work in the morning I see that he's managed to sit up and is drinking a little milk that Joaquín has given him. He props his arm up on his raised knee and looks into space. He sleeps on a piece of cardboard and covers himself with a large towel I've managed to get for him. I've spent whole nights near him, fearing that one of them might be his last. I must be there when it all ends.

He hasn't spoken since the night when he hallucinated for several hours, lying face up and constantly moving his hands.

I try to spend a lot of time with him, because the end is coming. He can only breathe with great effort, and sometimes his breathing stops for longer than normal, only to start again when it seems it's all over. I must take my place very close to him, because the columns block the light that comes from the only lamppost on the square and it's hard to see his face.

Tomorrow I'll send word to the office not to expect me for several days. That way I'll be able to sleep during the day and spend the nights with him. One slip, and all would be lost. Soon I must concentrate all my powers of vigilance and observation and be on guard against even the slightest distraction. If it all came to an end without my being alert and at my post, I'd never forgive myself.

There's no danger during the day. The day has the strange power to reinvigorate him; and in the afternoons, when I get up and go out for my coffee and a little stroll, I see that he's sat up, that he's resting with his outstretched arm laid on his knee, and that his yellowish eyes shine again. Perhaps the woman gives him something to eat in the morning, after I leave, knowing I can stay away till nightfall without worrying.

Night drains him of all his energy; I can sense that's the time of greatest danger. One careless instant would be fatal, or what's worse, unpardonable. The ground is uncomfortable, and it's cold; but the day is long enough for me to sleep and regain my strength. I don't know how many nights this will go on. I must be prepared; I have done my duty. I've brought him medications and even got a paramedic to come see him. Now all that's left for me is to observe.

VI

The other night I thought the end had come. His throat started to make a sound as though something were blocking his breathing and the air were scraping against the obstacle on the way out. I'd shifted away a little, but I could tell from the sound that something abnormal was going on. I took up a fixed position next to him and watched every detail. His face had become very drawn, his mouth hung half open, and his lips were dry. I know that dry lips are an unfailing symptom of the approaching end. Sometimes this dryness accompanies a quick end; but when the end is slow, the lips separate gradually and then draw back and a little up over the teeth, which become dry before the lips do. I've noticed that if the process follows its normal course the whole inside of the mouth dries out and the tongue, which tries in vain to moisten the lips, can no longer form sounds. Only a tiny amount of air enters the body; it gets as far as the bronchi, but hardly any reaches the lungs. Soon thereafter all sound stops, and the special instant is suddenly upon you, imperceptible sometimes for the layman, but never for the trained eye. This is the instant that requires a super-human effort of concentration: one little lapse of attention and life will have slipped away before my eyes, I will have lost it.

This instant is subject to endless variations. There is a backward movement of the head, followed by total inertness. The pallor that spreads from the ears toward the mouth sometimes signals the pre-cise instant and the moments that follow, when stiffness has not yet set in. Once that takes place, all further observation is useless. The most common form is the gradual sinking of the jaw, which is drawn toward the chest as the muscles lose their ability to hold it in place. Experience has shown me that in such cases one must watch carefully, because no sudden motion will signal the final moment, which will try, as much as it can, to pass unnoticed.

For testing, a candle flame achieves an accuracy unsurpassed by any other method. Impelled — ever more feebly, to be sure — by the weak flow of air coming out of the mouth, it will give very precise indications. If carefully applied very close to the lips, preferably placed on the chest, it will allow only the tiniest mar-gin of error. While life lasts, the sensitive flame, that most delicate precision instrument to which I owe such accurate measurements, bends slightly to one side; it burns erect once untouched by even the slightest breath. Thanks to it one can determine the moment of passage, the most elusive, which follows the last and most pre-cious of all; one can watch it approach, halt, approach again. By its light one can observe the face, which reveals the most subtle de-tails: the trembling of the eyelids, the sinking of the temples, the gradual sharpening of the cheekbones, the collapse of the cheeks, the inexplicable darkening of the nostrils, which have flared wider, and then, when the moment is over, the general shrinking of the features.

Still I must confess that the use of the mirror has one advantage. Often the breath has ceased to befog the glass, and then, when we think the drastic sharpening of the features that signals the end is going to begin, just then a surreptitious movement of the face — which always occurs in the eyelids — brings us a marvelous surprise: life has not ended. How richly we are rewarded at that point! Every possibility had seemed exhausted, and now we find ourselves obliged to renew our vigilance, because the process may continue. Such surprises are unfortunately impossible when we use a flame for our observation. When, almost touching the lips, the flame heads straight up and grows thinner, and when it stops trembling for several seconds, we can conclude that all is at an end and devote ourselves, in spite of our exhaustion, to observing other details that will soon appear. But these — extreme whiteness, incredible sharpening of the features, which normally become inexpressibly beautiful, a fixed expression, cessation of all change, a sudden display of profound calm — can be observed in a more leisurely manner once the extreme tension that precedes the final moment and forces us to focus on every detail has dissipated. At this point we know that we can expect few surprises, that the different stages may last more or less time but will inevitably be completed. The observer's nerves relax, and he can breathe deeply. One might call this the stage of serene contemplation, of a melancholy confirmation of details easily foreseen. The tears of family, the accusations, the angry voices, the laments — all this forms the background of these moments of resigned serenity that precede those others when stiffness, absence of life, the first appearance of yellowness, and other ephemeral details first come into view and force us to withdraw.

VII

Need I say that my greatest frustrations sprang from accidents and unexpected passings? Such occasions would arise suddenly without the least prior warning, making it wholly impossible to take appropriate measures. Unfortunately this happened several times during those months.

More than once I struck up a friendship with a neighbor whom I assumed to be in perfect health. Then one day I'd stop seeing him on my street or in the neighborhood, or there'd be a bit of a commotion by his house, and I'd know it was all over. Just like that, unexpectedly and abruptly, with no warning, no telltale sign, nothing that might have suggested that the end was coming. What a sense of futility came over me at such times, a sense of irreparable loss, weakness, helpless frustration!

Other times it was an accident, unexpected but no less annoying for that, a sudden flurry of activity on the street showing that something serious had happened. Although I always allowed for such occurrences and tried to be ready and alert at the least sign of something unusual going on, it often turned out that, no matter how quickly I rushed to the scene, everything had happened with lightning speed and I got there late, at the time of the final symptoms. This made me feel all the more useless, because if I'd come earlier I might have been of some help, might have held the trembling hand or dried the icy sweat on the forehead. Sometimes, however, not as often as I should have liked, I managed to arrive in time and to join others, who were less painstaking, less alert, in giving the care needed during the final seconds, those that precede the moment. Working at such tasks, I came across clumsy people who, in their frenzied desire to help, succeeded only in hastening an end that might have come slowly and perceptibly. I felt boundless contempt for such persons, born under the sign of haste and clumsiness.

It was different with Jacobo. He was an old friend; and if everything had developed as I expected, without the subsequent mishaps, I could have been with him.

I found out he'd had an accident. A serious one, I thought at first; but then I was somewhat disappointed to learn that it didn't amount to much, but that some complications had arisen from his having to spend weeks in bed without changing his position.

I went to see him. A relative of his answered the door; and without letting him announce my visit I went straight to the farthest room of the house, where I knew he was lying.

Jacobo was asleep and very pale. I came up to him to observe his breathing. It was almost normal, with an occasional slight irregularity, perhaps caused by dreams.

I sat down on a chair next to Jacobo, waiting for him to wake up. When the relative came to see whether he needed anything, and maybe also wondering why we were so quiet, I waved him away. I quickly calculated how many days it all might take, in view of my experience with similar cases. The best time, in every respect, is night. That's when even those closest to us are overcome by exhaustion and their determination flags. That is the time of the great silence, when the sounds of the city fall still and we hear the deep sleep of those lying in other rooms and the wings of insects drawn to the solitary light.

I decided to work days so I could devote my nights to Jacobo. I used to have surprising stamina for cases like this. No more — I think I've exhausted it. At this point, just remembering that time makes me feel incredibly tired. Now that I have unlimited leisure, I spend hours sleeping, trying in vain to make up for those other hours of sleep lost forever. I succeeded in working all day, sleeping a few hours, and then staying awake all night, never faltering for a minute. I was able to go to sleep and wake up at will, effortlessly, as though by clockwork, as my system marvelously adapted itself to each new case.

And who better than Jacobo on whom to exercise such remarkable talents? If I couldn't change my work schedule, I'd quit my job.

Since there was poor ventilation in the room, I climbed on a chair and managed to open a high window that, inexplicably, was almost closed. I pulled away a homemade curtain that was blocking the air, and I dragged a useless old piece of furniture to an adjoining room. That way Jacobo would breathe easier. I planned to bring an armchair in which to spend the nights and something to cover me in the early mornings. I noticed that Jacobo was waking up and then passing out again. Bending over him, I took his pulse and observed his breathing. It was even calmer than when I'd arrived. He was obviously breathing better. I felt satisfied.

"What are you doing here?"

The loud unpleasant voice made me jump. I looked up and saw

the tall, heavy body of Lucrecia, so near me that it almost blocked any movement.

I confess I'd forgotten her. I couldn't match what others have said about the secret mechanism that makes us forget what we dislike and that had wiped the disagreeable face of Jacobo's wife from my memory.

"Who tore away the curtain? Why's the room all changed?"

She asked these questions without getting very excited, in that calm way so typical of her fatness, pretending a childish surprise that clashed with her size and shape.

I tried to calm down and explain as best I could.

"It seemed to me he didn't have enough air in this little room."

Lucrecia stared at me.

"How long have you been here?"

"Not long. I came to take over for you; you must be exhausted, sick people are so much work."

"Jacobo is very little work, and what he's got will clear up with time. Don't you bother yourself."

"I can stay so you can sleep; you must have bad nights."

A mocking glint formed deep in Lucrecia's eyes.

"There's no need for that, he's fine at night. Nobody has to stay up with him."

The huge body came even closer.

"I'm going to wake him up so he can see you before you leave."

"Please don't, he's resting quietly."

I stood up nervously. The mocking expression of her eyes, which were very close to me now, became more pronounced.

"All right, come back another day," and she gestured toward the front door, gently pushing me with her body. "He'll be glad to know you stopped by," she said as I headed toward the door.

The last thing I saw was the thick smoke of a cigarette that, already forgetting me, she had just lit.

VIII

The first thing I did when I got up the next morning was call Jacobo's from a phone booth.

133

"Jacobo's just fine." I heard a note of triumph in the voice that answered. It was Lucrecia. "He's much better; the doctor's amazed."

"Glad to hear it."

The conversation dragged on for a few more minutes. I was crushed; I really didn't know what to say.

"Take care of yourself. You shouldn't worry so much."

"You're right."

"As soon as he's ready to travel we're leaving town. The house makes him sick."

"Good idea."

And then the *coup de grâce*, "Go see a movie."

"Goodbye." I hung up.

I realized I was facing a pointless day. I cursed the quick recovery and I cursed Lucrecia, who was denying me the chance to be with Jacobo and slowly bring him back to life. I'd have to go back to my office bearing the secret humiliation that her voice on the phone had inflicted on me.

I thought of the long day that would go by to no purpose, uselessly, while I wandered through the city with no one to talk to.

I felt defeated. Once again the bungling of a relative — in this case, stupid jealousy, petty frustrated posessiveness — was keeping me from my goals.

And what if I suddenly showed up at their house and surprised them and tried to find out how much of all this was true? I realized that would be imprudent. The most I could do was to let two, or better three, days go by before seeing him again, take him a present, offer to keep him company and take a little walk together while his wife was out.

I took the first bus going in the opposite direction from my friend's house. I watched the streets go by, the corners, the avenues, the bridges. Slowly I started to feel better.

Since an empty afternoon lay before me, I decided to go to a movie and got off the bus. As I walked along a tree-lined boulevard toward downtown I realized I could visit an aunt and uncle who lived near there and whom I never saw. They lived very quietly. They were in good health, but I hadn't visited them for a long time.

For all I knew they needed my help and my visit would be a god-send. Perhaps I was just what they wanted as their colorless lives drew to a close.

I vaguely remembered my uncle, a pleasant little man who on the slightest excuse broke out into nervous laughter and who was always putting his partial bridge in his mouth or in his pocket. It was he who answered the door.

When I saw him with his little crest of grey hair, his nearsighted eyes behind thick lenses, his shirt, buttoned to the neck as always but with no tie, his everyday pants, and the smell of old clothes that rose from his body, and when I heard his cracked, somewhat mocking voice and the constant laugh that sometimes brought him to tears, I realized that I hadn't given him a thought in ages. It seemed to me that if I hadn't seen him that afternoon I'd never have thought of him again.

He opened the door, which was locked and bolted, and asked me to come into the front hall. He'd recognized me right away. I noticed a certain reserve about him, but I attributed it to some peculiarity of character that might have developed over the years.

As I looked at him, my memories slowly came back to me. The noise of the traffic outside was deafening; I remembered that when I was little I'd be startled to hear the couple and their visitors shout at each other every time a streetcar went by, while furniture, hosts, and visitors all shook.

"No, not there, please! Over here."

My uncle seized my arm. He kept me from sitting on one of the armchairs that almost filled the little hall and placed me with my back to a small dark patio. As I sat down I noticed he was casting worried glances toward the inside of the house.

Within seconds a low harsh voice asked from one of the inside rooms, "Who is it?"

My uncle rushed toward the inside, popping his bridge in and out.

"You'll never guess," he answered, trying to adopt a concilia-tory tone and disappearing through the door of the study, which opened onto the little hall.

I was left alone. The breeze from outside reached as far as the small patio. For the first time that afternoon I had a sense of well-being and forgot Lucrecia's horrid voice. I was almost glad to have found my uncle in good health. The light, blinding out on the street, was filtered in the cubicle where my uncle received visitors. Before reaching the deep, narrow patio, it was further diminished until it took on a soothing greenish-grey tone from the humid walls that had never seen the sun.

Once my eyes had grown used to the feeble light inside the house, I received a sudden shock. In front of me, very dull and worn but enormous, stood an automobile. It was hard for me to believe that this vehicle was occupying almost the whole of the small living room next to the hall.

I recognized objects that I hadn't seen for years and that now appeared as though crushed against the wall by the enormous automobile: a lacquered sofa, two prints of Roman scenes, a fat urn that could be seen over the hood. The corner of an upright piano stuck out from behind the front door of the car and made opening it quite impossible.

After a bit my uncle returned. Speaking very quickly and in a very low voice he told me, "When she comes, don't shake hands."

"Why not?"

"She thinks everybody wants to infect her."

We heard steps, and my uncle took refuge in his armchair.

When his wife appeared in the narrow space between the bumper of the car and the study door, it took me a while to recognize her. I'd seen her maybe three times in my life.

She was wearing white gloves and carrying a canvas folding stool. As she came in she commanded me with her hand, "Don't get up."

My uncle made me sit down. She set the stool on the floor, placed one foot on one of the front hubcaps of the car, and with a rapid movement seated herself on the fender. Then she pulled up the stool with her feet and placed them on it. She crossed her gloved hands on her lap and sat there expectantly.

It seemed to me she'd aged. We exchanged the customary greetings and polite formulas. My uncle reminisced about long-gone relatives. I noticed he spoke fearfully, often looking at his wife, who spoke rarely and without looking at him, and who seemed to be vaguely impatient. The conversation reached a dead end and stood still.

"Do you play the piano?" I asked my uncle, just to say something.

She answered for him, "That's impossible, we'd have to take away the car."

My uncle, who seemed animated when I first arrived, fidgeted in his armchair and then lowered his chin onto his breast.

I realized I'd asked the forbidden question. I tried to efface its bad effect. "Do you go out much?"

She fixed her eyes on the floor. After a moment she answered, "Very little."

"Never!" my uncle shouted, abandoning his silence with the same abruptness with which he'd fallen into it. The woman squirmed on the fender. She started to take off her gloves but then remembered that I was there and quickly drew them on again.

"She never lets me go out!" My uncle became extremely agitated. "I've been waiting for you to come so I could tell you."

He'd jumped out of his seat and grabbed me by the arm. The noise of the buses that stopped in front of the open hall door drowned out his voice.

"Don't act like that!" she thundered, and her voice overpowered the noise from the street.

"I will! I will!" Hanging on to my arm, my uncle seemed like a hysterical child.

"Sit down!"

"I'm glad you've come. You don't know what goes on here! She doesn't let me go out because I'll pick up germs. When we're by ourselves it's as though everything were walled shut. She's dismantled the motor so we can't go out in the car."

I saw that an especially violent twitch was choking him.

"Come on, sit down . . ." I started to push him gently toward his chair.

"And I can't play, either!"

Exhausted by his effort, my uncle began to sob and dropped into the armchair.

"That's the way things go, it doesn't really matter," was all I could think of saying to calm him down and make myself feel less uncomfortable.

While I stroked his back I looked at the woman out of the corner of my eye. She was pale but had lost none of her aplomb as she sat bolt upright on the fender. She kept on adjusting her snow-white gloves.

I felt a powerful urge to go home and put an end to that disastrous day, which had begun with Lucrecia's hurtful voice.

I took my leave as best I could.

"Come again!" I heard my uncle say in a tired voice as I was rushing away from the house.

But I understood that they would still live a long time. Their mutual loathing sustained them. I definitely had nothing to do there.

IX

I found myself heading back to my place. But as I entered the building I thought of the narrow space enclosed among four walls that was awaiting me.

Walking slowly, I turned the corner and went to the square. It was past noon. The shadows of the buildings had reached the middle of the street. Feeling tired, I walked to the farthest arch and sat down on the steps.

As evening approached, a slight breeze began to blow from the direction of the harbor. Little by little I calmed down. I hadn't been in the square since my conversation with Joaquín and his wife. It seemed cleaner than usual, as if the recent rains and the autumn air had washed it down.

I glanced around me and was startled. I hadn't noticed that the young black man who used to argue with himself at the top of his voice was lying just a couple of steps from me, behind the column I was leaning against. He seemed to be sound asleep, or rather to be sunk into a lethargy that was beyond normal sleep.

Slowly, trying not to be seen, I came up to him, edging over from where I was sitting to where he was stretched out. It was the first time I could observe him from so close. He must have been a little under thirty. He'd deteriorated sharply since the last time I'd seen him. I'm familiar with that sudden collapse of energies, which occurs most frequently in the young. When I was a mere beginner I used to get careless in cases like that. Experience has taught me that the process can be slower in the old and atrociously rapid in the young. I realized that my bitter day was taking an unexpected turn and providing me with an opportunity not to be missed. If I was patient, everything might come to an end that very night. Luck was with me. The unpleasant events of the previous hours had been leading up to this unexpected encounter, still in full daylight.

Since I was in the shadow of the column, I drew as close as possible to him, trying not to be noticed. The pulsation of the neck had decreased to the point where it was almost imperceptible. I held the back of my hand in front of his lips. I found his breath weak.

Just then someone came walking, the steps gradually slowing down until they nearly stopped right by us. I looked up. It was a young woman. I met her questioning eyes.

"He's drunk," I said, speaking slowly.

The woman looked at him for a moment with a vaguely curious and somewhat condescending expression and then went on her way.

I realized I had to avoid attracting the attention of idlers, who are my personal enemies, bumbling enemies, stupid gawkers, people who are just killing time. I went back to where I had first sat down and prepared to wait and see what would happen. From there I saw that the man was making slight movements of his head and mouth, as though he were trying to breathe in a larger volume of air, only to fall back into his deep trance. His features were very sharp, and his face was calm, serene, a little bloated. I debated with myself for a long time whether I ought to intervene in the process. It grew dark.

There began to be fewer people under the arcade. Once the darkness was complete, I drew near again. The breathing was calmer, accompanied by little sighs. Through some incomprehensible coincidence the process had been reversed.

After a bit the man gradually awakened and stretched. Slowly he looked around him. Then, turning his head in my direction, by the weak light that shone on him, he gazed at me with a fixed and sly expression.

X

I have every incentive to be careful in observing the symptoms of those around me and thus, insofar as possible, avoiding surprises. An increasing paleness can be a valuable indication of many things, from financial difficulties to a fatal loss of energy.

I watch the eyes that cloud over, the skin that grows spotted, the cracked nails, the shortened breath, the darkening mole, the hair falling out in unexpected quantities, the unsteady walk, the persistent headache, the weight going down, the shaky thought process, the slowness of speech, the repetitions, the spreading discoloration, the serious expression, the awkward movement, the sweaty palm, the cold skin, the declining appetite, the sunken cheek, the fallen shoulders, the bonier hips, the transparent earlobes. The slightest detail can be an indication. The slightest distraction is risky. Neglect one clue, and you've wasted what may be a unique opportunity.

Those who suffer alone are so many that, with proper investigation, a sentence or a word heard in passing, a letter left on a table or falling out of a pocket, scraps of a conversation heard during a short trolley ride, a wrong phone connection, can all give us splendid leads.

With a minimum of skill it's easy to keep tabs on everything. I remember that once I was able to set up an emergency call service in the poorest part of town. It was summer, and for next to nothing the school children on vacation came to the office to tell me about possible cases in the neighborhood. It was a fruitful, rewarding summer. I remember it nostalgically. When the students went back to school I was exhausted. The start of classes cut off this productive vein of observations. I couldn't bring myself to repeat the experiment during the next vacations. I thought of Lot's wife and of what happens with sequels. Why use the same method twice, when the opportunities are as inexhaustible as life itself?

If only we visit our acquaintances with some regularity, keep a careful list of possible cases, setting aside the improbable ones to save time and effort, make inquiries about our friends and relatives, discreetly use the telephone—that useful invention, superb safeguard against misplaced hopes, to which I owe so much—to learn in passing, without undue curiosity, without unnecessary haste, the precise status of one situation, to discover the truth about others; in a word, if only we dutifully follow the lead of some clue that chance has placed on our path, not closing our mind, recognizing that the possibilities life generously offers us are numberless, we shall be abundantly rewarded.

XI

That was the time I began to visit hospitals and other such establishments. What hostility and misunderstanding I encountered there! But for that, how could I have given up such an inexhaustible field for observation? Intolerable, those insulting looks of animosity and suspicion that my mere presence drew from remorseful relatives!

Now I specially remember the lonely, the abandoned, the wretched, who never showed me an unfriendly face, and who, as their loneliness neared its end, received me with an expression of boundless gratitude, never daring to question my motives for coming, far-fetched as they might seem, and accepting my presence as the most natural thing in the world. I recall nothing unpleasant about them, no gesture of impatience or astonishment. My presence needed no justification; they were satisfied with the most trivial explanation. For them, and only for them, it was natural. Outsiders, however, when they were present, behaved with unbridled selfishness, as though they wished to monopolize the final minute, the most precious of all, guarding it with a narrow ferocity, and determined to share it with no one. How different were the old, the sad, the forsaken! They seemed to want nothing but to share it.

Before I was forbidden to enter such institutions I employed various tricks to create reasonable-sounding pretexts for admission.

I prepared a wooden case and bought a number of articles that seemed useful and attractive: combs, razors, paper napkins, small flasks of perfume, soap, lipstick, face powder, mirrors, nail files, nail polish, tweezers, hair clips, deodorants, and a selection of costume jewelry.

I used some of my purchases to set up a small traveling display in my case. One morning, with the display hanging from my neck for convenience, I entered one of the largest wings of what by some strange euphemism is called a convalescent hospital.

"Combs, razors, hair cream," I discreetly announced from the door of the first room I came to. I withdrew just as discreetly. At that moment its inhabitant was taking care of some very private business. He looked at me hesitatingly from across the room, like an animal from its cage, resigned to its fate, beyond all doubt and all certainty.

"Combs . . . , " I announced at the next room. I was met with a beatific smile rocking in a rocking chair. The face of its owner, a middle-aged man, showed no reaction whatsoever.

"Cologne, soap, cigarettes . . ."

The smile went on, back and forth, unchanged, as if its long-ago cause were also still operative, alive, perhaps eternal, though unknown to me.

I held a mirror up to him, but the face, reflected there with every movement of the rocker, gave no sign of acknowledging my presence, and the smile kept coming and going, into the mirror and out of the mirror. A trace of saliva caught the light at the corners of the mouth.

"Mirrors . . ."

I had better luck with the next room. It was shared by a young man and an old one, apparently healthy, who were passing the time playing a little poker. The older one ordered some talcum powder, which I promised to bring on my next visit.

"Come on Thursdays," he said.

I was pleased. I'd landed my first customer, who furthermore was asking me to come regularly, perhaps just so he'd have someone to be expecting.

"Thursdays, every Thursday at four o'clock sharp," he repeated as he cut the cards.

The younger man was busy studying his hand.

In the other rooms I visited I had the same luck, or worse. At the end of a hallway I saw some old women sitting in the sun, and I headed toward them in the hope of making some sales. They received me with a mixture of indifference and mistrust. A few of them showed some interest in the smallest flasks of perfume. They removed the stoppers with trembling hands, sniffed at the contents, offered each other scents.

They wound up making me open all my little flasks, which were none too many and which now went from nose to nose losing part of their contents, because more than one of the women, asking for my approval with a timid smile, placed a few drops on her handkerchief or her clothes. I was forced to gather up my merchandise.

I did a bit better with the lipsticks. As a sample, I made a little smudge on a wrinkled hand with painted nails, a trembling claw. This created quite a sensation. I had to test other shades on other shrivelled fingers. After long debate about the unusual shades that were coming into their lives almost at their close, the liveliest member of the group proceeded rather skillfully to outline her sunken lips. The success of this operation encouraged one of the others, who was watching us from her chaise. I set my box on her lap; slowly she went through its contents, one article at a time, and after much soul-searching selected a nail file that she carefully stowed under her clothes.

The probing looks of a nurse, who, dressed from head to toe in white and brandishing a hypodermic, was coming to administer the morning injections, forced me to close my box and call a halt to that day's operations.

More than once I encountered disappointing surprises. When after long wooing of a possible buyer, often accompanied by little presents, I managed to establish a relationship with him, I would arrive some day only to find that he was not in his usual place.

"He didn't make it till morning," was all his neighbor would say.

For instance, I was only able to see the talcum-powder man two Thursdays at the precise time he'd asked me to come. The following Thursday I found his roommate playing solitaire by an empty bed, bare except for the mattress and the uncovered pillows yellow from the last sweat of countless heads. I went on my way.

Another time, after a desperate citywide search for an odd shade of face powder, the sudden disappearance of my difficult customer made delivery quite impossible.

But besides not arousing much interest, these trinkets didn't allow any but the most superficial relations. Once the sale was made, there wasn't much to be said, other than some trivial comment on the weather. Besides, there was a kind of irreconcilable contradiction between the novelty of my merchandise and the greyness of the world in which I moved. My pretext for witnessing the end of those lives was something fresh and new that did not encourage those twilight conversations that lead to the detailed description of physical ailments and thus create friendships as sudden as they are ephemeral. I could not get my undecided customers to open themselves to me.

In view of my limited results, and since my display of samples was rather bulky and could be seen from far off, which made it familiar to the ever-alert medical personnel, I decided to get rid of it.

XII

On the other hand, I had striking success with books. The thought of setting up a small circulating library came to me in a flash. I was surprised by the last-minute interest in books that flared up in some cases. I suspect that some patients were really rediscovering something. I think that was the brightest idea I had.

Without any great expectations, and working in secondhand bookstores, I managed, at minimal cost, to form a limited but quite varied collection of worn little paperbacks. Nothing spectacular in quantity or quality. I figured that the patients were quickly bored with their diet of newspapers and trivial magazines, and that books would keep them entertained for a longer spell.

I decided — and experience showed it was a wise decision — to change my theater of operations and explore a large hospital, where there was less supervision. Thanks to a certain laxness in the regulations I was able to take up my station in the basement and organize my activities from there.

My plan met with little or no resistance. For a penny a day, desperately lonely patients could get to know brilliant salons or storm great estates with their arthritic joints. I suspect that in some of my customers, by providing them a brief respite from their daily routines, or between one routine and eternity, I fostered the sense of fulfilling an already doomed existence. Some cases were deeply moving. Some of the patients could only make out the texts of the greasy little volumes with great effort, but they held on to them, as though grasping a world glimpsed too late. Perhaps then, when it no longer mattered, they had found a meaning only they could gauge, a tenuous private paradise, a consuming hell.

Nostalgically I remember one morning when, after the tiresome doctors' visits and after all the enemas, serums, and injections had been given, I achieved my most splendid success: a whole roomful of the less seriously ill patients were engrossed in their reading. For a moment I felt I was the master of destinies. Certain coincidences that I shall reveal later confirmed this secret and delicious sense of power.

The first subscriber to my circulating library was an old man who coughed. I suspected that his cough was a way of reminding himself he was still alive and of drawing attention to himself. He returned my greeting with some anxiety, but his eyes did not reflect the slightest doubt about my motives for approaching him. I offered him some books, which he inspected very seriously, and explained my system. He looked at me, a bit perplexed; and I promised to come back the next day to collect the sum of one centavo as a first installment and to find out whether the book was to his liking. This seemed to delight him. When I left he was already immersed in his book. Perhaps he was just pretending to be interested out of politeness; perhaps he was grateful to me because for the first time in a long while someone had been willing to listen to the story of his ailments, the tortuous and complicated course of a process that apparently interested very few people. I don't know. I preferred not to delve into his true motives.

My lengthy effort to establish what I most prized and desired, a personal relationship, a relationship of dependency, had been crowned by success, partial and insignificant if you like, but undeniable. I felt that my field of observation was about to be vastly enlarged and that I'd discovered endless possibilities.

Time confirmed my hopes. Slowly, just by imitation or, in the more recalcitrant cases (I met with only two or three outright rejections), by means of persuasion, I was able to put my little library on a solid footing. All that was still required were perseverance, observation, patience.

I suspect that life in the hospital was enriched and that, without really knowing the origin of the little books that unexpectedly appeared in those yellowed hands, the staff was grateful for the sudden quiet of all those bodies that, engaged now in distant adventures, stopped reeling off their annoying complaints and passively offered up their anemic and apathetic buttocks to the needle.

Modest as was the rent I charged for the books, I was startled to see that this small transaction was slowing down the degenerative process. Long books allowed me to prolong some lives; and even the shorter ones, if they rekindled the curiosity of their readers, managed to stave off or at least draw out the moment.

I also noticed that in some cases, by simply keeping close track of the number of pages as yet unread, I was able to predict events and avoid surprises, and at the same time distribute my books without unnecessary worry or alarm.

Other patients developed a curious attachment to a volume without ever opening it and held it in their hands till the very end, delicately savoring this unexpected final acquisition with which I had provided them. How much gratitude there was in their last words, how much understanding in their glances, and how often did an inopportune relative come out of nowhere, feigning a tardy concern and interrupting our often unspoken dialogue!

One case seems especially worth mentioning, a hopeless case who had long been on the critical list without ever being declared terminal.

How did I detect a kindred spirit in him? I don't know; an instinctive force must have guided me to his bed. He, better than anyone else, seemed intuitively to understand my motives for being there. He was calm, quiet, a man of excellent character, still young; and with him I was able to forge a friendship none the less cordial for being ephemeral, or perhaps more cordial for that very reason.

Maybe it was the desire to be with him as long as possible that made me do all I could to find him a thick volume. I asked him to forget about the usual fee; if he managed to get to the end, the sum would be too heavy for his bony shoulders.

A pleasant surprise was in store for me, a touching coincidence that I had secretly considered possible, but without expecting, even in my most optimistic moments, that it would occur.

During the first days his condition seemed to improve very little; but as he continued to read, the improvement was clearly noticeable. It was a surprise for everyone. By the time he'd read halfway through the book, he was speaking animatedly. One morning I found him walking around his room. I was able to keep him in this condition far into the book. Toward the last pages he began to grow weaker. Only with great effort was he able to hold the book in his hands.

When the end came I was with him. He was terribly pale and breathed with enormous heavings of his chest, but with an admirable lucidity his eyes still managed to concentrate on the printed characters. Not one of his movements escaped me, not one anguished shift of position, not one nuance of skin color. It seemed useless to call anyone. If I had succeeded, even if only by chance, in prolonging his life beyond what anyone else could have achieved and in making him take a renewed interest in things, why should I now let others fumble their way in and ruin our last moments together? Fortunately, his relatives rarely visited him; and, after all, in terms of strict morality, didn't those moments belong to me? Forsaking the others, I had devoted myself almost exclusively to him. By his bed of suffering I felt, more than at any other time, that I was the master of life and death.

With great effort his eyes took in every word on the page, onto which I was shining the night light. Foreseeing that the end was near, I'd installed a brighter bulb. I saw his eyelids droop; the blood barely reached the icy hands. For some time I'd had to hold the book. I hope and trust that his vision was not clouded forever before reaching the last letter.

The circumstances of my friend's end were so moving that when I renewed my operations I gave up my little system of fines for late returns.

Less successful, and also less agreeable, was my relationship with an old man who received my proposal pleasantly enough one morning when I found him alone and discouraged.

There was no one with him, but when I revisited him the following day I found two relatives there. We looked at each other with mutual distrust. Long experience has shown me that you have to be prepared for anything from a relative. My new customer was reading quietly in his bed. He took one centavo out of his pajama pocket, handed it to me without a word, and went back to his reading. I explained my little system to the relatives, stressing my desire to entertain the patients. They seemed to approve. One of them accompanied me into the corridor.

"My father's perked up a lot," he told me when we were out of the room.

"Yes, that's the usual reaction."

"Have you been in business long?" I shuddered at the vulgarity of this question.

"No, not long."

"I see."

And after looking at me again, this time more coldly and probingly, he went back into the room.

The next day the number of relatives in attendance had doubled. My customer was sitting in a rocking chair, seemingly unaware of them. When he saw me he handed me another centavo. For a few moments we carried on a lively conversation in the presence of the silent relatives.

In no other case was the recovery so obvious. I decided that a stroke of pure luck was allowing me to give renewed purpose to certain lives and prolong them a little. Common sense told me that chance, too, has its laws and that once underway it could be carried to its logical conclusion. Having kindled interest in life, could I not extinguish it by simply eliminating its object? Wasn't this the same as shortening life? I was stunned by the extent of my powers.

On the fourth day, two of the relatives and a member of the hospital staff took me aside. They angrily accused me of having disturbed the sick man, who was back in bed and had the same despondent expression as on the first day. He'd been ordered to avoid any exertion.

Obviously, if I put up an argument I was bound to lose. The hospital official sided with the relatives, who, sure of victory and with an air of injured virtue, were shouting their outrage. I realized that my simple activities had delayed the outcome they wanted. They won.

Ominously, I was expelled from the hospital. One way or another I'd soon have had to liquidate the business. My small circulating library was shrinking rapidly. I felt that in return for the last moments they'd given me I ought to leave the worn little volumes with my ephemeral friends as a small sentimental souvenir, and I would insist on their accompanying them to their last resting place. When the end came, I never felt up to reclaiming my merchandise. I had to liquidate my business.

The other covers that I adopted after this failed miserably. They couldn't penetrate the barrier that the security staff set up against me; in spite of all my precautions, they always managed to detect me as I crossed the far end of some corridor. I think I became very well known.

XIII

One night on my way home I passed by a several-storied building whose façade looked familiar. Gradually a recollection of the place rose to the surface of my memory, pushing aside many others like it. I'd been there weeks, perhaps months, before.

The dark staircase smelled of humidity; as I climbed it, I reconstructed the scene. When I reached the topmost landing I found the woman on her way out, still busy, sweating, and confused. I was a bit ashamed as I looked at her. I'd promised I'd come back, but far more urgent obligations had made me forget my promise. She didn't seem to recognize me. She pushed me aside with her large body and rushed down the stairs, leaving the door open.

Inside the apartment nothing had changed. The same magazines were still lying on the same collapsed piano keys from which I'd lifted them during my earlier visit. In the gloom, the remnants of some recent or long-ago breakfast were visible on the table, still without a table cloth. The piles of newspapers were, if anything, more numerous.

Again I straightened the picture. The bed standing across the far end of the corridor still took advantage of every hint of a breeze, but it was empty now. Once more I went through the familiar rooms. In a corner, as though in a niche, with the light of a floor lamp shining on him, I found the occupant of the bed, his chin sunk onto his chest. It took me a while to recognize him. The past months had worn him away.

I feared I'd missed a precious opportunity, and this fear was confirmed as I drew near: it was much too late. With infinite care I raised the body and deposited it on the bed. It was very light, like a child's body; its weight seemed to have diminished to an extraordinary degree. The expression was that of someone engrossed in some profound idea; but seen from another angle, he looked like a disconcerted child who is perhaps annoyed at being denied some pleasure. I felt that a calm silent dialogue that needed no words was being established between us. It seemed to me that if I asked him a question he would answer politely from the depths of his eternal sleep.

To comply with ritual I started to look all over the place for a candle. I got as far as the kitchen, but to no avail. There'd been no preparations whatsoever. When I returned to the bedroom, I saw the woman come back panting. From the doorway she looked at the body placed on the bed. She seemed annoyed by the unexpected change and rushed angrily into the room.

"There you go again! How long are you going to keep this up?"

"He hasn't moved from where you left him."

My words seemed to deepen her customary confusion. The vast mass of flesh wavered and had to hold on to the bed. She looked at me and then back at the body as she poured out her anger on it. Then suddenly she seized me by the arm and began to hit me hard.

"What have you done to him? What have you done?"

When at last she understood what was going on she began to scream so loudly as to make the room shake. She threw herself on the bed and made it shudder and teeter on its none-too-sturdy legs.

I heard voices on the floor below, hurried footsteps on the stairs. I realized I'd come at a bad time, that I should leave as soon as possible.

As I reached the door I ran into several neighbors who were coming in.

"What happened?"

"I'm going for help. Stay with her!"

And avoiding their looks and their questions I dashed down the stairs.

XIV

I take note of the final signals as they appear in what we might call escalated form. The rupture is always gradual and verifiable. Laymen usually speak of a sudden wrenching away. Those of us whom long experience has taught how slowly the signals set in know that there is no such thing: the break comes at the appropriate moment. We could never make so superficial, so clearly frivolous and disgraceful a comment.

Secondary details can be extremely useful to the observer, but we must rely primarily on visual inspection to understand the full scope of the process. It, and it alone, allows us to track what is happening, tells us what will happen, and, when all expression suddenly disappears, reveals that the instant has passed. Sometimes in the instants before the last, those that require the greatest power of observation, we find an unexpected flaring-up. The pupils slowly grow bright, as if they were seeing everything for the first time, and a clear look of recognition appears. It lasts a moment and then is extinguished along with all the rest. It's a revealing instant, which can stretch on and which makes up for all the long hours of watchfulness. The consciousness is illuminated, the eyes look around and seem to understand the meaning of the hours of semidarkness, of the long labyrinth the mind has had to traverse. Consciousness rises to the surface to take note of every detail: the sunlight on the wall, the metal of the bed, the whiteness of the sheets, the windowpanes, the glasses and bottles on a table, the faces of onlookers, the crossed feet under the sheet, a towel, a book, a door that opens, a body that approaches and then goes away again, the shadow of a bird as it passes between the wall and the sun.

Usually the eyes brighten slowly; they gradually cease to be fixed. It's as though their fixed expression were diluted and replaced by another, more flexible one, through which the intelligence begins to rise to the surface. At those moments, we must intensify our power of observation to the utmost; no noise, no incident must distract us when we are granted this rare privilege. All too well do I know the value of such moments, which fate doles out to us so sparingly. They are the precious instants in which life returns. Once the last traces of fixedness have melted away, an expression of lucidity appears, weak at first, more marked as time goes on. The eyes recognize one object, then another. The lids open and close with a rapid, yet peaceful movement. The gaze now takes in details: the folds of a cloth, the edge of a glass. Then, drifting slowly, it proceeds to another detail. Perhaps it does not yet recognize faces, but the objects it encounters are clearly familiar. Once they have been explored, it can leave them for others, in a slow semicircular movement. The less concentrated expression indicates that the degree of lucidity is now more intense. The retina transmits familiar features, omits others. There is an almost imperceptible movement of the hands, instantly aborted; all energies are reserved for the efforts of the eyes. Memory has clearly returned and is partially recovering its powers. If the lips could move they would speak names.

Now the eyes no longer wander but rest on one point; there is an evident chain of thought that is interrupted when attention is shifted. The eyes are now able to leave a point and return to it without getting lost. No doubt they are making comparisons. Perhaps the effort tires them, because they close for an instant before resting on one spot for a long time.

At that moment, prolonged and deceptive, a clumsy hand might pounce on them before anyone can stop it. After waving back and forth, and unaware of the care and extreme precision with which these precious instants must be calculated, it raises a finger to some lips and urges silence, wary of the acuteness that hearing achieves at these moments. Then, with unconscionable tactlessness and with a movement that is meant to be firm and measured but is really foolish and awkward, it lights a match. The eyes leave their point of temporary rest, examine the walls and then the faces with an expression of incredible lucidity, with a searching circular motion that, though slow at first, comes to acquire dizzying speed.

My God! My God!

XV

I went back to Jacobo's house. I felt an urgent need to see him, to be with him. I hadn't dared to call again since the day his wife had told me so brusquely to go see a movie. More than a veiled suggestion that my presence might become unpleasant, her insinuation seemed to me a crude insult to my feelings of sincere friendship for her husband.

At the door of the building I hesitated for a long time as to whether I should go up. When Lucrecia came around the corner and started to approach the house, I quickly hid. I realized my blunder. If I'd gone up right away and rung the bell, someone, some relative, would have opened the door for me, and then it would have been too late for her not to let me in. Now it was too late; I'd lost my chance. With her slow heavy steps, Lucrecia came to the front door, went in, and disappeared inside the building.

I didn't know what to do. If I went up, I was sure to face another insult. But then, mightn't my imagination be leading me to invent situations that didn't really exist? I was torn between these two ideas for a long time, until at last common sense prevailed.

I calmly climbed the stairs. When I reached the door I rang the bell, which sounded somewhere at the back of the apartment. I heard hurried footsteps coming and then going off in different directions, but not toward the door. My ringing seemed to plunge the place into turmoil. I thought I heard stifled voices, muffled scurrying about. A door slammed.

I rang again, more insistently. One last scurrying sound, then silence. I pushed the button almost violently. I started to hammer with my fists. I had to have a talk with Jacobo. I realized that his wife was in control of the situation and capable of inventing anything that would discredit me. I knocked again, frenetically; the

153

only reply was the most obstinate absence of any sound. I went down the stairs.

I waited a while by the door of the building, vaguely hoping that if someone went in or out, I'd somehow manage to get into the apartment. I sat down to rest on the doorstep. I was too nervous. Moments later I crossed the street and headed off. Before I turned the corner I stopped and looked back at Jacobo's balcony. The door was closed, but after a few minutes I saw the shutter half opening and then closing again, very slowly.

I had no idea how I got to the square. Walking in a daze, crushed by what had happened, I got there somehow, perhaps drawn by the hope that the familiarity of the place would restore my calm.

It was still early. The first lights were appearing against a reddish sky. During the brief moments when day and night overlapped, everything grew more intense and took on an air of unreality and violence.

Near me someone spoke. Joaquín's wife was arriving. She settled down near him. Soothed by her presence, I drew closer. The woman didn't notice I was there until I stopped almost next to them. When she saw me, she looked at me fixedly. Following the direction of her eyes, Joaquín raised his until they met mine. He staggered to his feet and stood there silently, glaring at me with his bloodshot eyes.

After a moment I decided it was best to leave.

XVI

The night before last I made an extraordinary discovery.

The unexpected hostility of Joaquín and his wife, the look of hatred I received from the father and son, who were just arriving as I left, depressed me all day long. At the office I worked mechanically, aimlessly, feeling no impatience, paying no attention to the clock. Was I to stay away from the square, too? What was left? Where should I go?

I went home. I fixed something to eat but didn't touch it. For a long time I paced from wall to wall; then I threw myself on my bed. I awoke with a start. It was night.

I half opened a shutter and saw the square full of people. They'd set up a fair during the day. Deafening music was coming out of two loudspeakers placed directly opposite my window. I tried to read, then to go back to sleep, but I couldn't. The music came through the closed shutters and through the pillow I was pressing against my ear. I'd have to abandon even this, my only place of rest.

I stepped out. The stairway was deserted. I supposed that my neighbors were probably at the fair, unable, like me, to stay in their homes. Others, less easily disturbed, might be chatting or sleeping.

As I started down the stairs I suddenly felt like going up. What might there be on the roof? If I'd thought it was uninhabited I would have lost any interest in going there, an interest that, anyhow, I'd never felt before.

What a relief when I opened the door at the top of the stairs. A closed, narrow world remained behind me; neither the street noises nor the music of the fair reached the roof. I felt surrounded by silence, soothed by the pleasant breeze coming from the bay.

I looked over the wall on the street side. Under the corrugated iron roofs of the stalls, a dirty light was shining down onto the pavement. The music had temporarily stopped. In the unexpected silence, the fairgoers seemed to drift in and out of the booths aimlessly. People moved like shadows.

Behind me, toward the more distant walls that separated my roof from the adjoining ones, it was almost totally dark. I walked over to the farthest wall and sat down on the flat surface of the roof, which was still warm from the heat of the day. From far off, muffled, I could hear the din of the city.

A glimmer rose from a ventilator set into the roof. I went up to it. A yellowish light stained my hands. Voices were coming up the shaft. Down below, a forgotten puddle gave off a distant gleam. Someone coughed drily, a voice sang; I heard laughter, more voices. A door closed in the distance. The smell of steam and humidity reached me from below.

The walls around the rooftop were low. A very thick one separated the buildings. It occurred to me that many houses had leaned against it, and that it was still standing while sooner or later the houses had been demolished.

The roof of the next house was on the same level. I hesitated a while before jumping over, but once I was on the other side I regained my courage. Treading softly I explored the roof and looked over one of the side walls that faced an empty lot. Several cats interrupted their play to join me, and for a while we silently explored the roof together. Then they left.

I pulled a board from a pile of rubble and carefully slid it over the wall until it rested on the next roof. That house was older, with a large opening in the middle corresponding to the patio and to the corridors of the upper stories. I walked all around it. The sound of a musical instrument rose from the patio. When it stopped I could hear conversations and quiet laughter. Dark figures crossed the patio with a muffled clacking of heels.

The whole top story was dark, except for one room. I came close to it. It was brightly lit.

Through a door and grill that opened onto the corridor I could see part of the interior. Everything seemed very neat. The arm of a sofa and a section of the floor shone under the blinding light that must have hung from the ceiling. On the visible half of a dresser stood some bottles and a china angel; there were photographs under the glass top. On the floor, also very clean, there were bright-patterned cushions. The metal railing of a bed gave off a pale gleam.

Across the void that ended at the window, a pair of eyes was staring at me. I shifted my position to get a better view of the inside. The eyes followed me until I left their field of vision, then accompanied me again when I reentered it. There were feet under the bedclothes. The rest of the house was dark and quiet. I looked again at the eyes, open under their motionless lids.

I made several tours of the roof, where by now no sound was to be heard. I felt the coolness of midnight. I went back to my starting point. Down below, the fair was drawing to a close. The stalls were empty; the loudspeakers were silent.

When I looked into the patio once more, I again met the motionless eyes under the blinding light.

Last night I saw light in the back of the apartment. Two persons were talking by the corridor. It wasn't quite dark yet, but the light was already shining brightly in the room. Maybe it was always on. As on the previous night, no one else was there.

For a long time my eyes met those gazing up at me from the bed.

Except for a slightly more intense look when I entered their field of vision, I observed no change in them. Perhaps, I thought, the head hadn't moved all day, waiting for me to appear on the roof.

Suddenly the voices talking by the corridor grew louder. For no apparent reason, what had seemed to be a quiet, intimate conversation exploded into a stream of mutual insults. It was a man and a woman. Lights began to come on, room by room, in what had been an almost dark building. I heard heels clacking down in the patio, not slowly, as on the night before, but like those of people running.

Frightened voices rose above the noise: "What's going on? What happened?"

The corridor and the patio below filled up with people who, half surprised, half delighted, witnessed the altercation, as though the silence of the night had been too heavy and they were glad of this unexpected relief, this sudden interruption.

Those who were arguing went directly from words to violent deeds. The man seized the woman by the arm, pushed her against a corner of the corridor, and, with his hands on her ears and looking into her eyes as though he were about to kiss her lips, began to beat her head against the wall.

From my position directly above them, I could see her eyes close in bewilderment before every new blow.

The spectators in the corridor passed on the details of the scene to those below or at the front of the building, who, unable to see it from up close, were eagerly asking, "Hey, what's he doing to her?"

The woman managed to break free, and the quarrel went on, though less violently. As inexplicably as it had begun, it wound down. I heard loud laughter.

I went back to my place above the room, which was still brightly lit. The eyes had closed. I waited for them to open. When they did, they'd lost some of their inhuman expression. Thankfully, I saw that the light of recognition gradually came over them.

Perhaps as a reaction to what I'd just witnessed, I felt tears running down my face; I let them run, almost with pleasure.

I stayed a long time, my elbows resting on the wall, knowing that the eyes in the room below never left me. I felt that as long as I stayed there, motionless in the half dark, I was in a way protecting them from any new eruption of violence.

When I left, very late, I was very tired. I waved goodbye. By the harsh light from the ceiling, the eyes took on a mocking gleam.

Tonight, as I did last night until so late, I again roamed the rooftops, attracted by their vast silence. I'm thrilled by this world I've just discovered, a world apart, separate from that below, a remote universe of flagstones that give off in the darkness the heat that has burned into them during the day.

Unconcerned that I might be heard, I explored it joyfully, sometimes running as far as the walls would allow, looking down at the streets as at a no-longer-impending threat, holding my ear against the ventilation hatches to listen to the jumbled sounds that rose there.

Again, and for a long time, my eyes met those that were waiting for me, mocking yet grateful. I imagined they'd been watching for hours on end for me to come back to the roof. Perhaps they'd been relieved to see evening come and the light melt away, waiting for the dimly lit shadow that would look over the wall, disappear and reappear, and wave to them in a friendly way that they could answer only by remaining motionless.

I must have fallen asleep sitting on the rooftop, because when I woke up it was starting to get light. Before leaving, I looked over once more. The unrelenting electric light shone on wide-open eyes that blinked their goodbye.

XVII

All is lost. A criminal hand locked the door out onto the rooftop. For three nights I tried to open it and was forced to stop when I heard footsteps coming.

Finally I managed to break it open. I ran to the far side, climbed over the wall and crossed the next roof. Somebody had taken away the board I'd used to cross over on the first night; and I had to drop down to the building with the patio, hanging on to projections on the walls.

Once I was opposite the room, I saw to my chagrin that, for the first time, the light was off. The door was hidden in the darkness.

It was very late, and everyone was asleep. My heart beat violently. These eyes, too, were fading away; this door, too, was closing.

I waited all night, leaning against the wall, hoping that the light would once more fall on the bed. When I felt very tired, I slept a while on the stones of the rooftop. Perhaps the woman in the bed had taken a turn for the worse and someone had closed the door to let her rest better.

But by the light of dawn I saw that the door had been bolted shut.

XVIII

Now that I'm at last able to rest, I realize just how exhausted I eventually became. My repeated absences from work, the sleepless nights and consequent tiredness, finally made me lose my job.

The manager looked at me dolefully as he handed me my last pay envelope and a letter of recommendation. He was, in the best sense of the term, a kind soul, an upright man. Sitting at his somewhat pompous desk in an overwide leather armchair, he spoke to me calmly, almost affectionately.

"We don't have anything against you, but you've gone too far." And then, in a familiar tone, he added, "You always used to do such good work."

I thanked him, but preferred not to give any explanations. I couldn't have made him understand. As he spoke I noticed that his ears were very pale, to the point that the light from a window behind him almost shone through them. I looked at his lips, which were an anemic pink. The indications from the fingernails were no better: they were nicotine-stained and deeply cracked. Still, I'd thought of him as a healthy man. I decided we should stay in touch.

"May I phone you sometime?"

"Whenever you like."

I hesitated a moment.

"At home, if possible . . ."

He seemed surprised.

"I don't think that's necessary."

I didn't want to insist.

For several days I wandered around town aimlessly, trying not to return to my room, which I found overwhelmingly depressing. As I walked from one end of the city to the other I visited all-too-familiar places in silent homage to vanished kindly faces, to friends forever absent. I relived my failures of the last few months, my meager successes, my humiliations. I regarded them as worthwhile, but I couldn't help feeling deeply discouraged.

One afternoon—I'd decided to go back to the place where I was sleeping—I bumped into a large clumsy body passing by. I excused myself and kept on walking. Seconds later, I felt pushed, then dragged by a hand clutching my neck.

"This is the guy! This is the one!" someone shouted almost in my ear. I saw people stop in surprise and then also start shouting and running frantically. When I could finally turn around I recognized the heavy vulgar shape, the brusque movements, the clumsy rough vitality bursting from the dress. As in a dream I remembered the depressed piano keys, the crooked picture, the man sleeping as though in a niche.

Dazed, I heard the absurd accusations, saw heads looking out windows, arms wave, faces almost glad of the show.

Trembling and drenched in sweat, I gratefully took refuge in the policeman's arms that reached to me from inside a dark car, and so was freed from the hand that amid all the noise and confusion never stopped beating me, animal-like in its fury—yet perhaps the instrument of justice.

XIX

Shut in here, with no interruption in the long hours of forced rest other than those needed to eat what the guard brings me and to practice that other kind of meditation which is sleep, I can devote long hours to reviewing what I have done.

Lacking any evidence to support the charge of homicide initially brought against me, they've had to limit themselves to premeditated fraud. Not a serious charge, but I expect the maximum penalty. I'll spend several winters within these humid walls, stepping out at the prescribed times to see the sunlight and take an occasional bath. Since the sentence doesn't involve labor, the time will pass slowly. But no one is interested in making it pass quickly. From their point of view, they're in the right.

From their point of view, too, I did seriously abuse the trust or innocence of others. I must be prepared to hear the wildest and most atrocious accounts of my conduct.

I've seen a picture of the prosecutor. Such obesity in such a young man, the excessively dark circles around the eyes, the seriously hardened blood vessels, which I can sense even if the camera didn't capture them — these are certainly not good signs. I have to warn him somehow; maybe my lawyer . . .

The mind is fertile in inventions when it lacks the light of understanding. I of all people must comprehend that. The rules of this institution are strict, but not so strict that I couldn't find a way to write these lines. Describing my life during these last months gives me something to do in my enforced idleness. Laboriously — I'm incapable of steady literary effort — I've told myself the story of what has happened.

The facts will necessarily lead my judges to a conclusion that I shall make no effort to dispute. It will be interesting to hear it. At bottom, appearances are not deceiving.

Neither have I taken advantage of the opportunities I've been offered. The other morning, when a tall, pale young man who tried very hard to win my confidence came to see me, I calmly gave him all the answers he did not expect. Somewhat discouraged, he told me he couldn't help me. I sent him off with an affectionate, even tender, wave of my hand. He was the psychiatrist.

Of all the accusations against me, that of homicide was the only one that aroused my indignation. I will tolerate lack of comprehension, but not if it involves slander.

Beneath the truth revealed by appearances there is another, deeper truth that must also become known. I wouldn't have been much concerned about it if the possibility of being slandered hadn't first depressed and then infuriated me. History is made with the truth and with lies. Against the tons of paper and rivers of ink that will recount my case, printed along with other distortions of the truth so that it can be read by millions of eyes strangely eager for something new and different, all I can marshal are these pages that I write with difficulty by the poor light that reaches me where I work. The obstacles are tremendous, but I know that some day these words will become known. Let us hope.

The allegation that I've tried to cut off the lives of others could not be more vile. It shows a complete misunderstanding of my concerns and an unfortunate confusion of the means with the end.

Every morning I see the guard come in with my breakfast. His visit will be repeated several times in the course of the day. He's young and strong, he radiates vitality. In him I salute life, the supreme good, the most tenuous and imperiled and yet the only good we really possess, no matter for how short a time.

I am not obsessed with death but with life, that humble and magnificent treasure, always threatened, always lost. What intrigues me is the moment at which it is extinguished forever; I still haven't been able to understand it, it's beyond all understanding. I've tried to capture it. It always escapes me, it is elusive.

One moment we're alive; the next, life has been extinguished. In vain have I tried to capture the moment in which it really stops. How is it possible that the supreme good is taken from us? It's like a blasphemy whose meaning defies all explanation, an atrocity, an unspeakable outrage. As I tried to work out an explanation I've isolated myself, rejected all normal contact with my fellow-beings, and finally lost my freedom, for which — now I know — there is no substitute.

I am satisfied. I don't regret my life, the episodes that may seem sordid to some, and perhaps are. If I regained my freedom I'd start all over again. My obsession needs no justification; it lies at the bottom of every human action. I'd try again to capture the moment; perhaps some day its disturbing explanation would be revealed to me.

The guard has just come in. I can tell we'll be friends. It's too bad he's in this line of work. Everything in him announces the desire to live. In him, I salute life. But you never know . . .

Polonaise Brillante

Glad to be moving on, I've carried my suitcase down myself, asked for the bill I told them to prepare last night, and paid the clerk of the Francuski, who sent me off without unduly disturbing herself. Then I've stepped out into the cold May night.

I'm standing on the sidewalk, looking at the deserted street. After a few weeks of spring, an icy wind has descended on the city. Hardly anyone ventures out at this time of day. A sky I can almost touch throws back the murky lights.

They should be getting here any moment. They've asked me to be waiting in front of the Francuski. I look to the left, to where they should be coming through the park that fills almost all the space once occupied by fortifications.

The old doorman of the hotel signals to me that I can leave my single piece of luggage with him until they arrive. I accept, and along with the suitcase I give him my last coin. In the piercing cold I walk as far as the corner, cross the street, and follow the sidewalk in front of the Gallery. I button my overcoat up to my chin. Inside a barber shop with an advertisement painted on its glass front, the barber, with his back toward me, is sweeping up the day's hair. If I bend over a little, I can see, on the other side of the glass, the pile of blond, brown, white hairs slowly pushed by the broom. When I raise my eyes, I notice that the barber is watching me in a large mirror. He hides his bald pate under a wig. It occurs to me that he must feel nostalgic as he sweeps the floor every evening.

I cross the street the hotel is on. Walking slowly along the stretch of city wall that's been left standing, I reach Florianska Street. In the distance, somebody's turning out the last lights in the shop windows that form a silent row. There's not a soul on Florianska, which is always so lively. I spend a long time gazing at the deserted sidewalks.

I head back to the hotel as slowly as I came, but I avoid crossing the street again till after I've passed the barber shop, which sends out a pale light. When I finally cross, I find my suitcase on the sidewalk. The hotel entrance is closed.

A noise from the direction of the park makes me jump, grab my suitcase, and rush to the curb with my heart aflutter. The noise disappears on the other side of the wall. They must be running late; some car trouble, maybe. You never know. It occurs to me that they have my travel documents.

It starts to rain, so lightly that the pavement doesn't even shine. A gust of wind stirs up the dust of the day; it smells humid.

They could come down Florianska and then, since it's so late in the day, drive up the wrong way on the street with the hotel. If I wait for them on the corner of Florianska I can wave to them and keep them from getting a ticket. Quickly I walk back to Florianska. The light's out in the barber shop.

The walk from the hotel has made me feel warm. More calmly now, I cross from the corner with the barber shop over to the restaurant where I've been eating these days, but without losing sight of the hotel, just in case they come from the park after all. Just thinking they might come and not see me makes my forehead break out in an icy sweat.

Now I see that the ideal spot is where the wall opens to form an arch. If I stand a little to the right of that so as not to lose sight of Florianska even for a moment or turn my back on the other street, I can also be sheltered from the wind and rain under the projection of the wall.

There I stay till a noise from under the arch starts to make me uneasy. Slight explosions, or rather crackles, break the silence. On guard against any sudden gust of wind, I peer into the opening. I see right away where the noise is coming from: inside a glass, the flame of a candle is sputtering as it draws up the last of the wax and casts its light on two religious images that appear behind robes of blackened copper and above artificial flowers. The flame crackles one last time and goes out. The darkness is dreadful.

And what if they came by the side of the hotel and turned the corner and then, when they didn't see me, drove off in the opposite direction from the wall and from me? Skirting the wall I pick a halfway point from which they'll be able to see me whatever direction they come from.

Now I start to wonder whether they mightn't have come down the street where I'm waiting for them while I was looking at the altar, but I realize right away that it would have been impossible not to hear the sound of the car as it was coming up. The sun is blinding. Will you come? Will you? Perfectly calm now, I decide to stay at this spot, which is obviously the best of all. Yes, best of all.

The weariness of these last days starts to press down on me like a boulder. In the warmth of the car I'll fall asleep right away. My overcoat is an iron coil around my shoulders. I feel tremendously tired. I come to with a start, like someone shaking off a heavy load. For a moment I think they must have come and not seen me, but then I realize that with me standing here and turned a little toward the hotel, they had to see me. They had to, just had to.

It's very cold. A terrible wind is blowing down from Finland. When I look down Florianska again the storm pushes me against the wall. I slip and fall on the sheet of ice that covers the sidewalk. Touching the icy surface forces me to get up. From behind the steamed-up glass the barber is watching me steadily. His eyes shine in the darkness. Drunk with the perfume of the acacias, the blackbirds sing in the park flooded with light. I cross through the dense shadows. I look toward Wawel. The window is gone. I retrace my steps. In the opening in the wall there's a candle stub hanging on to a dusty wick.

"Sancta Maria, Regina Poloniae."

"Sancta Maria, Regina Poloniae . . ."

Meski Damski.[1] An endless wilderness opens before me. Huge yellow leaves fall from the trees, and the tepid smell of burning dry foliage comes from across the river. Exhausted by summer, people are leaving the city. The heat is killing. A snowflake drifts down my neck, I feel the first shudder: a freezing vapor rises from the crust of ice. A yellowish moon shines weakly. In the full sunlight the blackbird calls again. Eyes watch me through the acacia leaves. Meski Damski.

---

1. Polish: Męski Damski, apparently marking public toilets for men and women, respectively. Trans.

There's nobody in the city. Amparo is in Milan. Theo, too. Clemente's in Norway. Although I know they won't answer, I dial their numbers. Nobody will come out, but in that warm half-light, behind the drawn curtains, there, right there, the phone will ring, with a sound triggered by me. That's something, better than nothing, much better than nothing.

"Sancta Maria, Regina Poloniae!"

Who's been in the house? Who turned on the light I left off? Who knocked over the leather suitcase? Whose cigarette's been left burning?

"Sancta Maria, Regina Poloniae!!"

"Sancta Maria, Regina Poloniae!!"

I'll still be walking between the hotel and Florianska Street when the villa hidden in the park where the lady and her nephew offer me tea, the children that were running toward the Groteska Theater tomorrow, the icy train, the puppets, the single huge wet footprint in the room that I left dark (positively, dark—I turned on the light in the hall, everything had turned so dark, but not in the room, that one I turned out, for sure, long before they did, for sure), the aristocratic brothers who will take me out for supper last night, the red Bronzino,[2] the enormous chestnut tree, the bass player, the cripple who will try to sell us obscene postcards, the city wall, the eyes of the barber, the riverbed, the nightclub ticket, the nightclub, the Aula Leopoldina, ah, the splendid the splendid Aula Leopoldina (definitely) the splendid Aula Leopoldina, are all reduced to blinding ashes.

2. Sixteenth-century Italian painter. Trans.

Goodbye . . . and Thanks for Everything

There was death in the air, but not sadness . . . and even the human heart acquiesced. E. M. FORSTER, *A Passage to India*

Since I'm alone so much, and sometimes my face and my shoulders hurt and I realize that it's the loneliness that makes me cringe with shame, I've invented Marta. I've invented her just the way I want her. With nothing but my imagination, I've endowed her with life, so as to get some relief for my inexorable loneliness.

Marta's hair is silky and light in color; the skin of her arms is very smooth. Her face and neck turn pale when she talks seriously; and when she laughs, they're tinged with delicate pinks.

Everything about Marta has that inexpressible quality of beauty. I was going to say that golden quality; but no, it wouldn't be quite right to limit it to one color, one material, when beauty is something elusive, indescribable. Marta's beauty includes the delicate healthy skin of the ears and the clean pink of the nails; it's in the way she places her feet, puts her hand on her cheek, in how the lips are set into the cheeks, in how the smoothness of the cheekbones continues into the temples, in how a delicate down spreads from the other side to cover the temples; in her, as in all those who possess that strange and mysterious gift, it's in the way her clothes drape her body, in the very clothes she chooses. Above all, it's in her voice. Marta's voice—its timbre, its rising or falling pitch, the sound of her laugh—is almost half of her being. An incredibly childlike tone when she wants to convince me of something, a smiling seriousness when I press her on a point and she doesn't want to give in.

I don't know how old she is. I don't dare to ask her; it's a silly habit, not asking young women—or other women—their age. By tacit agreement we never bring up the subject. Any comparison would be upsetting, perhaps melancholy. Sometimes I think that if I'd had a child when I was very young, Marta could be my child's daughter. But then, people don't really marry that young, it seems to me.

Beneath perfect dark eyebrows, her eyes sometimes seem on the verge of tears. At such moments they become clear to the point of transparency. The face, for all its beauty, gives no hint of the skin of the shoulders, which must be honey-colored, almost golden.

In the evening I go to a library in the old part of Havana; and to avoid getting home early to my insomnia, I stay till they close, at eleven. The employees can hardly wait for closing time. At ten-thirty they start to look at the clock, put the dictionaries back in place, run off to the ladies' room, and make phone calls. From then till they close, it's impossible to read.

I'm never in a hurry and am always the last to leave. I'd like it if they closed later; that way I could stay a little longer and so go to bed after midnight and be able to sleep, because when I get home, since I don't have anybody to talk to, I go to bed and start feeling wide awake.

One night I was, as always, waiting for the librarian to close before leaving. I noticed she was a little better dressed than usual. I held the door open for her.

"Going for a walk?"

"At this time of night? Not a chance! I'm going home."

"I see. Good idea."

Slowly, as every night, I started off for home. Long sleepless hours lay ahead of me.

That's when I decided to invent Marta.

She was in a fluster when she got there. She'd obviously been running to make it into the library before they closed.

"Just a minute, please don't close!" she said, almost out of breath. "I forgot a book here this afternoon."

The librarian, just coming out, looked at her sternly.

"Is it yours?"

"No, it's not mine." She seemed distressed. "And I've got to give it back."

"What book is it?"

She was flurried for a moment before she answered. "*Sexual Pathology*, by Stevens," she said.

"We've just closed. Why don't you come first thing in the morning? If somebody's turned it in, it'll be here."

"It's just that I've got to return it tonight."

I decided to step in.

"Maybe somebody's found it and it's sitting right there. I'll watch the door for you."

The librarian looked daggers at me. She pushed open the glass door, which she had not yet locked, and said, "Wait a minute."

"Thank you so much," Marta said to me.

We stood there waiting. She half-smiled at me, between anxious looks through the glass door.

"Things like that happen," I said, just to say something. "But they're very efficient here; if it's been turned in at the office, they'll have it for you."

The librarian reappeared on the other side of the glass door. She came out, and then locked the door before saying, "There's just one copy of Stevens's *Sexual Pathology*, and that belongs to the library."

"And nothing's been turned in with that title?"

The librarian gave me a look of cold satisfaction and said, drily, "Nothing."

And without a "good night" she left.

Marta was crushed. I tried as best I could to calm her.

"Don't worry; come early tomorrow and ask them to look again. It's a little late now, and the employees have to leave."

"I can't tomorrow."

I took a sudden decision.

"Look, I live near here and I can come tomorrow as soon as they open. I'll say the book belongs to me."

She seemed hesitant, surprised.

"I'd hate to impose like that. Why should you bother?"

"Please! It's no bother. Don't you worry. You'll see, they'll find your book."

She looked at me for a moment, evidently curious as well as touched by my concern. I realized that this was no time to lose ground.

"Tell me where I can contact you, in case they find it."

She gave me a phone number, and my hand trembled as I wrote it down in my address book. I didn't want to push it, and after a few more soothing words I left.

"Good night, Marta," I said.

"Good night."

Before the library opened I was out in front, waiting. But in spite of all their efforts, the staff couldn't find any other copy of Stevens's *Sexual Pathology*. I felt deeply discouraged.

I decided to wait till the bookstores opened for the afternoon. I had lunch earlier than usual; and when the first bookstore opened on the Calle Obispo, I was there asking for the book.

Between Obispo and Reina I found every kind of pathology, in new book stores and used, but not the one by Stevens. I was tired when I got home, and I went to bed without dinner. But the following afternoon, just walking aimlessly, I saw it in the first store I'd gone to the day before. The buyer's interest in pathologies had lasted exactly two days, after which he'd sold it, and there it was in my hands, almost brand new!

I rushed to a telephone. Unfortunately Marta was not home, she wouldn't be back till dinnertime. I was on pins and needles all afternoon. I called again at four, hoping to reach her. The same voice answered, drily this time, "I told you when she'd be back."

I killed time as best I could, and at seven Marta's gentle voice answered. Yes, yes, I'd found her the book. No, it had cost next to nothing, she shouldn't worry about that. No, not at all, she shouldn't even mention it, I'd be offended. But where could I see her? All right, at the library, at nine. Not before that? All right, very well, at nine.

And at nine a jubilant Marta received her book, which I handed to her the moment she arrived, next to one of the reading tables. There was a special gleam in her eyes.

"Why, it's the same one! It's a miracle!"

We tried to muffle our voices so as not to bother the other patrons, who were looking at us, vaguely curious.

"No, just luck. I knew I'd find it for you sooner or later."

Marta was sorry to have to excuse herself, but she had to leave. We spoke for a moment, she held out her hand, I shook it, and she was gone. I assumed I'd never see her again.

I went home slowly, and an exhilarating mixture of joy and sadness kept me awake a long time.

But I saw Marta again. I invented her again many, many times.

One afternoon I gathered up all my courage — after several rash attempts that ended with my hanging up before anyone answered — and called her from a pay phone. She was very cordial and said I could meet her that same evening, after class. I wrote down the address. I got ready very early, and a little before the agreed-on time I was already there, waiting for her. When I caught sight of her she was coming out with several other young people. She seemed to hesitate a moment when she saw me; but she quickly said goodbye to the others and walked, almost ran, toward me. She shook my hand in the warmest possible greeting.

"I'm so glad you called me!"

Marta's hair is always lovely, full of life; she has a special way of arranging it with her hand, of running her fingers through it.

We walked a while; then I treated her to an ice cream — I never eat anything in the evening — and she let me walk her home.

From then on we saw each other very often. Several times we met after her classes. Other times I waited for her and we chatted briefly before going our separate ways. I offered to run errands for her, get her books. I barely managed to get her to accept. How nice it was to meet Saturdays on a crowded downtown street, go shopping and then not buy anything, meet at a movie house and then, a moment before going in, decide that we wouldn't, walk feverishly to no particular place, feel my blood hot in my veins.

Sometimes we wouldn't see each other for two or three days, and then every hour became a torture for me. With her presence or with her absence, Marta changed the meaning of time and of things. Days could pass like lightning when all things seemed focused on the evening's rendezvous, which always had something magical about it: Marta waiting for me in front of a store window, lost in contemplation of the latest fashions; Marta sitting in a park, reading; Marta having something at the small marble table of a café; Marta at the door of a theater, standing amid the people rushing in, offending me — making me secretly happy — with the already-purchased tickets in her hand; Marta alone in the vast courtyard of the Museo de Bellas Artes, lost in the music. Or they could pass with maddening slowness because we wouldn't see each other that day, or the next, but the day after that, and all that lay before me were pointless mornings and afternoons and evenings. Everything took on a very clear meaning: before Marta, and after Marta. I admit that I neglected my best friends; but the fact is that what they had to say, their little problems, real or invented, their sicknesses, had come to annoy me.

One Sunday — Sunday afternoons had stopped being so long, so lonely — we were to meet on the boulevard, the Prado, to see the carnival. But she didn't come. Or maybe she did, maybe she came and we couldn't find each other in the crowd. She might even have passed right by me without seeing me. I walked up the Prado, distraught, looking in every direction just in case I might suddenly catch sight of her, confetti raining down on my face, into my mouth, even down under my collar. I thought I'd go home, but I put off leaving in the hope we might still find each other. For a moment I felt panic. Perhaps I'd lost her, perhaps forever. Unable to control myself, I shouted, "Marta!"

The boulevard, as I neared Monte, was at its finest that warm winter evening. All around me people were having a good time; some girls were dancing on top of an illuminated float, some of them tied to very tall platforms and performing the most astonishing balancing act. It was a beautiful sight. Each float had its orchestra. The street was bathed in light. Stimulated by the music and the bright colors, people were rushing in uncontrollable waves into the middle of the street, dancing. The noise was terrible; but beneath or above it and the blinding light and the laughing couples walking with their arms around each other, I sensed a profound harmony, a serenity, that soothed me. For a few minutes I managed to forget Marta. The girls were turning and twisting on the tall platforms; each carnival would bring new ones, ever new ones, who would make their gaudy cheap costumes to show them off on

February evenings. Tears came to my eyes, I don't know why. It seemed to me that happiness was possible.

The next evening, in a café, as I told Marta what I'd been through, her lovely eyes glistened. Never had I invented her so beautiful. I instantly forgot my distress of the previous day. Our lively conversation went on for a long time. It got to be late for Marta. I mentioned it to her, but she shrugged her shoulders in a delightful little gesture. On other occasions she had seemed in a hurry, but that night she wasn't concerned about time; she simply ignored it, perhaps to please me and blot out the previous day's disappointment. For the sake of my company she forgot about her friends, her duties, in what seemed to me an infinitely delicate gesture.

On the way home I felt deeply happy. I looked at the city as though I'd never seen it before. Other times its noises bothered me; now it seemed to me radiant, full of charm. I thought of her; I repeated her name as I walked across the city, covering enormous distances without noticing it, without getting tired. Once again time was becoming meaningless.

Patiently I waited for her birthday, the date of which I was able to find out without her knowing it. I had her name, Marta, embroidered in very delicate little letters on some small handkerchiefs. That day I invited her to my house. I told her she should come with a friend — anything else would have been impolite.

A few hours before their arrival I realized how oppressively ugly my home was. I moved the furniture several times, and each time I found it more dreadful. In despair I had everything thoroughly cleaned and polished. I plundered a whole florist's shop — maybe it would all look better with flowers. But everything looked just the same.

At five, exhausted, I took a bath and then sat down to wait for her. But five o'clock came and went, and then six, and finally night fell and Marta did not come. I was crushed. I didn't turn on the light. I stayed on the balcony, not daring to go back into the apartment, which was slowly sinking into darkness and silence. I decided that I'd never imagine Marta again.

I must have fallen asleep on the balcony. Toward morning I felt cold and went to bed without taking off my clothes.

The next day I dressed carefully and went to wait for Marta. She greeted me with what seemed to be genuine affection. I didn't want to say anything about the visit; and she, perhaps out of tactfulness, didn't mention it either.

"I won't be here tomorrow," she announced after our first greetings. "We're going to the country, and when I get back I'll have to rest."

I felt crushed.

"Couldn't I go, too?" I asked timidly.

"It's a long trip."

"At least we'd be together."

Never had I dared to be that outspoken with her.

When I got home I was ready to collapse. I had to spend a whole day in bed. But I'll never forget her sunlit face against the rich green of the countryside, her encouraging smile when I was exhausted and our eyes met, her fine hair in the wind on the road. Marta, Marta!

Two days ago, in the afternoon, she was here. I was surprised to hear the knock at the door, because I never, or almost never, have visitors. I opened the door and there she was. When I saw her, my heart skipped a beat. I didn't know what to say; I wanted to do a number of things all at the same time and couldn't manage any of them.

A man was with her.

"Come in."

Marta introduced us.

"We were in the neighborhood and thought we'd drop in. We've been walking for hours."

"Come in, please, this way . . ."

"I'm afraid it's an imposition, just showing up like this."

"Not at all!"

I opened the door to the balcony and a weak breath of air came in. We sat down. There was a brief silence.

Marta's companion was a tall young fellow, dark, intelligent.

He seemed friendly, maybe too friendly, and his broad smile proclaimed an almost offensively good health.

"Marta's told me about you," he said. "I was looking forward to meeting you."

"I'm glad to hear that, but now you've been walking for so long . . . Just wait a minute and I'll fix you something."

"Please, please, don't bother," Marta said.

"Oh yes, as long as you've come all this way you'll have to let me get you something."

"But we'll be going right away."

"I'll just be a minute," and I dashed into the kitchen.

While I was making coffee, I heard them talking in a low voice, with interruptions, as though they were continuing a conversation they'd begun long before. The boy's voice was pleasant, deep yet cheerful. I didn't remember having noticed him among the friends I sometimes saw with Marta.

"Do you live nearby?" I asked him when I poured them their coffee.

"No, quite a way off; I come when I can."

"We can't meet at my house; it's very small, and there are a lot of us," Marta explained. She stopped a moment and then added, "And in this heat . . ."

There was another pause. We drank our coffee.

I looked out the balcony door. Lord, what a beautiful afternoon . . . The shadows had begun to fall, and a purple tint was suffusing everything. Something, perhaps the imminence of night, was accelerating the rhythm of life, filling everything with an exaltation, a violent ephemeral joyfulness, a sense of deep and at the same time tenuous well-being. You could weep or shout for joy. I left the house.

When I returned, much later, Marta and the boy were on the balcony. They were talking calmly in a low voice, leaning on the railing, very close to each other. They smiled at me. I turned on the light. Under its brightness Marta's hair glowed palely. Her skin gave off a freshness as though it had just been washed. An expression of infinite sweetness was in her eyes.

"We're going, it's a little late," the boy said.

His arm was around her waist; one of her hands, with its delicate veins, rested on it, contrasting with its darkness. The soft line of her neck and her hair were silhouetted against the light.

"Goodbye." There was a serious and tranquil tone in Marta's voice.

She placed her small warm hand on mine and left it there for a moment. I saw the golden flesh of her arms, the exquisite texture of her skin, the deep eyes.

"Goodbye," she said, "goodbye . . . and thanks for everything."

In Partenza

FOR ESTHER JUDITH, CONSOLING MOTHER OF THE TRIBE

A few days before I left on my trip, my cook decided it was time to consult the dead.

My priceless Angela! How you worried about that short sentimental journey as you watched me prepare for it unenthusiastically, in fact with a certain sadness, uneasy about my true reasons for crossing the sea.

Angela was conspicuously absent during all of my last day at home, and I had to go without lunch. In mid-afternoon I caught sight of her in the old part of the city. She was laboriously getting off a bus. She was loaded with packages wrapped in newspaper. Not without feeling a bit guilty, I guessed what she had in them. She bustled off into the crowd of vehicles and people; and I didn't see her again till it was time for dinner, which she didn't prepare either. She'd forgotten about eating, and she forced me to obey her rigid laws.

At eight the guests she'd invited began to arrive from the neighborhood where she lives. I heard a knock at the door and was going to go open it; but Angela rushed out of the dining room, where she'd shut herself in for a long time, and shouted, "I'll get it!"

I heard the sound of greetings, conversations, nervous laughter, and then silence. Angela came for me.

"Come meet them."

In the living room I was introduced to the guests. In response a fat mulatto woman struggled to her feet, perched on wood-platform shoes. Her son was a young black man, short and stocky, and exceptionally intelligent-looking. I thought I recognized him from having seen him in some government office a few days before. A blonde woman stepped up and introduced her daughter, almost a child, and apologized for her presence saying she couldn't leave her alone. The fifth person was a black woman, well along in years, well groomed, and dressed in spotless and stiffly starched white, who walked with incredible elegance on enormously high heels and greeted me with poised cordiality.

We sat down, exchanged comments on the weather; and pretty soon Angela said, "Let's go."

Slowly, still chatting and laughing a little, we trooped off toward the dining room. As I stepped inside, I saw that Angela had sacked the whole city. Mountains of roses and gardenias were arranged on the table. From beneath it, huge bundles of grass gave off an intense fresh odor that blended with that of the incense.

Angela placed us as best she could on the chairs she'd brought into the small room. She tightly closed the balcony doors, turned on the dimmest lamp, turned off the overhead light, and we started.

Need I give a detailed account of my last evening at home? I especially remember the exquisite discretion with which Angela and her friends received everyone, their courtesy toward the congenial and their terrible harshness with the unwanted. How can I forget the polite words of welcome, the wishes expressed with such moving sincerity, the swearwords, the violent gestures, the hard thump of bodies thrown to the floor, the icy hands of the heavily sweating young man, his wild squinting eyes, and above all the sincere and gracious interest in my well-being?

Among my memories of that night, one stands out above the rest and stays with me.

At one point the mother of the young man stood up on her wooden platforms and greeted us. We all answered her greeting. Her son stood up, laid his hands on her shoulders, and asked, "What's your name?"

The mother placed her arms akimbo and tilted her head sideways—unnecessarily, I thought.

"Blanca."

The boy stared steadily into her eyes and asked again, "Are you sure?"

"Positive! Everybody knows me."

The boy shook his head. "That's not true. You're a man, and your name isn't Blanca."

"Of course my name's Blanca! Of course it is! Everybody knows me as Blanca."

There was something repulsive in her gestures.

"Your real name!" The boy had suddenly turned furious.

Her voice choking with laughter, the mother of the young girl remarked to the well-groomed thin woman, "It's a fairy!"

"Your real name!" the young man bellowed.

"All right, then: my name isn't Blanca." And pointing toward me, also suddenly furious, she added, "But that guy, I hate him!"

We all stood up and holding hands formed a circle around the woman as she tottered on her wooden platforms.

When the unwanted visitor had left the house forever, we walked over roses and gardenias back to the living room, where Angela lit a large cross drawn with alcohol.

The sweat pouring down our faces glistened in the light of the flames.

Before I set off on my trip, Angela taught me a song to calm rough seas; but when a storm tossed our ship around in the Bay of Biscay, I shook with fear, and when I wanted to sing that song, I realized I'd forgotten it.

On the Avenue

When he opened the balcony door, the harsh light of an overcast morning struck his eyes.

Covering them against the glare, he contemplated the city spread out on a monotonous plain punctuated by abortive would-be hills.

Several floors below him lay the avenue, very wide. At one end of it stood a pseudo-Roman monument, massive and pretentious: a curving row of columns with heroes, matrons, vestal virgins, charioteer and chariot, all of it protecting the almost invisible great man, a little fellow in a cutaway, carved in marble. It gave the illusion of being the source of the avenue, which then ran down to end in the sea.

The monument struck him as frightful. When you saw it like that, taking it all in at once, sitting on rising ground that came to an abrupt end behind it, there was something theatrical, unpleasantly operatic about it, especially on bright days or at night, when a glow rose from the other parts of the city and the sky seemed like a background especially illuminated to set it off, waiting for the tenor ferried by the swan: *Leb wohl, du wilde Wasserflut* . . .

Below the balcony the avenue made an attempt at a garden, with rickety shrubs, doggedly pruned, amid sad-looking open spaces trampled by thousands of feet. Farther on it was shaded by dark luxuriant trees as it went its way toward an ever-lovely sea whose intense indigo he found exhilarating on certain afternoons.

He looked at the charioteer, the matrons, the virgins, the angels, and the ridiculously small prow of a galley. With its tiny marble oars, it gave the impression that any moment now the huge monument would start a journey down the avenue over the grass.

Then, before the assault of the glare, he closed the door and went back into the room.

Lying there exhausted on the bed, in the half-light that filtered through the partly open shutters, she seemed almost beautiful. He gazed on her for a long while, afraid of destroying that rapt expression, concentrated in the total forgetfulness of sleep, indifferent to the deafening noise that rose from the intersection below the window.

As he watched her sleep, it seemed to him that moments like these, and those others when she was quiet, were her best. Not that her conversation, in which she invested the same unnecessary degree of intensity that she devoted to each of her acts, annoyed him. Far from it: he was intrigued by her capacity for pouring so much energy into the most trivial affirmation, the most humdrum act; it seemed to him to betray a passionate inclination worthy of infinitely greater causes, to reveal hidden treasures that he might never come to discover, an infinite potential for goodness, for work, for resentment.

But when she was still, with her hair hanging softly against her cheek, absorbed in what others were saying or in what she was reading, a profound calm came over her that made him desire her more than anything else. Or perhaps desire her company above all things. During these last weeks he'd been telling himself that that was all he desired, ever since the morning when, on the way to meet her, he'd wondered with a burning in his eyes why it had all been spoiled so quickly, why everything was always spoiled so quickly. But desiring her or desiring her company, weren't they almost the same thing?

He asked himself whether that capacity for devotion, that irrepressible energy that governed all her acts and that had run up against him as against a bulwark, threatening him with its surge, flooding him with tenderness in the same determined way in which it could have swamped him under countless layers of loathing, might some day turn into a capacity for hatred, and whether the adoration that at the outset had flattered his vanity would gradually end up destroying him by means of a simple shift from one fanaticism to another.

He placed one hand on her warm round shoulder, tanned by a whole summer's sun, and it gave way beneath the pressure of his fingers. Gradually, she awoke.

"I'm going," he announced, caressing her sweat-dampened hair. She really was beautiful like that, half-asleep in the twilight. "It's late; get up," he went on.

Without opening her eyes, she merely smiled vaguely.

"Goodbye." Again his fingers brushed against her shoulders. She took hold of them with a soft and slender hand, hot, almost burning, from its contact with the sleeping body beneath the sheets. At first she squeezed them with the tremulous pressure of first wakefulness, then she played with them, and finally she let them go.

He waited for the question that he knew she was afraid to ask but that in an awkward way she always did ask, and that he wanted to hear, from a secret wish to annoy her, perhaps to torment her.

"When will I see you again?"

"One of these days."

There was a brief silence during which he savored his small victory, a little regretfully. She neither stirred nor opened her lips.

"Aren't you going to get up?"

The answer took a while in coming.

"In a minute. I don't like you to see me in the morning."

"Nonsense!"

She gestured as though resigning herself to her fate. He touched her hair again and bent over to kiss her, but then he held back.

"Goodbye," he said again, and left the room.

He walked down the hallway whose perpetual darkness annoyed him and which he always lit with an angry punch as he passed the switch. But this time he didn't notice the darkness. He opened the door, stepped out onto the landing, went down the stairs without waiting for the elevator, and quickly reached the front door, eager to breathe the outside air once more.

"When will I see you again?"

It was another woman now, asking him the same question from the landing of another staircase. Trite and innocuous as it was, it had the power of producing a wholly disproportionate irritation in him.

He had reached the first landing. He stopped, trying to identify the cause of his irritation. Just what was it that brought it on:

the implication that he had a duty to come back, the veiled demand that did not, after all, exceed the traditional limits of family obligations? Or was it the cracked and quavering voice, the body standing at the top of the stairs, clumsily leaning against the wall?

The figure up there put a hand on her waist in a gesture reminiscent of what a half century earlier must have been an elegant, even coquettish posture. He felt a terrible pity for her.

Seeing her there, several steps above him, patting down her hair with a tremulous hand with bulging veins, he called up his memories of her, which the photographs he sometimes asked her for, as though in a desperate effort to corroborate an ever more questionable and elusive reality, helped him to confirm. Especially the oldest photos, those taken before he'd been born, which had dazzled him the first time she'd shown them to him.

He evoked his first memory of that woman, his mother: her slender figure, her confident movements, her firm walk (for him, majestic), the often aggressive gaze, the calm voice, which could so easily turn hard, the frequently sarcastic laugh, the clothes that seemed to him beyond reproach, the excursions, the men who rarely reappeared.

His relationship with her wavered between pity and anger, between helpless despair and repentance. There were no neutral or uncharged intermediate points to make it bearable, to relieve the constant tension.

As he observed the fading of her intelligence, betrayed by the stories he'd heard a thousand times but which she doggedly repeated as though they'd just happened, he sank into a sullen despair that turned into violence, into ill-controlled outbreaks. Her childish reactions to things, the pettiness of her narrowing life, her infantile tricks, the ill-concealed, almost unhealthy, curiosity, the incipient addiction to vicious gossip, the pathetic lies, the vexing little malfunctions of the body . . . It seemed to him that his relationship with her had been reduced to observing this malignant process. He closed his eyes.

Quick, bring the photos! he was tempted to beg of the decrepit figure asking him the question from the top of the stairs. *Let's look at them again together!*

But all he answered was, "Soon."
And he went on down the stairs.

For a long time he looked at the comings and goings on the street and the slate-colored water of the bay that stretched out before him and then disappeared around a bend that hid it from his view.

What was there about this day that forced him to look at things as though he'd never seen them before? There were days like that, when even mere objects forced us to think of them afresh.

He looked at the walls of the room where he was working. It was an ordinary, ugly room that hadn't been touched by paint in many a year; but it was not altogether disagreeable.

He heard the woman who was coming to make his lunch. She was late; she was coming from the far side of town. He heard her put her key in the lock, open the door, close it carefully, and enter the little hall quietly so that he wouldn't hear her. At noon he'd feel hungry; but he'd wait for her to finish her preparations and then eat without scolding her, pretending he hadn't heard her get there, especially today, when the world was covered by that low sky that cast a glow on everything and brought out even the most insignificant details.

He came to think of those who would some day occupy the space where he now lived. Someone would paint the room, only to leave it again. Lovers, children, old people, young girls, lonely men — for each generation the walls would be covered with successive layers of color that would inevitably fade and eventually turn black.

The floor tiles, in appallingly bad taste, would bear bodies that he would never know and that would not suspect he had walked there. Beautiful young feet, children's feet, tired or deformed feet, feet coming from sad and cold or warm and cheerful beds, armies of feet coming in for the first time or leaving forever; men or women going to open the door to happiness or close it on sadness — all of it on those same solid ugly tiles, and no one would ever suspect (no, never, never!) that he had suffered there, loved there, thought there.

He walked all afternoon. A crushing heat hung over everything. The pointless din in which the city delighted grew more intense as

184

the sun—hidden all day long, but implacable—began its descent. Annoyed by the fierce glare, the mass of men and vehicles made ever more noise, which only irritated it more.

Suddenly lightning flashed and the sky almost immediately began to darken. The light grew a little dimmer, but the heat increased and the air grew thicker. Human beings, vehicles, and thunder were now competing in the production of noise. The air felt sticky.

"Maybe it'll rain," he thought. "I hope so."

When he reached a street corner he looked toward the south. A black cloud had covered a great part of the city and was advancing slowly, accompanied by thunderclaps.

He stopped in the middle of the sidewalk, savoring the relief the rain was about to bring, its moistness, its coolness.

"It's going to rain," he said out loud.

The street took on a dark tone, a leaden gray on the verge of black. The wind came to life and drove clouds of dust along the pavement. The cloud was now above his head.

"Thank God it's going to rain," he said to a passer-by. "Thank God."

The man looked at him and went on.

He stood on the sidewalk a long time, waiting for the rain, planning to walk across town, slowly, letting himself be soaked.

But the wind stopped and bit by bit the sky began to clear, although not completely. The same thick cloud still hung over the city with its purplish glare.

He walked about aimlessly. Then, from among the countless possible acts he chose the easiest: he dropped a coin into a telephone and waited.

He embraced her beneath the trees, where the avenue made a turn, behind the monument, where they couldn't be seen so easily. Again he saw the warm bare shoulder.

Beyond the monument, where the ground sloped sharply downward, they had cut through a low hill to make way for the avenue, which now continued there between two high walls of chalky soil, yellowish white in color. Somewhere he'd read that these long veins of white and yellow tint were marl deposited in the Lower Eocene.

As he felt her body press against his, trembling, he thought that perhaps some geologist, piercing the dust with his pick thousands of years in the future, would destroy his member, erect now.

The idea first saddened but then elated him. As long as this planet that was roaming through space to no apparent purpose did not explode, he'd be forever encrusted in some layer of marl. And even if the planet did explode, he would continue to float in the void, converted into particles of dust.

He saw that he was eternal.

Piazza Margana

I have now entered your bloodstream. I have gone beyond urine, beyond excrement and its sweet, acrid taste, and have at last lost myself in the warm recesses of your body. I am here to stay. I will never leave it. From my vantage point, where I have finally attained bliss, I see the world through your eyes, hear the most frightening and the most enchanting sounds through your ears, taste all tastes with your tongue, feel all shapes with your hands. What else could a man desire? Forever and ever "emparadised in thee." "Enveje-ceremos juntos, dijiste," and we will.

My fate is to be envied by generations of lovers for all time to come, till the end of Time.

It all came to me while you were shaving one day, between spells of mutual hatred. The blade cut a small, deep gash into your chin. While I squeezed the wound in order to clean it, as your blood oozed out from the severed vessels, I felt a terrible urge to have a taste of it.

From that moment on, my mind went down an irresistible slope, out of control. That night and many nights after, while you breathed peacefully in your sleep next to me, I thought of the red raw tissues of the stomach, crossed and recrossed by veins, forever giving out their juices at the slightest provocation. I saw myself touching in awe the hard red tendons, the white inside of the spine, your tender throbbing brain, the meaty muscular tissues of your heart, the outer dressing of your bones, so silky and pink, where vessels intertwine, endlessly bringing out new cells to replace the dead ones. I saw the inlets of your mouth, the dark embedment of the tongue, and beyond it the brittle cartilage and cords from which your voice stems. I wondered what the smell and taste of it all could be, what biting at the tendons would feel like: to lick the bones, to chew the soft, tender flesh, lay the scrotum open, deplete the blad-der, gash at the penis; having previously dislodged the lungs, let my cheek rest forever against the raw bloody tissue of the rib cage; lay out the long thick muscles of the thighs and buttocks, feed on them, have an actual taste of all your glands, diet for weeks on the genital cord; ever more earnest, ever more eager, feed, feed slowly on the eardrums, the eyes, the tongue, gnaw at the rectal opening, use your hair and all the hairs on your body for dental floss, bite deep into the armpits, replace lost energies on the ganglions, eat slowly from the fingers up until the arms are gone, uncap the knees and drink patiently and carefully (lest one drop should flow out) from the rich lubricants cupped up in the joints, dislodge the thigh, slit the bone and feed on the marrow for a whole season of delight, gulp down the eyes as one gulps down an egg, look into the empty sockets for nights on end, unhinge the ankles, feed on the feet for weeks, draw strength from the ligaments, lick the tendons white, pluck out the toenails and fingernails, nibble at them for calcium having disposed of the teeth reserve. But above all, eat slowly, deliberately and in rapt fervour from inside, where the heart beats undaunted, into the richly red, luscious tissue, right under the long-digested nipples.

But then I thought I knew better. As I said before, generations of lovers will for centuries to come turn green with envy. *We will rot together.* As I write, travelling at ease in unspeakable merriment through your bloodstream after a protracted summer in the mastoids, always ready to forsake the lymphatic for the parotids, where the frantic humming of your brain reaches and reassures me, I know that I will be with you, travel with you, sleep with you, dream with you, urinate and generally defecate with you, make love *with and through* you, hate with you, think, cry, grow senile, warm, cold and warm again, feel, look, jerk off, kiss, kill, pet, fart, fade, flush, turn into ashes, lie, humiliate myself and others, strip, stab, wilt, wait, wail, laugh, steal, quiver, waver, ejaculate, linger, backscuttle, pray, fall, doublecross, triplecross, ogle, browse, goose, suck, brag, bleed, blow with and through you.

My feat is yet to be equalled, so completely new and unparalleled is it. It has no precedent in history and will go down in the annals of mankind, lest they forget, until all trace of human existence will be wiped out from earth. My freedom of choice and sojourn knows no limit. I have attained what no political or social system could ever dream of attaining: I am free, utterly free inside you, forever free from all fears and cares. No exit permit, no entry permit, no passport, no borders, no visa, no *carta d'identità,* no nothing! I can choose to settle on the right nipple where the vein ends and nerve ends blossom into a delicate tender pink tip. There I can wait indefinitely. I'm in no particular hurry. Time has been obliterated. *You are Time.* It was only last century that I held on like mad to the slimy walls of your bladder to avoid being flushed out. So I can wait, typewriter and all, cuddle myself to sleep under the marvellous soft hairy hill on your chest and wait until some idiot wakes me up and makes me tingle with it. I can climb up your tongue and lick and squeeze myself into someone else's mouth, reaching out for all the delights that Heaven can hold. It is then that I take a wild plunge down the spinal cord sending out shiver after shiver of divine pleasure, until your pulses beat so savagely that I let myself be dragged by the torrent and travel with the speed of light inside the thick, quickening fluid of your blood.

But no hurry, no hurry. For days, weeks, months, I can roam up your retina, take leisurely trips down the pupil for a glance at the outer world, while methodically organizing the more demanding, infinitely more exacting trek into your brain. What delights then, what joy, as I slowly penetrate the grey labyrinth, the pulsating maze, taking an occasional lick at the white membranous partitions, the taste of which could hardly be equalled. The biggest stock exchange in the world on Crash Day, the largest railway station in the world could never approach what goes on inside your head.

The delights of the medulla oblongata! The endless ramifications of the arbor vitae! The harsh caresses of the dura!

How shall I begin? How shall I begin! How can I enter that seeming chaos, that supremely orderly anarchy without being crushed to death (everything in time) by the million shattering tremors, swifter than lightning and deadlier? How shall I begin! With love! How else? With love! Let love guide my exploration, my fabulous trip, the trip no man has taken before; let it be torch and compass to help me find my bearings through the frightening maze teeming with vibrations, forever bouncing and rebouncing at a fantastic frequency.

In silent reverence I start a trip which is to lead sometimes closer to the surface, sometimes into the heart of the highly organised wilderness. Using up days, weeks, even months, I take to the depths: periosteum, outer table, diploe, inner table, sutures, calvaria (next to the dura, for warmth and compassion). But again: no hurry, no hurry. In due time (who cares about time?) I will reach the falx cerebri, the charming softness of the meninx, bow to the optic nerve, squeeze myself into the infundibulum (the infundibulum, *O Paradiso!*), feel my way like a blind man through the substantia nigra using both arms for antennae, like a bat, gallop across the bridge of Varolius, like a happy playful child, and after a long dip down the aqueduct of Sylvius fall exhausted upon the sella turcica gasping for air. Sleep, sleep is all I want after this first exhausting leg of my trip. The thalamus, the thalamus! Where is the thalamus after the horrors of the claustrum, the lunar light of the globus pallidus? The terrific reverberations zoom through me, newly loaded with electricity. Sleep, sleep . . . Who can sleep when the pathetic is so close and I must take a long detour lest I kill your sources of compassion forever?

If overpowered by excitement I can always find shelter in the silence of the grey matter. But not for long, not for long. Who wants silence now that I have reached your innermost brain? Let the roaring blasts coming from the tympana deafen me for life. Who cares! Haven't I said that I am here to stay? There is always the olfactory nerve to take refuge in when everything else fails. In what wealth of odours I shall bask forever! There are always the sinuses for complete protection. Somebody is hammering at the petrous one. Let him hammer. There is room for everyone. If he gets too nasty, a good kick in the ass and away with him into the fathomless depth of the fossa. That's for a lively grave! No one has reached here; no one has gotten this far and survived the blasting of the neurons coming from everywhere, the terrific pressure, the awful charging and discharging, the supremely harmonious, supremely maddening tutti. Only I have come out unscathed and will go back again and again into the grey hell, the breathless heaven, to listen to the murderous roaring that no one has heard without being himself murdered.

But as I said before, it is in your bloodstream that I attain the state of bliss reserved to the chosen ones, the sage. I roll inside it, revel in it, bask, rise to mythical heights, reach the ultimate, become, cease to be. I am no more myself. I am your blood: I feed your pulses, cross and recross the threshold of your heart, glide up and down, rush from ventricle to auricle, loiter in the atrium, switch from vein to artery and back to vein, take the tour of the lungs and retrace my course into your heart. Your heart! At last I am your heart! Not only the soft hair on your pubis but also your heart. Sono il tuo sangue! Quello che senti rimbalzarti dentro, questi brividi, questa strana gioia, questa paura, questa bramosia, sono io, sono io, galleggiante nelle tue arterie, è la carne che rammenta, dorenavanti rammentiamo insieme per l'eternità, amore, amore, pauroso amore mio![1] You need not be afraid, we will never know loneliness again, the awful, shameful loneliness of the flesh. Loneliness is gone forever, discarded, thrown out, done away with, burnt, buried. Can you hear me? Can you hear me as I sail full speed inside your blood, singing and shouting at the top of my lungs, intoning strange songs of joy, sobbing, whining, wailing in a frenzy of happiness such as no human being has known before? Sono io, sono io! I will die with you, turn into lifeless matter, run the gamut of preorganic and postorganic existence, and be reborn again and again, a million times, ad infinitum, with you.

When in a less intellectual, more adventurous mood, I embark on long safaris into your intestinal flora.

The portal vein throws its doors open and I let myself into the rich darkness. I could use a shortcut through the mesenteric but I prefer the roundabout way, which makes me shake with anticipation.

After a long descent I find myself in the thick of mysteries. No Amazonian basin, no Nigerian watershed could even approach its wealth. To find its equal one would have to go back to the days when the sources of the Nile were unknown, or even earlier, much earlier, when the great river began to flow, a thin stream at first, winding its way down the bottom of a terrifying cleft, then growing, some million years later, into a middle-sized peaceful brook, aeons before man arrived with a glaze in his eye.

---

1. I am your blood! What you feel bounding within you, these shudders, this strange joy, this fear, this desire, is I, is I, floating within your arteries, is the flesh that remembers, as from now on we shall remember together, my timorous love!

As I get deeper and deeper into the jungle, I am endlessly attracted, embraced, and rejected by the myriad shapes, the tentacular beings of the uncharted forest, the tiny monstrous flowers, the endless process of creation and destruction, the thousand karmic wheels no one could have suspected down here, repeating themselves millions of times along the long descent.

I could write endlessly about my passage through the semilunar folds, the opalescent light where the strangest creatures, half-animal, half-vegetal, open and close, degenerate and regenerate, disembowel in mass suicides only to swap fragments and reunite, seconds later. That part of my trip takes years, so strong is the fascination of the sickly glare, which takes on a subtly different shade under each fold. I let myself be embraced by the billion creatures swarming through me, crowding in the thick juice through which I swim in silence. I choose one at random, perhaps the most attractive, perhaps the most horrid one, and let myself be engulfed and swallowed like a corpuscle being devoured by a white cell. What infinite quietude, what peace then . . . How come I had never thought of this? This is happiness. There is no other word. In the depth of the innermost fold I have found it. This cancels and obliterates years of exhausting and useless search. I am happy. At last!

Not one sound, not a single regurgitation is heard from the remote spot I have reached. It is the silence of oceanic depths, ever surmised, ever unfathomed. It is only here that I can be myself. Peacefully and endlessly, I gyrate among the silent throngs entering and leaving through every orifice of my body. Millions of deaths and births take place without a wail, a stertor—nothing.

At a junction, after sliding for months in mortal agony down the almost impracticable sigmoid, the landscape changes abruptly. What Umbrian quietness among these mammoth trees, suddenly out of proportion with any imaginable species of any kingdom. The never-ending process of swallowing and ejecting stops, and another, a thousand times more deadly, more majestic, begins. I feel lost in this forest of giants moving slowly into treacherous embraces, utterly ignoring me in their greatness. I walk close to what I take to be a wall of the sunken forest, only to discover that I have awakened another giant and must dart away for dear life. (I could now take a respite before it is too late and make the long voyage down to the tip of your cock, with a brief stopover inside the testicles which might turn into a protracted stay — first on the right, then on the left, for the always welcome change in altitude. Who could stop me except death and then it would be *our* death? Should I decide to hibernate in the glans, sleep forever inside the prepuce, book space under the tunica, I could do so, but I decide otherwise.) Death is right here and so is life, and it is here that I feel closest to you. They could put up whole armies, legions of armored cars, ever replenished, ever updated planes sputtering fire to dislodge me from here. It's no use. This is Paradise. I have found it. Unlike Columbus I will not be shipped home in a hold with bound feet. No Canossa for me either. I have entered the Kingdom of Heaven and taken proud possession of it. This is my private claim, my heritage, my fief. I am NOT leaving.

John H. R. Polt is Professor of Spanish
Emeritus at the University of California, Berkeley.

Ilan Stavans teaches at Amherst College. His books
include *The Hispanic Condition*, *Art and Anger: Essays on
Politics and the Imagination*, and *The Riddle of Cantinflas:
Essays on Hispanic Popular Culture*.

Library of Congress Cataloging-in-Publication Data

Casey, Calvert.

[Short stories. English]

The collected short stories / Calvert Casey ; translations from

the Spanish by John H. R. Polt ; edited and with an introduction

by Ilan Stavans.

p.   cm.

ISBN 0-8223-2153-X (alk. paper). — ISBN 0-8223-2165-3 (pbk. : alk. paper)

I. Polt, John Herman Richard.   II. Stavans, Ilan.   III. Title.

PQ7390.C3A6   1998

863—dc21   97-32272

Opera Que Supersunt Omnia, vol. 7 (Brunsvigae: Apus C. A. Schwetschke et Filium, 1867; reprinted New York: Johnson Reprint, 1964), 170–71.

25. Christian Reformed Church, *Psalter Hymnal*, ed. Emily Brink (Grand Rapids: CRC Publications, 1987), 5–8.

26. Refer to Robin Leaver, "The Failure That Succeeded: The New Version of Tate and Brady," *The Hymn* 48, no. 4 (October 1997): 22–31; see also Louis F. Benson, *The English Hymn: Its Development and Use in Worship* (New York: Hodder & Stoughton, 1915), 131.

27. Benson, *English Hymn*, 130–31.

28. *Gloria Patri . . . or Hymns on the Trinity* (London: Strahan, 1746) included 24 hymns and *Hymns on the Trinity* (Bristol: Pine, 1767) included 136 hymns plus a section of 52 additional hymns and prayers on the Trinity, according to Barry E. Bryant, "Trinity and Hymnody: The Doctrine of the Trinity in the Hymns of Charles Wesley," *Wesleyan Theological Journal* 25, no. 2 (1990): 64–73.

29. Ibid., 66–72.

30. Ibid., 65.

31. Susan Drain, *The Anglican Church in Nineteenth Century Britain: Hymns Ancient and Modern (1860–1875)* (Lewiston, Lampiter, Queenston: Edwin Mellon Press, 1989), 67–68; and Erik Routley, *Church Music and Christian Faith* (Carol Stream, Ill.: Agape, 1978), 98.

32. Drain, *Anglican Church*, 483.

33. Ibid., 59–76.

34. Brian Wren, *What Language Shall I Borrow?* (New York: Crossroad, 1989), 195–215.

35. Thomas Troeger, "Personal, Cultural, and Theological Influences on the Language of Hymns and Worship," *The Hymn* 38 (October 1987): 7–15.

36. I wish to acknowledge the assistance of Robin Knowles Wallace in this aspect of the research. Bibliographical data on hymnals studied is as follows: Christian Church (Disciples of Christ), *Chalice Hymnal* (St. Louis: Chalice Press, 1995); Church of the Brethren, General Conference Mennonite Church, and the Mennonite Church of North America, *Hymnal: A Worship Book* (Elgin, Ill.: Brethren Press; Newton, Kans.: Faith and Life Press; Scottdale, Pa.: Mennonite Publishing House, 1992); Episcopal Church, *The Hymnal 1982* (New York: Church Hymnal Corp., 1982); Presbyterian Church (U.S.A.), *The Presbyterian Hymnal* (Louisville, Ky.: Westminster John Knox Press, 1990); Reformed Church in America, *Rejoice in the Lord* (Grand Rapids: Wm. B. Eerdmans Publishing Co., 1985); Southern Baptist Convention, *The Baptist Hymnal* (Nashville: Convention Press, 1991); United Church of Christ, *New Century Hymnal* (Cleveland: United Church Board for Homeland Ministries, 1995); United Methodist Church, *The United Methodist Hymnal* (Nashville: United Methodist Publishing House, 1989).

37. *Presbyterian Hymnal*, 158–258.

38. All hymns mentioned in this chapter are listed by categories in the Appendix, "A Sampling of Trinitarian Hymns." The list indicates where the hymns appear in the eight hymnals we studied.
39. Marilyn Kay Stulken, "Singing the Trinity," *Liturgy: The Journal of the Liturgical Conference* 13, no. 1 (winter 1996): 32–33.
40. David Tripp, "Methodism's Trinitarian Hymnody: A Sampling, 1780 and 1989, and Some Questions," *Quarterly Review* 14, no. 4 (winter 1994–95): 372.
41. Benson, *Hymnody*, 147.
42. I quote the version in *Piece Together Praise* (Carol Stream, Ill.: Hope Publishing Company, 1995), 7, not the version in *The Presbyterian Hymnal*, because Wren's 1995 version is more sensitive in its language related to people with disabilities.
43. Wren, *Bring Many Names* (Carol Stream, Ill: Hope Publishing Company, 1989), 35a.
44. Wren, *What Language Shall I Borrow?* 210.
45. "Somos Uno en Cristo," *Chalice Hymnal* (St. Louis: Chalice Press, 1995), number 493. Translation by Ruth Duck.
46. Tripp, "Methodism's Trinitarian Hymnody," 375.
47. Ibid., 372.
48. Richard L. Christensen, "What Language Shall We Recognize: A Critique of the *New Century Hymnal*," *Prism* 10, no. 2 (fall 1995), 44.
49. Ibid., 45.
50. Ruth Duck, *Circles of Care* (Cleveland: Pilgrim Press, 1998).
51. I am drawing on the analysis of Tripp, "Methodism's Trinitarian Hymnody," in determining where trinitarian hymns fell within the subject index of the *United Methodist Hymnal*, as well as on my independent research of that volume. Further, I am suggesting topics that coordinate with my suggestions of key places where trinitarian theology is and should be expressed in Christian worship, as discussed in chapter 4.
52. Catherine Mowry LaCugna, *God for Us: The Trinity and Christian Life* (San Francisco: HarperCollins, 1991), 342–48.
53. Ibid., 367–68.

CHAPTER 6: SOPHIA AND THE TRINITY

1. Elisabeth Schüssler Fiorenza, *Jesus, Miriam's Child, Sophia's Prophet: Critical Issues in Feminist Christology* (New York: Continuum, 1994), 133.
2. Ibid., 132.
3. Ibid., 134.
4. Barbara Newman, "The Pilgrimage of Christ-Sophia," *Vox Benedictina* 9, no.1 (summer 1992): 12. Her book on Hildegard of Bingen is *Sister of Wisdom: St. Hildegard's Theology of the Feminine* (Berkeley, Calif.: University of California Press, 1987).

5. Ibid., 13.

6. Fiorenza, *Jesus, Miriam's Child*, 136.

7. David Winston, "Wisdom in the Wisdom of Solomon," in *In Search of Wisdom: Essays in Memory of John G. Gammie*, ed. Leo G. Perdue, Bernard Brandon Scott, and William Johnston Wiseman (Louisville, Ky.: Westminster/John Knox Press, 1993), 150.

8. Ibid., 153.

9. Fiorenza, *Jesus, Miriam's Child*, 137–39.

10. For examples, refer to Jack Suggs, *Wisdom, Christology and Law in Matthew's Gospel* (Cambridge, Mass.: Harvard University Press, 1970), and W. D. Davies and Dale C. Allison, *Matthew*, vol. 2 in *International Critical Commentary* (Edinburgh: T. & T. Clark, 1991).

11. Fiorenza, *Jesus, Miriam's Child*, 139; Suggs, *Wisdom, Christology*, 57–58, 96; Davies and Allison, *Matthew*, 272.

12. Scholars have commonly identified this as "Q" material, although theories about the "Q" material are currently being debated. Emphasis is mine in both passages.

13. Fiorenza, *Jesus, Miriam's Child*, 151.

14. Suggs, *Wisdom, Christology*, 58.

15. Tertullian was writing in Latin, but he wrote *Logos* and *Sophia* in Greek. Refer to *Against Praxeus*, in *Ante-Nicene Fathers*, vol. 3, ed. Alexander Roberts and James Donaldson (Peabody, Mass.: Hendrickson, 1994), chapters 5 and 6.

16. Tertullian, *Against Praxeus*, 602.

17. Origen, *On First Principles*, trans. G. W. Butterworth (Gloucester, Mass.: Peter Smith, 1973), 15.

18. Ibid., 109.

19. Gregory of Nyssa, *Against Eunomius,* Book III, section 2, *Nicene and Post-Nicene Fathers,* series II, eds. Philip Schaff and Henry Wace, vol. V (Grand Rapids, Mich.: Wm. B. Eerdmans Publishing Co., [1954]), 137.

20. Here the present author has substituted "begotten" for the NRSV's "was brought forth," because Gregory understands Proverbs 8:25 to mean "begotten."

21. Gregory of Nyssa, *Against Eunomius*, 140.

22. Ibid., 140–41.

23. Newman, "Pilgrimage of Christ-Sophia," 10.

24. Saint Hildegard of Bingen, *Symphonia*, trans. Barbara Newman (Ithaca, N.Y.: Cornell University Press, 1988).

25. Julian of Norwich, *Showings*, trans. Edmund Colledge and James Walsh (New York: Paulist Press, 1978), 285. Refer to pages 293, 294, 295, and 299 for additional associations of wisdom with Christ the Mother. Julian does not, however, appropriate wisdom exclusively to the second partner of the Trinity, but can speak of wisdom in relation to the Father, the Lord/Spirit, or the whole Trinity.

26. Henry Suso, *The Exemplar, with Two German Sermons*, trans. and ed. Frank Tobin (New York: Paulist Press, 1989), 213.

27. Susan Cady, Marian Ronan, and Hal Taussig, *Wisdom's Feast: Sophia in Study and Celebration* (San Francisco: Harper & Row, 1989), 13.
28. Elizabeth A. Johnson, *She Who Is: The Mystery of God in a Feminist Theological Perspective* (New York: Crossroad, 1992).
29. Ibid., 147.
30. Ibid., 162.
31. Ibid., 179.
32. Ibid., 273.
33. Jann Aldredge-Clanton, *In Search of the Christ-Sophia: An Inclusive Christology for Liberating Christians* (Mystic, Conn.: Twenty-Third Publications, 1994).
34. Ibid., 30.
35. Ibid., 55.
36. Ibid., 57 and 52–55.
37. Conversation with David Furniss, the church musician at Saint John's, and the author, October 1995.
38. *The United Methodist Hymnal*, ed. Carlton Young (Nashville: United Methodist Publishing House, 1989).
39. Patrick Michael, "Who Comes from God as Word and Breath?" in the *Chalice Hymnal* of the Disciples of Christ (St. Louis: Christian Board of Publication, 1995), number 258.
40. In the *New Century Hymnal* of the United Church of Christ (Cleveland: Pilgrim Press, 1995), 740 in the Psalter (numbered separately from the hymns.)
41. *StreetWise* is a paper distributed in Chicago by homeless or formerly homeless people. The paper is full of hope and encouragement, whether people are seeking secure homes and jobs or more healthy relationships. The sermon refers to the community outcry when an off-duty policeman shot and killed a *StreetWise* vendor.

CHAPTER 7: LIVING THE TRINITARIAN LIFE

1. Gordon Lathrop, *Holy Things* (Minneapolis: Fortress Press, 1993), 15–20; Patricia Wilson-Kastner, *Sacred Drama: A Spirituality of Christian Liturgy* (Minneapolis: Fortress Press, 1999), chapter 2.
2. Richard D. McCall, "Liturgical Theopoetic," *Worship* 71, no. 5 (September 1997): 411.
3. Margaret R. Miles, *Image as Insight* (Boston: Beacon Press, 1985), especially 139–54, offers a provocative and informative interpretation of images as reflective of and informing culture.
4. Giuseppe Bovini and Leonard von Matt, *Ravenna* (New York: Harry N. Abrams, 1971), 122–25; Barbara C. Raw, *Trinity and Incarnation in Anglo-Saxon Thought and Art* (Cambridge: Cambridge University Press, 1997), 78–81.

5. David Coomler, *The Icon Handbook* (Springfield, Ill.: Templegate Publishers, 1995), 10, 31; A. Kostova, *The Subject of Early Russian Icons* (St. Petersburg: Iskusstvo Publishers, 1991), 110–13.

6. Coomler, *Icon Handbook,* 10, 30; Kostova, *Subject of Early Russian Icons*, 112–13; Kurt Weitzman, et al., *The Icon* (New York: Dorset Press, 1987), 270.

7. The Nativity also offered opportunity for portraying the Trinity, although I have seen few examples. One is found in a Belgian Book of Hours from the 1460s, in Roger S. Wieck, *Painted Prayers: The Book of Hours in Medieval and Renaissance Art* (New York: George Braziller, 1997), 66.

8. Coomler, *Icon Handbook*, 74, 107; Kostova, *Subject of Early Russian Icons*, 36–37.

9. Gerhard B. Ladner, *God, Cosmos, and Humankind* (Berkeley, Calif.: University of California Press, 1995), 20–23; George Ferguson, *Signs and Symbol in Christian Art* (London: Oxford University Press, 1954, 1961), 88–89; Kostova, *Subject of Early Russian Icons*, 40–43.

10. Raw, *Trinity and Incarnation in Anglo-Saxon Thought and Art*, plate XVIb.

11. Coomler, *Icon Handbook*, 28, 89.

12. Raw, *Trinity and Incarnation in Anglo-Saxon Thought and Art*, 143.

13. Ibid., 144–47.

14. Ferguson, *Signs and Symbol in Christian Art*, 94, E. J. Hunt, *English and Welsh Crucifixes: 670–1550* (London: SPCK, 1956), 86–87; Janet Backhouse, *The Illuminated Manuscript* (London: Phaidon Press, 1979), 57.

15. Hunt, *English and Welsh Crucifixes*, 25–26.

16. Coomler, *Icon Handbook*, 11–12, 32–39.

17. Ferguson, *Signs and Symbol in Christian Art*, 94; *The Calendar of the Prayer Book Illustrated* (Oxford: James Parker & Co., 1870), 182–84; Frank Bottomley, *The Church Explorer's Guide* (London: Kaye & Ward, 1978), 144–45.

18. Leonard Swidler, *Biblical Affirmations of Women* (Philadelphia: Westminster Press, 1979), 61.

19. *The Calendar of the Prayer Book Illustrated*, 182–84; Bottomley, *Church Explorer's Guide*, 144–45.

20. *Book of Common Prayer* (New York: Church Hymnal Corporation, 1976), 301–7; *Book of Worship* (New York: United Church of Christ Office for Church Life and Leadership, 1986), 134–44.

21. Thomas J. Talley, "The Structure of the Eucharistic Prayer," in *A Prayer Book for the Twenty-first Century*, ed. Ruth Meyers (New York: Church Hymnal Corporation, 1996), 83–85.

22. Ibid., 86.

23. Ibid., 87–89.

24. Ibid., 91.

25. Bard Thompson, *Liturgies of the Western Church* (Cleveland: Collins World, 1961), 132–37.

26. Ibid., 154.

27. Ibid., 172–79.
28. Ibid., 197–208.
29. Ibid., 278–82.
30. Ibid., 204–5.
31. *Book of Common Prayer*, Holy Eucharist II, 363, 369, 371–72, 375.
32. *Book of Worship,* 44–49.
33. Ibid., 68–75.
34. *Saint Joseph Sunday Missal* (New York: Catholic Book Publishing, 1977), 31–43.
35. *The Divine Liturgy of St. John Chrysostom of the Eastern Orthodox Church* (St. Louis, Logos Mission, 1966), 15.
36. E.g., Saint Hilda Community, *The New Women Included: A Book of Services and Prayers* (London: SPCK 1997), 89–90.
37. Elizabeth Johnson, *She Who Is: The Mystery of God in Feminist Theological Discourse* (New York: Crossroad, 1993), 192.
38. Catherine Mowry LaCugna, *God for Us: The Trinity and Christian Life* (San Francisco: HarperCollins, 1991), 379.
39. Ibid., 388–400, especially 399.
40. Jürgen Moltmann, *The Trinity and the Kingdom* (San Francisco: Harper & Row, 1981), especially 191–222.
41. Leonardo Boff, *Trinity and Society* (Maryknoll, N.Y.: Orbis Books, 1986), especially 123–63.
42. Geervarghese Mar Osthathios, *Theology of a Classless Society* (Guildford, Surrey: Lutterworth Press, 1979).
43. Gail Ramshaw, *Words around the Table* (Chicago: Liturgy Training Publications, 1991), 13–14.
44. Johnson, *She Who Is*, 58–59.
45. Dante Alighieri, *The Divine Comedy: 3 Paradise*, trans. Dorothy L. Sayers and Barbara Reynolds (London: Penguin Books, 1962), canto 23, p. 346.
46. John Pope-Hennessy, *Paradiso: The Illuminations to Dante's Divine Comedy by Giovanni di Paolo* (New York: Random House, 1993), 176–79.
47. Janet Morley, ed., *Bread of Tomorrow: Prayers for the Church Year* (Maryknoll, N.Y.: Orbis Books, 1992).
48. Ibid., 75 [22].
49. Ibid., 132 [10].
50. Ibid., 168 [3].

EPILOGUE AND INTRODUCTION
TO THE LITURGICAL RESOURCES

1. The closing words are based on a trinitarian formula proposed by Letty M. Russell in "The Credal Basis of the World YWCA and the Practice of God's Hospitality," background paper, August 1998, 13. Used by permission of Letty M. Russell.

GENERAL LITURGICAL RESOURCES

1. Julian of Norwich, *Showings*, long text, trans. E. Colledge and J. Walsh (New York: Paulist Press, 1978), 279–82.
2. Ibid.
3. This formula comes from Riverside Church in New York; refer to the discussion in Ruth Duck, *Gender and the Name of God: The Trinitarian Baptismal Formula* (New York: Pilgrim Press, 1991), 163–66.
4. Hymn and Worship Resource Committee, United Church of Canada, in its *Services for Trial Use: 1996–1997* ([Toronto], 1996) uses the traditional baptismal formula ("in the name of the Father and of the Son and of the Holy Spirit") but asks the church to discuss the use of the alternative formula given here.
5. The remembrance of the Last Supper is intentionally abbreviated to avoid the traditional sacrificial imagery and to place the Last Supper in the context of other meals that Jesus shared. Further, recitation of a long narrative in the midst of the prayer tends to shift the address from God to the people. See Marjorie Procter-Smith, *Praying with Our Eyes Open: Engendering Feminist Liturgical Prayer* (Nashville: Abingdon Press, 1995), xxx.
6. Formula from Riverside Church; refer to Duck, *Gender and the Name of God*.
7. The Anglican Church in Aoteoroa, New Zealand, and Polynesia, *A New Zealand Prayer Book / He Karakia Mihinare o Aoteoroa* (San Francisco: Harper & Row, 1989, 1997), 181.